For April, you are my universe.

In Memory of David Farland.
Beloved and irreplaceable mentor.

RED TEMPEST

BOOK TWO OF THE ANGELSONG SERIES

KEVIN A DAVIS

Inkd
Publishing

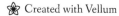

RED TEMPEST

CONTENTS

This is *Red Tempest* Book Two of the AngelSong Series. This is the story of Hadhira Dawson, Haddie, as she struggles to accept her powers and her place in an increasingly wonderous, yet dangerous world.

A law student in Eugene, Oregon, Haddie and her father have the power to spread matter back into time.

In *Penumbra*, Book One, Haddie saved her friend Liz from a woman with the ability to twist people's desires and who commanded the mysterious demons, both somehow connected.

PART 1

The Seroveilm brought us here to protect the timelines of this place from their enemy, and in abandoning us, forfeited this world.

CHAPTER 1

Haddie tried to ignore the hot, humid air in Liz's home-made lab, steeling herself for their experiment while twisting her hair into a knot.

Behind her, ahead, and to the right, unpainted drywall covered the three sides they'd framed in. The air smelled and tasted musty and dusty from the new construction.

"Relax," she said out loud to herself. Nerves could've accounted for some of her sweat.

A polished steel table awaited Haddie on the far side of their makeshift lab.

Liz's house stretched overhead, overhanging an open porch before they'd begun construction. Measuring twelve by twenty feet, the lab had been mainly Liz's doing.

Since Haddie had opened up to her friend about her powers, Liz had wanted to experiment. Not that Haddie didn't want to know more about how her abilities worked. Their first test a month ago had proven the theory that her powers scattered matter back in time. However, the pain she had to endure — and worse, the visions — made the project difficult to embrace.

A green camping chair sat opened behind her; Haddie remained standing, avoiding the urge to pace.

Dad doesn't like these tests, but he's interested in the results.

Today she had hoped they would do something different. It didn't look promising though. Liz tried to keep her in the dark. Part of the scientific method. However, something was wrong.

Haddie was stripped down to a sports bra and panties for Liz's post-power exam. Her hands showed no marks from last month's test. *No purpura.* David and her coworkers had accepted her excuse of a rash when she'd worn gloves. After today's attempt, she'd be back to wearing gloves and a bucket of makeup.

Inside the house, Liz's cart clattered along the hall, bringing a rising sense of dread into Haddie's chest. Slowing at the threshold, an assortment of vials and needles slid toward the front lip. A red camera lay on its back, its stand attached and protruding from the bottom. The object of the experiment, a plastic, 3-D printed brick that had "H2" stamped on it. The first had been "H1."

Liz wore lightly tinted glasses that barely seemed to hold onto her button nose. Brown shoulder-length hair dropped strands over one of her eyes. She wore faded jeans and a casual blue blouse with short sleeves rolled up.

"Sorry, didn't mean to leave you waiting." Liz maneuvered the cart beside Haddie. "I want to run a test fifteen minutes after an electrolyte infusion." She lifted a blue Nalgene bottle.

Great, more blood samples. Liz had been intent on getting Haddie a CT scan. It hadn't happened.

Liz began setting up the camera on the stainless-steel table. "Technically, we've already failed. I find no evidence that the object has been scattered back in time, as we tried with the last experiment. Our object has never shown up whole in the seven years I've lived in this house." She shrugged as she grabbed the plastic brick.

Haddie raised her eyebrows. Liz hadn't mentioned anything over the past month, but she'd been avoiding the topic for obvious reasons. *A waste of time.*

Haddie's voice squeaked. "Then why try?"

Liz motioned her silent. Placing the brick onto the table, she viewed the camera screen and adjusted it. "I'd say wait another month, but that might be the reason I didn't observe any results." She returned, tucking a random strand of brown hair behind her ear, and unwrapped a needle. Her head tilted as she cleaned and tied off Haddie's arm. As she searched for a vein, she said, "Not doing it at all would certainly explain the object never appearing."

Haddie winced at the pinprick and focused on the table. For the second time, she vowed not to do any more testing. Liz's pep talk wasn't helping.

"Any theory for moving matter in time is so — theoretical. We could do the experiment now, and everything I'm saying, which would be in the past, is changed when the brick appears farther in the past. Maybe we'll never have this conversation?" Liz shook the vial and arranged it with the empty ones.

She clicked on a tiny, black recorder. Her own nervousness showed as she aligned vials and plastic-wrapped needles.

Haddie's brain hurt when she tried to follow any thoughts about time travel. "So?"

"Blast away." Liz gestured toward the plastic brick.

Haddie's stiff joints had finally worked down to a dull

ache over the past couple of weeks. She was about to kick them all up again.

They'd hoped she could focus her intent and keep the brick whole. Move it in one piece through time, rather than scatter it throughout the past and destroy it in the process. Liz had already planned their next attempt with a living plant. If this had worked — which it hadn't. *Shut up — you're procrastinating.*

Nudge it. Haddie growled.

The air around her rang with a tone and the brick disappeared.

The nerves of her skin crackled and burned with what felt like electric fire. Joints burst with searing pain that threatened to buckle her knees.

The gray lab and metal table faded into a dark moonlit night wet with humidity. A flash from the trees in the distance sparked, and she heard a grunt from the soldier beside her. There was a second flash from the muzzle of the gun. She growled, and far across a wide river, the enemy faded from his perch in the trees. The world swam around her into dizzying brightness. Then, a helicopter beat the air above her. Bullets rang against metal. Wounded friends fired from inside the helicopter. She turned toward the two enemy soldiers racing across the field. A yell and they vanished, leaving tall grass waving in the wind.

The lab returned around Haddie.

Liz helped her sit down in the camping chair. Her hips screamed out, but she couldn't have imagined standing any longer.

"Okay," Liz said. "Almost there." She began working Haddie's left arm to draw more blood.

Haddie could barely feel the needle. Her skin crawled

with residual pain. The first test had some merit. It had proved to Dad that she'd been right. Their powers scattered their targets back in time. It didn't seem she could control it enough to send something back whole, at least not in a short time span. At the moment, it hardly seemed to matter. She wouldn't be — didn't want to be — doing any testing, at least not anytime soon.

"Drink this." Liz shoved the blue water bottle toward Haddie.

Haddie's phone buzzed in the cup holder of the camping chair.

"Ignore that." Liz shook the vial of blood she'd just taken.

"You get bossy, you know that?" Haddie winced as she popped the lid.

"It's my crime lab persona, sorry." Liz tucked back her hair and nodded toward the bottle. "Drink up."

Two red vials sat together on the table; the third, empty, waited for fifteen minutes after the electrolytes. Liz had explained her theories after the last round of blood tests. She'd wanted Dad's blood as well, but Haddie hadn't asked. Liz hadn't outright questioned whether her dad had powers, but the questions were close. Dad didn't want it known, and Haddie respected that. He'd tried to discourage these experiments.

When Liz had mentioned Meg's blood, it had struck home that Haddie's distant cousin — grandniece or what-ever — might develop these powers. It disturbed her that she might have to go through this someday. Haddie's throat tightened, and she focused on not choking on the water. *No one should have to go through this.*

Haddie handed the bottle back and motioned toward her phone. "May I please?" She needed a distraction.

Liz blushed and smiled. "Of course. Sorry. I just want this timed."

Terry had texted. "Livia wants to change up her character. No more cleric. Wizard. Still on for Thursday?"

"Cool. Yes." Haddie typed, adding an emoji. She had hoped to get David involved in their little group; he'd even stopped by one night. *I'll turn him yet.*

Livia had turned out to be a fun addition to their D&D group, except she wanted to play all the time. She'd taken the summer off classes, along with Terry. *Love.* They were good together. Their relationship kept Terry from getting too focused on the internet forums and conspiracies. He'd stopped nosing around about what Haddie knew of the demons. Terry had even started hinting about moving in with Livia, something that David and Haddie hadn't even come close to.

David added a sense of stability to Haddie's life. He liked scheduled meals and planned activities. He said that she added spontaneity to his life. She wasn't ready to move into a situation where David's order would crash into her independence.

Liz started collecting her camera, reviewing the images. "I've got a couple new supplements to add, to help with the joint aches. Still want to get you in for a CT scan." She paused, watching the screen intently and pressing buttons, then shook her head. "Still that interference to the recording right at the moment you — do your thing."

Haddie didn't know if the supplements helped. Dad had been interested in *that* part of Liz's studies. The nightmare visions were the worst for Haddie. Why had she agreed to Liz's experiments? Curiosity? Her life would be fine if she never used her abilities again — despite Dad's doom and gloom about a war.

Liz straightened her equipment on her cart and checked the time. "I'm really tempted to go back to Portland. The chance to get some trace of those demons. Next time could you just 'poof' the head and leave me the body?"

Haddie swallowed, pinched her lips shut, and closed her eyes. Her mouth tasted sour. Liz meant well. Haddie just wanted to get up and leave. She couldn't think about killing anything, even those demons. *Too much death. Like in my nightmares.*

Demons had died in Portland around those raves. But so many people had died, and Haddie blamed herself for most of them. How did someone live with that? Is that what Meg had to look forward to?

"How 'bout that Aaron? I'd be surprised if he hasn't already done some analysis." Liz paused.

Haddie felt her friend's hand on her forearm and she jumped. Tears welled up. "So many people, Liz," Haddie choked.

"I'm sorry. It's not your fault." Liz had put up with Haddie's outbursts for the past two months.

It is, Haddie thought. She didn't have to use her powers. There had been less of a choice when Liz was in danger. But, she'd made the decisions, and people had died. No more. She had school coming up this fall, and she'd taken a bear of a schedule. Like punishment.

Dad had no more issues with people hunting for Meg, that Haddie knew of.

Right now, all she had to focus on was her job. It hadn't been the same at the office since some of her issues had taken her out for days, but that wouldn't happen again.

Her phone buzzed and she pulled it up, expecting Terry. She didn't recognize the number.

"Barnes & Noble. Valley River Dr. Cookbooks. Two hours. W."

W? Haddie swallowed. It could only be Special Agent Wilkins of the FBI.

She typed, "Ok."

CHAPTER 2

Kiana Wilkins absently rubbed her ear and flipped another page. Sunk into the oversized easy chair, she had an excellent view of the entrance without highlighting her presence.

Haddie had walked in a minute before, noticeably tall, and the white hair made her stand out even more. She had a confident walk, if not a little slow today. Even when she'd been attacked outside the hotel months ago, she hadn't lost it. She would have made a good agent with some training.

No one tailed her into the store. Haddie stood in the cookbook section browsing books and looking obvious. The store had four other customers for Kiana to keep track of: two older women browsing in the mystery section and a mother with a young boy arguing about the children's books.

Haddie's powers were baffling, more so than the mutants that seemed to be popping up around the world. Those could be explained. Considering the FBI's interest in covering up the incidents with mutants, there could be a government program. Super soldier attempts. The conspiracy forums called them demons. Those same forums hadn't found Haddie or her strange abilities. No one had. *Except me.*

Kiana would have filed a complete report, including the impossible. However, superiors far removed had been clear about the account they provided. They didn't want to know the truth. They hadn't even asked any questions until much later. By then she'd begun her own discreet investigation, wary of her own department.

This leave of absence had been a risk. It would flag all through the FBI's administration. Anyone involved in the cover-up would surely notice it.

Drawing in the scent of paper and dust, Kiana took a deep breath, slid her receipt from the back of the paperback, placed it where she'd been pretending to read, and went to meet Haddie. She didn't see a better option at this point. Who could she trust?

Haddie wore a faded pair of jeans and a thin navy jacket over a pale blue-green T-shirt. Oddly, she wore a pair of thin leather gloves and sun-glasses. With the white hair, no one could help but remember her. A wig would help.

Kiana walked past and noted as Haddie flinched. She reached up and selected a small book on cooking shellfish. "Ms. Dawson." She made sure to focus on the book in her hand, hoping Haddie would take the cues.

After a brief start and an awkward glance around the room, Haddie turned back to her chocolatier book. "Wilkins. What's going on?" Her tone carried a sense of concern. She'd been worried at their last meeting as well. For good reason.

Kiana turned so she could keep an eye on the entrance. "The FBI, among other government agencies, has been systematically removing any indications of these demons, especially since our incident. I've taken a leave so that I can pursue my own investigation. I've got a couple weeks left and have located what I believe to be a viable lead. However, I would need assistance. I've staked the location out for the past week." Kiana didn't really want to involve Haddie, but there was no one else. If she had to go alone she would, but at a greater risk.

They stood silent for moment. Haddie wore a heavy base of makeup. Her skin, a lovely light brown from her mother's mixed heritage, had been dulled. Her father's pure Anglo-Saxon genes seemed recessive.

"You want me to help with a break-in, looking for information on the demons?" Less than a question, Haddie spoke reluctantly.

"Yes." Kiana had come to this decision over the past few days. She didn't expect a definitive answer immediately.

Haddie's jaw tightened. "Okay." She sounded resolved, almost angry.

Kiana touched her lips, surprised at the quick response. She had a lot to learn about this woman. Cold analytical data didn't give you a true sense of people. "Thank you. We need a secure place for me to go over the details." She drew out the slip of paper with the address from her purse, and dropped it to the floor between her and Haddie. "Tomorrow afternoon? 4:00 p.m.?"

"Yes." Haddie's response seemed pensive. Regret?

"I'll explain everything, then you can decide." Kiana returned the shellfish book, though the chipotle and tequila dish had made her hungry. "Don't use my name on the phone, or in texts. Lose my old phone number. Make sure you aren't followed."

No one new had entered after Haddie, and the original customers hadn't moved. Kiana smiled and nodded to the young cashier and headed out into the daylight. She had less than an hour drive back to her Airbnb just south of Salem. *Am I making a mistake?* Did she have a choice?

She couldn't just let this go, even if it put her job, her career, in jeopardy. But the conspiracy tainted the FBI already — could she accept that? It had plagued her for almost two months.

Haddie might not be fully committed, but the alternative would be risky.

CHAPTER 3

Thomas pulled the Mini Cooper onto Route 99 amid afternoon traffic that rumbled through the hot summer afternoon. Heat waved off the tar ahead, distorting the cars. The plastic of the interior of the car had baked all day and stunk.

He'd gotten used to the increased outings that came with a tween like Meg. It didn't make the constant rush and angst of city traffic any easier or his dislike of the entitled driver any less. He'd reached the era where speed equaled purpose. Money and hustle drove people's reasoning. Even in Goshen, along 99, they surged toward the denser city of Eugene, thriving on the condensed proximity of fellow humans. Then they cried and moaned about their stress and anxiety. He'd experienced the slower eras of life when an afternoon interacting with one another could bring true peace. How much longer could he face their drive for frenzied masses who went nowhere?

Haddie thrived in the chaos. On the rare occasion, he could force his daughter to slow down and take a ride, to visit the peaks and slopes of the surrounding mountains.

Once she got near the city, her peace faded into the background. He'd watched it over two months ago when they'd rescued Meg. Those first few days had turned long and lazy on wide stretches of road, then the turmoil over Meg's pursuers had interrupted that. Still, she settled down for the trip back west, until they reached Eugene and the pressure of people and city life had come crashing down on her again.

Meg sat in the back and kept Louis from climbing between the seats to him. The puppy, still all legs, whined and squirmed, bouncing against the back of the seat. He'd been exactly what Meg had needed — someone to care for. She'd kept to her part of the bargain, as Haddie had when she was the girl's age, walking Louis regularly, feeding him, and keeping his water fresh. Thomas hardly had to help at all. Biff had taken to their new mascot at the garage and helped clean the grease out of his fur when Louis got too curious.

Meg's next step, school, was faced with resistance. Not active rebellion. She just didn't engage when he tried to collect school supplies or discuss their upcoming schedule. He'd even tried to offer the opportunity she'd have with an art class; she had a talent for it but no interest in the school's offerings. Despite the planned movie night at Haddie's, Meg had brought her satchel for drawing.

His own reservations made it more difficult for Thomas to put Meg in school. He already had enough concern regarding those who hunted her. A public school offered more exposure, more risk.

His other option, to leave Haddie and his present life behind and homeschool Meg, didn't sit well with him either. Instead, he kept track of her pursuers.

There was a war going on. He didn't know the players or the stakes, but he'd been in enough wars to smell them.

"Will Sam be there?" Meg leaned between the seats. Straws of auburn hair dangled across her face. She still didn't smile much.

"Of course," he said. "She wouldn't miss it." At least once a week he tried to get Meg out to Haddie's, more for Sam and Rock's sake than anyone else.

"Did you call her?"

"Haddie did." He pulled onto I-5 and joined the throng. On the western horizon, lightning crackled in the dark clouds. A storm would be moving into Eugene tomorrow tonight.

When they arrived at Haddie's apartment, Louis had already been leashed, and Meg's satchel was wrapped over her shoulder. She didn't wait for him to put it into park before her door opened.

Wincing at his complaining joints, Thomas climbed out, glancing over at Haddie's Fat Boy parked under the overhang. The RAV4 needed a wash, though it looked better than after that demon had torn into it earlier in the summer. His body man had not asked too many questions, and he'd gotten zero answers.

Haddie's apartment sat on the upper floor inside one block of three-story apartments that crowded into a square at the end of a city block. They'd planted bushes and trees everywhere as if to block out the city itself. The dogwood had stopped blooming this late in the summer, but the evergreen huckleberry bushes misted flowers along their edges. He passed a trail of earthy, growing scents.

He climbed the stairs slowly. Already, Sam's voice greeted Meg, and Louis yapped. Someone had recently scrubbed the walls with a perfumed cleaner; he preferred the baking plastic.

Haddie popped out the door, white hair falling over her shoulders. She needed to get that dyed.

"Hey, Dad. Coffee's brewing."

He grunted. "Not that flavored crap."

Haddie snorted. "No. That was my fault, didn't even look at it."

She'd caked on the makeup again.

Thomas stopped and nodded toward her, dropping his voice. "Liz again?"

"Yeah." She seemed distracted, unsettled. "Later."

He nodded and climbed up the rest of the way. Holding the door, he motioned her ahead of him.

Sam sat on the floor as Louis bounced and wiggled over Haddie's black Pitbull, Rock. Dyed black hair hung straight down over her shoulder. She wore a pink, blue, and white trans pride T-shirt and jean shorts. "Hey T. Louis has grown since last week."

He grunted and closed the door. Wiping his hair back, he could smell the coffee mixing with some spiced bean dish. Haddie's apartment looked like a mess, as usual. Clothes scattered across most of the available surfaces. Her desk on the far wall had stacks of folios and books piled beside and behind the monitor.

Her room at the garage had been worse. Meg tended to keep it neat, though Louis didn't help.

Rock shook off Louis and came to sniff Thomas, who began scratching him behind the ears where he liked it best. They both ignored the puppy running around them and jumping up with a whimper at being left out.

Haddie brought out a cup of black coffee and waited as he patted Rock. "He likes that you visit more."

They'd had a rough spell for a while; Thomas hadn't been particularly welcome at the apartment. That was last year. A lot had changed since then. He sipped the coffee. Black, but with an inherent creaminess, and rich enough that he nodded in appreciation. "I come for the coffee."

She smiled, but something bothered her.

Liz and Meg ignored them, playing with Rock and Louis.

He nodded toward Haddie's bedroom.

She grimaced, but led the way. Passing through the short hall made by the bathroom and closet, she kicked clothes out of his way.

"What's going on?" he asked. "Liz's experiments?"

Haddie dropped down to sit on the bed. "Yeah. That was a bust." She shook her head. "No. I met up with Special Agent Wilkins today. Actually, she's on a leave of absence."

Thomas waited, quietly. He'd always been suspicious when nothing had come from Haddie's display in front of the FBI. It had made no sense, cover-up or not.

"She's still tracking the demons," Haddie said. "Found out something that she wants to investigate — I don't have the details. I'm meeting with her tomorrow."

"Why?" he asked. She didn't need to get involved with the FBI. They couldn't be trusted.

"She needs my help."

"Don't." He bit down as soon as he said it. *Mistake*.

Haddie's jaw tightened. "I'm just going to see what's going on."

No, she'd end up on another disaster like the raves. He couldn't fault her for wanting to help her friend Liz, but this was no friend. He knew his arguing with her would just set her in motion in the opposite direction. He couldn't blame her, though; he'd raised her to be independent.

"Okay. Sorry. I get worried." He glanced back toward the living room. "You'll keep me up to date on it? When do you meet up with her?"

"Tomorrow." She still seemed annoyed. "How's your little war going?"

He sipped at his coffee. Meg and Sam chattered excitedly in the other room. "Nothing new. The two that we have eyes on are still searching the area and the dead uncle's family. Haven't led us anywhere."

Thomas had hoped that those who still searched for Meg would lead him up the organization of those that had killed the descendants of his last identity. The people he could find were just grunts. Haddie disliked his search, much like his present concern with her FBI agent. He needed to find the leaders. Then he could make sure they weren't sniffing around Eugene.

He tilted his head back toward the living room. "Let's go watch a movie. Take a break. You look like you need one."

He'd have to keep track of Haddie again. She'd get herself on a cause quicker than he could follow, and without warning. He didn't trust Wilkins. Any authority. Even if she had broken with the FBI. Might be worse. They could have their eye on Wilkins and catch Haddie in their sight.

Thomas walked out to find Sam looking through Meg's drawings. Haddie stepped up beside him and put her hand on his shoulder.

Sam had stopped on a pencil sketch of Thomas. It looked like Meg had added drooping wings. Dragon, devil, or angel?

CHAPTER 4

HADDIE SORTED through the printouts and tucked them into bright yellow folders. Her face felt stiff from the heavy makeup covering the purpura. The room smelled of electricity and ozone from the copy machine as it groaned out the last few pages.

The firm's copy room, an alcove at the back of the office, had a smell that reminded Haddie of her dad's garage. Not the same scents, but it had a work aroma — a mood of its own. Metal shelving lining the walls added to the effect, except here they held paper and ink instead of oil cans and parts.

She ached still, but the workload this morning required standing and filling boxes for a case that had just closed. Andrea had left a note on Haddie's keyboard before heading off to the courthouse. The list looked light, and Haddie needed to get out early to meet with Wilkins.

The copies had begun fading across the law firm's logo, so Haddie had left her own note for Josh. He usually handled everything in the copy room, if he showed up.

Haddie labeled one of the boxes and lugged it into the back office.

"Josh — will be late." Grace spoke from her cubicle without looking up, the blue light of her monitor highlighting her cheeks and nose. She had beautiful, brown features that could have served her well as a model or actress. She didn't smile, but her tone held a smirk. As Andrea's paralegal and backbone of the company, she kept a discreet work demeanor that Haddie could learn from. However, they all looked forward to Josh's excuses.

Dropping her box in front of Josh's cubicle, Haddie stepped over to lean on Grace's. "Do tell."

"Evidently, a semi carrying an extra wide snowplow jackknifed on Josh's street. He's helping the paramedics." Grace never broke a smile, but her tone hinted at her amusement.

"In the middle of summer?"

Grace paused her typing and looked up. The slightest hint of a smile around her eyes. "That's your only concern?" She shook her head. "I've loaded the Dickens brief on the drive; Andrea wants you to proof and look up some information. I've bracketed the spots."

"She left me a note." Haddie straightened up, preparing to head back to finish her first task on her list.

"My niece, Cathy, is moving to Eugene." Grace leaned back into her chair. "She's enrolled at the university and is looking for an apartment. She's staying with me until she finds one."

Haddie paused. Grace never talked about her personal life, not even when Haddie or Josh prodded for information. "What major?"

"Business." Grace absently tapped her armrest. "Would you be willing to give her some pointers? Some parts of town are better than others, and some apartments are better than others."

"Of course." Haddie smiled. "There are spots open in my complex." Grace had never asked for a favor in all the time Haddie had interned at the firm, but she'd helped Haddie plenty.

"Thank you." Grace reached down and took her phone out of her purse. "I'll send you both contact information."

"I'll be happy to help." Haddie headed back to the copy room, still smiling. She could hear her phone vibrate in her cubicle.

It would be nice to help Grace and maybe learn a little about her. The paralegal's personal life had remained a closed book. Haddie had respected that. With Josh's fantasy world and Grace's close-lipped aspects, Haddie felt like she showed everything. But, she didn't. In fact, she had deeper secrets than either of them likely ever would.

Her phone vibrated as she carried out the second box. Their back office had been emptied last Friday. Only two banker's boxes shared the room with the three cubicles. Often there were stacks. The room always stayed musty, unless Josh brewed his earthy, pungent teas.

Haddie grimaced and sighed as she dropped into her seat. Her hips felt stiff. She wouldn't be doing any of Liz's tests any time soon. Grace had never asked about the gloves, but everyone knew about Haddie's supposed rash. Andrea hadn't commented.

She flipped over her phone. Grace had sent her niece's contact. Cathy Carter.

Below, Haddie had a text from Aaron. It had been a month since she'd last heard from the scientist. "Check out this link. I've found a connection to this group. Have you seen or heard anything about them?"

Haddie clicked on it. While she waited for the website to load, she glanced at the work on her screen and the yellow note stuck on the side of the monitor. She needed to clear Andrea's list so she could get out early and meet with Wilkins. Andrea might not even be in today. The last two weeks she'd been heavy on a case — the one Haddie just boxed up.

The site loaded. The header had the name in bold red letters across black, "Unceasing." Her lips tightened. She'd seen this somewhere. The logo, an infinity symbol with a double-cross, looked familiar.

The page had one statement. "Our unending goal: A civilization reprieved of the psychosis of war and without the manacles of technology, where man is free to prosper and rise to a greater glory and purpose under the care of their true and eternal gods."

Haddie raised her eyebrows. How did this tie into the demons? Or raves? Or whatever the yellow-hazed faces were controlled by? Eternal and unceasing had an eerie resemblance to Dad's immortality. So, someone like him who considered themselves a god? He'd want to know about this.

Unceasing. She'd seen it spray-painted on a wall near the first rave site. Something about neon gods. It had been a rough day; it was surprising that she remembered that much.

Haddie texted, "Remember seeing it as graffiti near one of the rave sites. The first one in Portland. There was a second tag about neon gods. How did you find it?"

Aaron didn't respond. It had taken her a few minutes to get to his text. She would mention the website to Wilkins as well as Dad. Had Aaron mentioned it to Terry? He'd go nuts over it.

She texted Aaron again, "Does Terry know about this?"

Haddie slid the phone to the side of her mousepad.

Focus. She needed get Andrea's work done. Her internship had suffered with everything that had gone on over the past few months — distracting her. There had been days she expected Andrea to let her go.

Should she mention Wilkins to Aaron? Maybe after the meeting.

Haddie opened the Dickens brief on the firm's drive. Easiest task on the list. A quick line through her list. She'd begun proofing when Grace's phone rang.

"Done," Grace said. "Done and done. Haddie has it."

Haddie swallowed. Andrea.

"He's late. No idea." Grace leaned closer to the wall between their cubicles. "Haddie, Andrea."

The light blinked on Haddie's office phone. "Hi," she answered.

Andrea's tone sounded exasperated. "Haddie. I'm taking over the Dickens case. It's mid trial so I need the case notes from the previous attorney — Charles Seism. I'll need them in the morning. Go get them after you finish the list. You can bring them with you to work tomorrow."

"Of course." Haddie raised her eyebrows. She wouldn't have to explain leaving early for Wilkins.

Andrea had paused. "Thanks."

The line disconnected and Haddie put down the phone. This would be a good chance for her to win some bonus points. Josh usually ran these kinds of errands, but Haddie could get her work done and his. She'd never heard of the attorney.

Her email flashed. Grace had sent the address; it was across the river in Springfield. Not too bad. "Thanks," Haddie said.

She had lunch planned nearby with David. Haddie avoided overnights the first few days after Liz's experiments, but he was working in Eugene today and it would seem odd if she hadn't accepted. He'd seen the purpura before and appeared to believe the rash excuse. She imagined he did from the way he would check up on her and offer suggestions. *I hate lying to him.*

Her cell vibrated; Grace's niece called. Haddie took a deep breath, eyes flicking back up to the brief on her screen. "Hi, Cathy?"

"Hey. Yes, this is Cathy, Gracey's niece. She says you go to the University and might know some decent areas to look for apartments. Is it okay that I called?" The woman had the same solid, confident tone that Grace did. Sparkier though.

Haddie smiled. "For Gracey's family, anytime."

"Don't start," Grace said quietly from the other side of the cubicle wall.

"In fact," Haddie said, "there's spots open in my apartments. They're close and safe. Great neighborhood." The break-in at her apartment didn't count; that had been an attempted hit.

"What time are you there after work? Could you introduce me? I mean, if that's okay."

"Sure." Haddie blinked. She had expected to offer some sage words of advice, but if it meant helping Grace, then she'd do it. "The office is open 'til nine." Haddie planned on meeting with Wilkins at 4:00. An hour? Then, she needed to head back to Springfield and pick up the Dickens files. "How about 6:30 to be safe?"

"That would be great. Thank you. I mean it." Cathy paused. "Really weird, all this out on my own stuff."

"Happy to help. You'll like Eugene." Haddie scrolled down the briefing, proofing as she went. Her back ached.

"Okay, thanks. See you tonight. Bye."

Haddie looked forward to meeting Cathy. Forthright like Grace, but a lot chattier.

"Thanks," Grace said.

Haddie smiled. It felt good to be able to help Grace for once. She'd covered Haddie on so many occasions that she couldn't keep track.

Aaron responded before she finished proofing the brief. "Terry was the one who found the original graffiti tag in a picture from one of the California raves. We've got a group now that's been posting sightings of the graffiti wherever it shows up. That's why I asked you. Did you get pictures? You mentioned neon gods."

"Yes, but no pics." She waited a moment, unsure if they were done.

Terry was still digging around about the raves. He called *her* obsessive. They hadn't discussed much since she'd met with him and Aaron. Keeping him shut out of the details was for his own good. There'd been no option with Liz.

She spun her hair in a ball at the base of her neck, staring at her phone. Starting, she realized her cell screen had turned off and her actual work on the computer sat unattended. *Focus.* She had a list of things to do tonight.

Haddie managed to get all but one item on the list done by lunch. Toby had left the reception desk empty to eat with her sister. Andrea had no appointments and hadn't shown up; she probably worked from home after court. Grace ate Thai take-out that momentarily filled their office with spice and curry that Haddie could taste from the smell alone.

Haddie stood and stuffed her phone in her pocket. "I'm going to go grab Chinese. I need some fresh air."

Leaving Grace alone, the office felt empty. Toby's reception desk, neat with only a rinsed coffee mug and her computer, protruded into the waiting area.

Hot humid air wrapped Haddie as she stepped outside. The west had darkened with clouds and lightning, but above, the sun shone through light wisps of white.

Josh's black Jeep Cherokee was parked in the lot, not far from the front of the office. She always smirked at the antique license tag - an '87 if she remembered correctly. Dented, he'd kept it painted, though it looked like he did it by hand.

He sat in the front seat; she could tell from the silhouette. Why hadn't he come in? She approached along the driver's side and could see his face in the mirror. Unusually somber, as if deep in thought. She stood by the window and he didn't react. Windows up and engine off, it had to be getting hot inside. In the back seat, a cardboard box had piles of paperbacks, fantasy or science fiction from the covers. He wore a lime green and pink Hawaiian shirt.

Haddie tapped the window and Josh jerked toward her.

Instantly a smile came to his face and he cranked down his window. "I was trying to remember the lyrics to a song."

Haddie raised her eyebrows. Whatever odd feeling she'd had faded. "What song?"

"That's just it, I don't know," he said.

Haddie sighed. Normal Josh. "Are you heading in?"

"No. We've got a sinkhole that I need to check on down south. I'll be done by tomorrow morning though. I thought I could squeeze in a little work, but I got caught up reading. Your rash again, I see. We need to protect the aquifers."

Haddie glanced at the books, opened her mouth, and stopped. "Bye, Josh. See you in the morning."

He cranked up his window. "Less TV Haddie, that's what Eugene needs."

Across the street, a Black woman leaned against a tree, turning as Haddie looked. She wore a dark green cap that pushed her curls out and around her face. Regretting the minute she'd wasted standing in the sun, Haddie turned toward the alley behind the law firm. She'd be done with her work early, then she could get with Wilkins. Curiosity had gotten the better of her, but if this led to some information about the demons, it might be worth it.

Dad said it was war. After what she read on the Unceasing website, maybe he'd been right. However, it felt more like a hostile takeover by a corporation. The raves had been all about money. The demons and the coerced men were just their muscle. But who was behind all this?

Haddie looked back as she reached the corner. Josh still sat in his Jeep. Odd. *Okay, a different odd.* Had she glimpsed some part of him that he didn't normally show them at the office?

She cut through the alley and headed toward a hedge of young bamboo. Behind, in the outdoor seating, the smell of burgers and fried food hung under the umbrellas. David had already gotten a table for them. A cup of hot tea sat beside a glass filled with ice; he had his usual espresso.

"Thank you." Haddie motioned toward the tea as she approached.

David bounced up with a smile and kissed her. "I got here early. She just brought the tea." His bright eyes narrowed, inspecting her makeup. "A flare-up?"

Haddie nodded and sat down. "Yeah, no big deal." She grabbed the menu off the table, though she'd be ordering the mac and cheese. "I'm starving. Work is crazy this morning.

I've got to run over and get some files this afternoon, but have to finish everything on my desk first."

"Are things better with Andrea?" he asked.

David had listened to her griping last month when she'd gone back to work after the raves. Andrea had accepted the story about the car accident, but had still seemed offish. "Better. Today she's got me doing Josh's work while he's out."

"Again?" David gestured into the air, palm up, as if incredulous.

Haddie shrugged. She'd gotten used to Josh's absences and forgot how much she mentioned them. "No big deal. I don't have a lot on my desk." Putting the menu down, she poured the hot tea over the ice. "What's your schedule this week?"

"Off this afternoon, south Tuesday and Wednesday. You want to have dinner at my place tonight?" He offered a sweet smile.

Inside, Haddie winced. She didn't want to do the whole overnight without makeup considering how soon it was after using her powers. "I've been craving pizza, but I don't know how late I'll be." She had no idea what Wilkins wanted or how long meeting with Cathy would take. "It could be as late as 7:30."

"The place in Springfield? You want to call me after you get out of work?"

Haddie nodded, then took a sip of her tea. She wanted to be with David, but she already had Andrea's files on her list, then the meetings. *I'll make it happen.*

PART 2

The Gates are locked, so we have known only these wives and husbands, these children of ours.

CHAPTER 5

HADDIE DROVE her RAV4 west toward the address that Wilkins had given her. She would have ridden her bike, just to relax, but a storm moved in with a bank of dark clouds sparked with lightning.

Rush hour hadn't started yet, so 11th Avenue still ran smoothly. Work had gone well — quiet with just the three of them. All of Andrea's list had gotten crossed off, and Haddie had until seven to get the Dickens files. The day had gone well, and still her chest felt tight with dread.

Did she really want to get caught up in Wilkins' plan? She couldn't really let go of wanting to know more about the demons. There seemed to be some connection between them and people like her with power. She didn't have much to base that on, other than their presence around the woman, Sameedha, who'd run the raves. Aaron had introduced demons to Liz and Haddie when they'd first met him, and Terry had been gathering his own information. Sameedha hadn't been the source. Haddie believed it still had to do with someone who had powers, like herself and Dad.

She took a deep breath as she passed the cycle parts store with their scooters out front. They'd always looked like children's toys, but she'd considered them differently after a trip to the Bahamas the summer after her first year in college — Derrick had been her boyfriend at the time. Fun.

Her turn would be at the next light. Waiting, she took a sip of still warm tea while she watched the convenience store.

Terry had been apologetic for not letting her know about the Unceasing forums. Rightly, he thought she didn't want to be reminded of the raves or demons. *And yet, here I am, about to meet with Wilkins.* Terry ached to know more. Her secrets hurt him, but he said he understood.

She turned left and the sky divided into two halves. The right, toward the west, hung low with dark clouds and lightning. Above and to the east, bright blue stretched to the rolling horizon in the south. The road cut through a rural industrial area where yellow equipment clustered at the edge of a fence, as if waiting to graze freely. The buildings were mostly warehouse-sized with spacious parking lots, wire fences, and plenty of fields between.

Early for their meeting, she turned left into the parking lot of a small gray-blue office building with a "For Sale" sign leaning against the front. It seemed small compared to the warehouse of a carpet cleaning business on one side and what looked like a large medical complex on the other. A bay window in the front of the office showed a dark, empty interior.

She started to park in the front until Wilkins detached from where she leaned near the back and gestured for Haddie to park behind the building. The agent wore a blue tank top and jeans so faded they almost looked white. Despite the heat, a dark green shawl draped over her shoulders, possibly to cover a holster. Over her shoulder she had her small purse. Her black curls had grown out a little since their encounter at the Portland hotel.

Haddie parked in the back beside a silver Ford Fusion, a rental from the sticker. She grabbed her phone and texted David. "Running a bit late. Call you soon." The air hung heavy, smelling of the promise of rain.

Wilkins watched the street from her position at the corner of the building. A brown patch of wet gravel and dirt lay glistening on the drive beside the agent.

"You think someone's following me?" Haddie stepped up beside the woman.

"Not likely. The FBI would have contacted me if they had any interest in you." Still, Wilkins watched as she walked along the side to a red door.

A lock box hung from the knob, but Wilkins already had the key. She pulled a pair of nitrile gloves out of her purse and put them on. Were they breaking in?

"How'd you get the key?" Haddie asked.

"Found a lazy realtor. They gave me the lock box code." Wilkins opened the door. "I told them I wanted to open a tattoo shop."

An FBI Special Agent had conned their way into a meeting place — why would she need to do that? Haddie knew that Wilkins didn't trust her superiors anymore. That had become obvious. Otherwise, Haddie might have ended up with government testing far worse than Liz's. She still didn't trust the situation. However, if Wilkins wasn't being honest, they wouldn't have to trick Haddie; they'd just pick her up and no one would hear from Haddie again. She needed to know about the demons, and Wilkins seemed to have some information and needed Haddie's help. Perhaps they could work with each other.

As they entered, cool air with the scent of pine cleaner welcomed them. A short hall led to an empty room ahead, but Wilkins turned right into an office with a desk pulled into the center. A swivel chair sat in the corner. She didn't turn on the fluorescent light above.

David texted back a quick response, "No problem, I love you. See you soon."

Haddie replied and tucked her phone away.

Pulling a folded paper from her purse, Wilkins studied Haddie. "Why did you agree?"

"To meet you?"

"Yes."

Good question, thought Haddie.

CHAPTER 6

Kiana held the plans, waiting for Haddie's response. Sweat trickled along her side, under the holster, and down her stomach.

Haddie seemed nervous. From what Kiana had seen, this law intern could make people vanish. And, she had handled the shooter better than expected. *Can I trust her?* The woman seemed intense, yet scattered somehow. It was a dangerous mix in a pinch. However, the abuse the woman had gone through around the Harold Holmes case had given Kiana some respect for her.

What were the gloves about? They didn't go with the blue business blouse. She owned a bike; riding that, they would make sense, but she'd driven up in an SUV. Did she bleach her hair white? Her records stated black hair. She wore heavy makeup.

Haddie seemed to deliberate her answer before she finally spoke. "I'm here because I want to understand what is going on."

Kiana snorted. "You know more than I do, I'm sure."

The end of her statement sounded bitter. She hadn't meant it to.

She hadn't dared use FBI resources to investigate Portland. Even coming to Eugene had been a risk. It had been obvious that Haddie didn't intend to offer any information when she was approached over a month ago. Everything Kiana had done since had been as low-key as possible. Her last assignment had been in north Washington state, before she'd requested leave.

She had to admit, part of the reason she'd asked Haddie to help had been a faint hope that the woman would open up. It seemed they were on the same side, though Kiana couldn't figure out who the players were.

Haddie stood awkwardly obstinate, silent, and waiting.

Kiana opened her sketches of the building. "I followed the shooter from the incident at the Portland hotel. His real name was Don Mack. An equipment operator out of north Texas. Nothing to lead anyone to believe he would end up as hired muscle." She paused, waiting to see if Haddie reacted to the name or description.

Kiana continued, "He rented a car on the east coast of Oregon. A town called Coos Bay." She watched Haddie's expressions as she flattened out her drawings. "The car was abandoned in Portland, after –"

"After I threw him into a passing car," Haddie finished.

Kiana noticed Haddie's jaw tightened and her lips flattened. She might have had some regret. *Good.* "I got into the car's GPS, and he had frequent stops at this building. I thought at first he'd been going to the bar across the street, but after staking out the area, I'm sure it was this office upstairs. They have a lot of odd visitors during all hours of the day and night. Part of the reason I need your help."

"What do you expect to find there?" Haddie nervously

twisted her white hair into a knot, tilting her head as she looked down at the sketch.

A question I've been asking myself. "Something, anything that will give me another lead on who these people are." Kiana pointed to the office on her drawing. "I'll need time for that. There don't seem to be any regular employees. The lock is a keypad, and I don't see any indication of an alarm system. People just come and go; sometimes they're in and out, other times they stay for eight hours. If I had resources, I'd track their license plates or use facial recognition. Some are regulars, some are one-offs. But I've only watched for a week."

Kiana had initially expected to figure out the employees' schedule and plan an opportune time to get inside.

"Why me?" Haddie asked.

"Because they wanted to kill you." Kiana shrugged. "I figured I could trust you not to be working with them." Paranoia had struck the moment a supervisor above hers had provided an alternate report. Kiana's entire world had been turned upside down. Everything she'd believed about the FBI fell apart, but she still hoped that only a small portion had rotted. "Do you know why they were after you?" she asked.

Haddie scoffed. "Sticking my nose where it doesn't belong — like now." She pointed to the drawing.

Kiana felt a stab of guilt. "Are you okay with taking the risk?"

"Depends. What do you want me to do?"

"Watch the entrance. Nothing else." Kiana gestured over the drawings. "Call me if I get company. I've got a couple back escape routes available."

Haddie nodded. "So, maybe you end up with names, locations — what then?"

"Investigate. Find these people if I can. Stake out any locations." Kiana shrugged. "It really depends what I find and if there's any context."

It sounded like Haddie had decided to go. Even her response yesterday had been a bit hasty. Was the woman naturally rash? That could make for a disaster. She seemed less nervous – still intense, but not as scattered. Her questions were reasonable, logical.

Kiana had learned that Haddie had been investigating something in Portland that day. What though? There had been nothing in the police blotter to indicate any disturbance, except for the attack in front of the hotel. A fire had taken down an abandoned building.

"Why are you wearing gloves?" Kiana surprised herself with the question. "You wore those yesterday."

Haddie looked away as if blushing. "I get a rash." She seemed about to says something else, then stopped. "When are you looking to do this?"

Kiana sighed. "Soon as possible. I don't have much leave left. Tomorrow night? Around midnight?"

Haddie raised her eyebrows. "Sooner than I expected, but okay." She tapped the table. "Just lookout. Call you if someone enters?

"That's it."

At least Haddie played it safe. Kiana had been concerned that the woman would come up with some plan of her own and want to barge into the office to interrogate someone.

After a few more questions, it had barely taken thirty minutes to go over the details. Their meeting had gone well. Haddie seemed curious about the activity at the office and the man she'd killed in front of the hotel. None of it gave Kiana any hint of what Haddie had been involved with in

Portland. The more they talked, though, it seemed Haddie might loosen up.

Kiana had a little while to investigate before her leave ended and she had to return to the FBI. They seemed to have forgotten her. Maybe by the time she went back, she might know who influenced them, have some answers at least.

Thunder rumbled outside as they made to leave. She had a plan, and it looked like they were committed for tomorrow night.

CHAPTER 7

Haddie answered her phone, walking down the hall behind Wilkins. Cathy called just as they were preparing to leave.

"Hi," Haddie said.

"I'm sorry to call. I know we're meeting in two hours, but I'm thinking of stopping off at a place west of the university before then. Wanted your thoughts on the area." City traffic in the background around Cathy muffled her voice.

Ahead of Haddie, Wilkins stepped out the red door into a gray afternoon with a darkened sky. The wind roughed the grass bordering the next lot, and the scent of rain blew into the hall on moist air. The storm was moving into Eugene. Haddie would have just enough time to get Andrea's files and be back home before meeting Cathy.

The traffic rumbled through the phone in one ear, and the wind whistled into their meeting place. Wilkins held the door, waiting to lock it.

Haddie stepped out and didn't immediately recognize

the sound of a gunshot. Splinters off the corner of the door burst from the red paint, sprinkling into her hair.

Wilkins jumped away, reaching for her gun.

A man in a black T-shirt fired again. Haddie dropped her phone and crouched. She was close enough to smell the gunpowder and see the gun in his hand clearly.

Standing farther back, by her car, a second man wore red. She flinched as his muzzle flashed.

Bullets tore into the door.

Reacting, Haddie yelled. She could have jumped inside and left Wilkins to herself; instead, her tone rang in the air around her. Familiar and eerie, it pushed through the wind.

The man in the black shirt faded along with his gun and the flash from his muzzle.

Pain crackled along Haddie's skin. The clothes and wind against her added to the torture. Kneeling, her joints throbbed. The visions blacked out the blue sky above the man in the red shirt. Gunfire came with her manifested images, somewhere in the dark jungles of southeast Asia. She, through her father's eyes, watched more die with her family's powers.

Disoriented, she sagged.

Wind and gray sky flooded back around her. The moist smells returned. Wilkins had killed the other man. His body lay on packed gravel and dirt.

Red and brown splinters scattered the ground around Haddie. Trembling, she grabbed her phone. She rested on one knee, joints burning. Why had she automatically used her powers? It seemed to be a natural reaction to danger.

Who had they been after? *Wilkins or me?*

"Let's go," Wilkins said, heading toward their cars and the dead man. She stopped and offered a hand as Haddie delayed. "We need to get out of here. Someone in one of these businesses will have called the police."

Grimacing, Haddie pushed aching joints into standing. The clouds above held back the rain, but the air smelled like mist. She shoved her phone in her pocket and lumbered after Wilkins. They passed the brown, wet patch where the shooter Haddie had killed had been standing. This time, Haddie carefully walked around it.

Her skin chafed and protested under the gloves. It would ease soon, leaving another round of purpura to add to those left from Liz's experiments.

"Follow me," Wilkins said.

The man in red lay behind a white Chevy Malibu with rear-end damage that had been cheaply repaired. Should they check for ID? These hadn't been demons or coerced — she would have seen that.

Haddie glanced behind the office, where the yellow vans of carpet cleaners parked. She couldn't see anyone watching. Behind the lot where they parked, past blue dumpsters, a privacy fence blocked the warehouse behind them. How could they have not heard the gunshots? Did it sound like thunder?

Wilkins had already climbed in her rental as Haddie fumbled with her door handle to the RAV4. Follow Wilkins where? Haddie did have questions, and they certainly couldn't stand here and talk.

As Haddie pulled in behind Wilkins, the storm wall approached from the west. Black clouds dropped a sheet of rain halfway across a brown grassy field across the street. Trucks parked farther away disappeared under the gray.

Wilkins turned right. Haddie followed, driving past the carpet cleaner's warehouse. A pair of men stood in the open bay, looking at the storm.

Still shaking, she reached for her tea. Where was Wilkins going? The plan to break into the office suddenly seemed rash and dangerous. *What am I doing?*

The rain hit. Crawling across the road, the downpour slowed Wilkins ahead. They joined rush hour traffic at 11th Avenue and Wilkins continued north toward Bethel. The same questions repeated in Haddie's head, but she couldn't know for sure that their attackers had been after Wilkins. Did this mean they'd abandon the break-in? Somehow, despite Haddie's reservations, this disappointed her.

Learning the truth about the man she'd killed, Don Mack, stoked her curiosity. The news had reported him under a different name, Seth Jackson, a parolee who had done time for drug trafficking. Haddie trusted Wilkins more than the news. All of it had been fabricated.

Wilkins turned them east, toward the railroad and the river. Ten minutes after they left their meeting place, they pulled into a parking lot behind a takeout coffee business. Haddie pulled into the space beside Wilkins' rental. The rain blotted out anything a few feet from their cars.

Wilkins jumped into Haddie's passenger seat, dripping water. Rain dotted the woman's curls. "I'm sorry," she said.

Haddie raised her eyebrows. "Why?" Had Wilkins suspected they were in danger?

"I didn't think they were that close to finding out what I was doing. I've been a fool." Wilkins rubbed her ear and frowned. "I'm still going through with the break-in, but you should reconsider."

Perhaps. However, she couldn't drop the idea of finding out who had been behind the raves, other than Sameedha. Who had sent Don Mack and the demon to attack her? Sameedha, or her mentor? In that one quick conversation, there had seemed some organization. The demons and the coerced as their muscle supported that. Dad's idea of a war had merit.

Wilkins continued, "I'm assuming that those men were connected with the people I've been trailing. I've got to assume that my rental car is what led them to us. I'm only using a burner, so it's not my phone. That means my Airbnb south of Salem is at risk as well. I'll have to be careful and get everything out. All my files are there." She seemed shaken from the attack.

Haddie expected an FBI agent to be emotionless and controlled, but this was just another woman, one exposed to the strange impossibilities that surrounded Haddie's life. Did the FBI have something to do with the attack, or the people she investigated? Were they the same? Either way, Wilkins would most likely have to go into hiding. Maybe Dad could help.

"Wilkins," Haddie said, "I might have someone who can help. Find a safe place, that is."

The woman looked over, searching Haddie's face. Her expression withered, suddenly seeming broken. "Thank you. Call me Kiana, please."

Haddie understood how the woman felt. Sometimes she hated asking for help, or accepting it. It made her feel less capable. Less than. She'd gotten used to it since all this had started with Harold Holmes. Without the people in her life, there would be little chance she would have made it. Wilkins — Kiana — had no one.

"I'll follow you, so we can pick up your files, and leave your car there. On the way, I'll call my friend. We'll get through this, Kiana."

Kiana stared out at the downpour. "Okay. We'll need to be careful. They could be watching my place. The rain might help. I've got a spot you can park out of sight; I'll leave my rental there and walk over. I'm running out of options, so — thank you."

Haddie's joints wanted to lie down and rest, not drive. Traffic on I-5 would be a mess with this rain.

"What is it that you do?" Kiana asked. "To make them disappear?"

Haddie shrugged. She had tried to explain to Liz. "I don't know. Something comes through me, like a song, a single note. Sometimes, I don't even think about it — just react. It's instinctive, like blocking a punch."

Lightning froze the rain into a static moment, and silhouetted the vague shape of a building ahead of them.

"We should go," Haddie said. "I've got files to pick up for work tonight."

She groaned and reached for her phone. David expected a call. She took a deep breath and texted, "I've got to cancel for tonight. Work. Still haven't picked up the files." *A partial lie.*

Haddie waited, knotting damp hair in her left hand.

It took a moment for David to respond. "Ok."

She winced. He never texted that. Haddie hadn't cancelled any of their plans since Portland and the raves. David had been understanding, hadn't pushed too hard for answers, and had seemed to let it go, but she imagined he'd been upset by the whole situation.

"I love you," she texted. She almost promised to call tonight, but resisted. *No promises to break.*

She dreaded his response, imagining a simple "ok."

Instead, he followed with, "I love you."

Haddie stared for a moment. *He deserves better*. Taking a deep breath, she tucked her phone away. "Let's do this."

CHAPTER 8

THOMAS PULLED off I-5 at the exit for Creswell in the pounding deluge. Traffic had devolved into cars with emergency lights flashing, barely able to keep their lanes. Riding in it wasn't bad, if the cars could keep a constant pace and avoid drifting across lines. As much as it rained in Oregon, he'd have thought they would learn to drive in it, or at least pull off for a cup of coffee and wait it out. Instead, they crept along to avoid careening into each other. There were always those, however, who blindly raced at full speed, surprised to find some car blocking their path when they only had a few car lengths of visibility. He'd kept a steady pace and managed to avoid any real concerns on his Shovelhead. A cleansing storm like this did his soul good. Still, it would be good to stop for a minute, maybe get a cup of coffee himself.

Creswell straddled both sides of I-5. On the east it formed a neat grid of streets with shops and neighborhoods. A few trees scattered along the RV park next to the off-ramp, but most of the property held neat rows of campers hunkered in against the rain. Lightning splashed in the rain above, adding a quick level of detail to the community; vehicles, suddenly distinct, displayed various colors and designs. A table with an attached umbrella had blown against a silver RV and struggled to search out another resting place.

Water pooled and flowed along the gutters at the traffic light, and Thomas turned west. At the corner of the entrance to the park, a takeout restaurant had used an old gas station overhang, and two cars waited there. The field on the other corner had flooded and threatened to spill into the street. He rumbled into the entrance of the RV park and veered left for the little office. The dull brown shanty had a beat-up Ford truck parked close to the front. Miguel worked today. Good news. He didn't go for too much banter.

Thomas pulled up and killed the bike, checking the stand before he got off. Rain had seeped through his gear around his neck, so he paused on the porch to loosen his jacket and look through the windows. Miguel waited inside alone, busy with his phone.

Thomas opened the door with the slow creak of a hinge while the wind fought to tear it from his hands and slam into the office. Stale snacks lined the wall by the door. More expensive supplies, like chargers and aspirin, were kept behind the counter. The compressor on the soda cooler complained about the heat and humidity.

"Hey, Mr. Regis, haven't seen you in a couple months. Nice day for a ride." Miguel barely glanced up from his phone.

"Working south. New Mexico." Thomas stepped up to the counter. "Should have expected rain this far north."

Miguel nodded, absently trailing a finger along the mailboxes. "Think you just got something yesterday."

Thomas eyed his box, waiting until Miguel found it. USPS had sent the alert last night. He had two contacts that used this drop. Both monitored the people searching for Meg. Today, he expected a name from Crocus, his man from Utah.

"Here it is." Miguel flipped open the box and pulled out an envelope. "How long you here for?"

Thomas shrugged, taking the letter. Postmarked Idaho. "Who knows? They said I got a week, but you know how that goes. Trish working the diner today?"

Miguel smiled. "Yeah, but she got a darling now."

Thomas waved the letter over his shoulder as he headed out into the storm. "You're trying to break my heart, Miguel."

He'd kept this drop for five years, and Miguel had worked at the park the entire time. It helped keep the identity Thomas had created viable with the newer staff. Even if he didn't get a message, he checked in every other month.

The porch kept the worst of the rain off as Thomas opened the letter. Two pages, one blank, and the inner one had the name Barbara Stevens. Hell, could it have been a more common name? Folding it back up, he slid the letter into his rain pants and found his pocket.

The rain pounded the lot with vengeance, scrubbing off the oil and litter and pooling it into rivulets that ran into the grass. A coffee was in order. The storm intended to move quickly according to the radar. If he took a few minutes, the ride home might be easier.

Crocus had come through with their first real lead yesterday. Thomas hadn't gotten to messages on their online game until late at night, and focusing on the letter arriving today had cost him some sleep. Crocus watched the two men who monitored Meg's old family members. Somehow, he'd gotten the name of someone paying their bills.

Thomas would have to see if the name came up with

any viable leads.

He stepped off the porch into the rain as his phone rang. Swearing, he circled back up the steps and dug for his phone. Biff knew he was riding and wouldn't call unless there was a problem with Meg at the garage.

Haddie called. Was she still working with the FBI agent?

"Hey, what's up?" He loosened his chinstrap as he talked.

Wipers pounded in the background; she was driving the SUV. "Dad, I got a favor to ask. You're not going to like it."

Great start. "Okay." He glanced back in at Miguel who had returned to his phone.

"Kiana — Wilkins — needs a place to hide out. Do you want the whole story?"

"Probably best." He pulled off his helmet and smoothed back his hair.

"Someone followed us to our meeting. She thinks they tracked her rental." Haddie paused, leaving the thumping of the wipers. "I had to use my powers; they were shooting."

Hell. She needed to lose this agent. This new obsession of hers would end up in a mess, and they couldn't trust anyone who had decided to work enforcing authority. Bad news all around. His jaw tightened, waiting.

Haddie continued, "So, we're going to clear out her place and leave her rental car there."

She would be driving there now, of course. Had the agent not thought this out, or were they playing Haddie?

"Don't." He winced, and tried to calm his tone. "What makes you think they won't be watching her place? Think about it, Haddie."

"She knows what she's doing," Haddie replied sharply.

He'd gotten her hackles up. Thomas stared into the

storm and waited. Lightning sparked across clouds, lighting the back of the takeout restaurant on the corner. She wanted him to hide a federal agent? Why? Did they think the government had attacked them? He didn't want to start this conversation on the phone.

"She'll need a place to lie low for a while. I know you said that you had some properties . . ." Haddie let the comment drift off.

I should just say no. What would Haddie do? Put the woman up in a hotel under her — or my — credit card? Have her stay at one of her friends? Any connection could lead back to himself, Haddie, and Meg.

"Devil in hell. I've got a place she can stay." He shook his head. "I'll text you the information on a different number."

He'd have to burn the identity for that property. It meant moving other properties out of the name. *I'll have to be careful.* He had avoided the FBI and any of the security agencies' attention, but their methods became increasingly efficient.

Barbara Stevens would have to wait. If he did find a location for this woman, he already had someone to investigate her. The contact had come with solid references, discreet and careful with good results. So far, there had been no hint that Meg had been tracked back to Eugene. However, he didn't intend to leave her safety to chance. Someone had systematically killed any member of his previous identity's bloodline. They wouldn't give up on Meg easily.

"Thanks, Dad. Love you."

"I love you, Haddie." *Otherwise I wouldn't have to make rash moves.* "We're going to have a long talk about this. All the details."

CHAPTER 9

HADDIE FOLLOWED Kiana down the off-ramp at the town of Turner. The worst of the storm had passed, leaving dark skies, a few more car lengths of visibility, and torrents of runoff.

Her skin still felt raw under the gloves, but the ride had reduced much of the pain to a memory.

There wasn't much of a town visible, except a church that stood on the hill to her right. When they reached the stop sign, she could make out a couple buildings on the other side of the overpass to her left. Haddie hoped for a gas station, someplace she could get a drink. Instead, Kiana turned right.

They'd only gone a few yards down the road before Kiana turned onto the road leading up the hill toward the church. Haddie followed as they pulled off the road beside a fenced-in lot with some highway construction supplies piled at the end.

Kiana jumped out of her rental and moved quickly to the passenger door of the RAV4. She glanced around as she walked, but the only cars were passing on I-5. Sliding into the seat, she took a deep breath.

"I don't know what I'm going to find here," Kiana said.

Haddie nodded. If the man she'd just killed had been working for someone like Harold Holmes, or Sameedha, she worried that they'd have people waiting to ambush Kiana at her Airbnb. "Do you want me to follow you?"

Kiana shook her head; beads of water shifted in her curls. "Stay here. I'll text when I'm sure it's clear. If I come back in a hurry, don't follow." She waved off her last comment. "If I come back at all, don't follow."

"Okay." Haddie rested her hand on her empty bottle. Her chest tightened even more, and her tongue felt dry.

"When I text you the all clear, head up this road. At the top of the hill, take the first left; the Airbnb is on that street. Turn into the church parking lot, find a parking spot where you can see the road, and you'll see my car parked in the front of the second house on the street. There's an NA meeting at six every night in the back of the church, so you won't be the only car in the lot." Kiana looked off into the rain. "I'll walk over with my stuff if everything is okay."

Did she expect trouble? Haddie would find it difficult to just sit in her RAV4 if someone attacked Kiana.

Her phone vibrated with a text from Terry.

"Is this a good idea?" Haddie asked.

Kiana continued to stare out the window. "I've got to try, and now is the time. I'll take a lap through the church parking lot and the neighborhood before I attempt anything." She nodded and opened the passenger door; thunder rumbled in.

Lightning cracked the sky beyond the church as Kiana ran for her rental. The cross mounted on the hill made a distinct silhouette. Haddie sat in her RAV4 watching Kiana drive up the hill.

She checked Terry's message. "You were asking about Unceasing groups. I've gotten into a fan group. Aaron's joining now. Want the link?"

She raised her eyebrows. Did she really need something else to obsess on? Even this trip to Kiana's had her chest so tight she could barely breathe.

"Sure," she typed.

Killing a man and then driving for nearly an hour had given her time to question her life. She kept putting herself into situations where she had to defend herself or others. The man had been trying to kill Kiana, and would surely have killed Haddie. But she had placed herself in that situation. Maybe she should take Dad's advice and disappear. Forget about the Unceasing, the demons, the coerced, and her powers. What then?

She wouldn't make a good lawyer, that had become obvious, but what was she supposed to do while hiding out in the woods somewhere? What if she were immortal too?

Terry sent the link to a forum she'd never heard of. It would have to wait. Haddie placed her cell on her lap, waiting for Kiana's text. She tried to swallow away her thirst.

Dad texted, "Be careful." He followed with a map link to a property west of Eugene.

Haddie took in a deep breath, held it, then tried to release her anxiety with her exhale. He'd found a place for Kiana to lie low. Would this end up being her life? Would she start a new identity, as Dad did? She'd lose all her friends. It might be better than the constant chaos and killing. How had Dad been in all those wars?

"Thanks," she texted.

"House key by the water spigot. Under the brick. Truck in the back, key under the mat."

She hadn't expected a vehicle. Dad always thought things through. She'd grown up believing him just a simple bike mechanic and never realized everything he had going on.

He texted again, "Be careful. Call me when you're done up north."

She typed, "Will do."

Haddie didn't look forward to that conversation. She could see her Dad's face now.

His help eased some of her concern, but added more stress. He disapproved of her helping Kiana. Haddie could understand that. She'd already killed another man, and they hadn't even broken into the office in Coos Bay yet.

Another text from Terry popped up. "Did you sign in?"

She couldn't focus on that right now. "Not yet. Maybe tonight." Should she ask Kiana about the Unceasing?

"They've got a seminar coming up in Eugene," he texted.

Haddie paused. It *would* be interesting to find out more about this group. What connection did they have with Sameedha and the raves?

Haddie thought about a response, when Kiana texted. "OK."

"Damn," Haddie swore and dropped the phone into the passenger's seat. Terry could wait.

The RAV4 kicked some of the gravel from the side of the road and splashed through the stream of water along the edge as Haddie headed toward the church. The storm hadn't fully passed yet, but she could see to the top of the hill.

The church nearly disappeared behind the slope of the

hill and some pines, but the huge cross hung in the sky to Haddie's left. It almost seemed she was passing it before a small side street cut up the incline. Turning, a house and driveway appeared on the right, and through the rain she could make out the entrance to the church ahead on the left. Torrents of water flowed down from the church, making the driveway a river.

Kiana's rental was parked in front of a small house farther up on the right side.

As the agent had promised, cars were parked in the lot, but in the rain they had clustered close to the church and left her to park alone, facing Kiana's rental. Haddie picked a spot where she could see through a cluster of trees planted along the hill. Not the best vantage, but if anyone approached the house or car from the street, she could text Kiana. She turned off the wipers and the RAV4, sliding down to be less noticeable and still have a view.

The only activity were those coming for the meeting. They glanced toward her, but didn't take any time to notice her. Haddie had seen similar crowds on the few occasions when she'd accompanied Dad as he dropped off Biff or picked him up.

Watching the house, Haddie doubted she would see anyone who approached on foot, not in this rain. She tried to take calming slow breaths, but her heart raced. The attack after their meeting had her on edge, and they risked another ambush. If it went well, though, they had a place to hide Kiana.

Haddie sat up as she spotted motion at the front of the house. Grabbing her cell, she leaned up until her chin found the steering wheel.

Kiana, carrying a large duffel bag, jogged across the

street and splashed through water as she made for the driveway of the church.

Haddie didn't sit back until Kiana opened the back door behind the passenger seat and threw in her belongings.

"I haven't seen anyone. Did it look okay inside?" Haddie asked.

Kiana slid into the front seat, wiping her face. "Inside the house? No one's been inside."

She sounded sure. Did she have special spy cams? Motion sensors?

Haddie opened her mouth to ask and shook her head, firing up the RAV4. "Dad's got a place for you to stay. And a truck. Damn, it might be manual."

Kiana offered an appreciative smile. "Thanks. I can drive a manual. Army."

Haddie backed up in the church lot. Rain flooded across asphalt, pouring over the edges of the slope. The dash clock read 5:22. "I'm just going to drop you off and run. I've got something I need to pick up by seven." She would just make it, unless I-5 had an accident.

Kiana buckled in, dripping from the rain. "Okay. We can go over the plans for tomorrow night on the ride."

Driving forward, Haddie slammed on the brakes. "Damn."

She'd forgotten about Cathy and their 6:30 meet-up. *Worse.* Grace's niece had been on the phone during the shooting. Haddie winced, grabbed the phone, and dialed Cathy's number. What was she going to use as an excuse for the gunfire?

"Hello?" The call hopped to Haddie's car speaker, and Cathy sounded apprehensive.

"Hey, Cathy. Sorry about that. Storm is horrible here.

Lightning, nasty thunder." Haddie grimaced, glancing at Kiana.

Cathy took a moment to respond. "And gunfire?"

Haddie twisted her hair in a ball behind her head. "Uhmm, long story. What I'm calling about is our 6:30 meeting. I'm running late, and I've got a package to pick up for work. If the rental office is open when I get home, want me to call you?"

"You're okay?"

This would get back to Grace. Likely, not much farther if Haddie talked with Grace first. "I'm fine. Want me to call you?"

"That's okay. I came early." The background noise had been quiet. "I'm sitting in the office now. I'll let them give me a walk through. I would have liked to meet you. Maybe another time?"

Haddie sagged, guilt forcing her eyes into a long blink. "Yes. I wanted to meet you too. Maybe tomorrow." Even as she made the comment, she hoped there would be time.

"Okay, bye. Be careful." Cathy hung up.

When Haddie looked over, Kiana tilted her head and said, "Looks like you've got a lot on your plate. Still sure about tomorrow night? I could have been made there while I was staking it out; I hadn't thought so, but I can't explain why else they attacked us."

Haddie paused with her hand on her empty bottle. They would have to be careful. Someone had been willing to try and kill an FBI agent over this. "Yes, but I'm stopping for something to drink before we get on I-5."

CHAPTER 10

Haddie turned onto Oak Hill Drive, a small paved road that led deeper into the rural part of west Eugene. The thunder and lightning had stopped, and the rain had thinned to a drizzle. Pools and puddles remained at the sides of the road, occasionally stretching under the wheels of the RAV4.

When they reached the odd assortment of mailboxes that marked the drive for Dad's hideaway, water still ran down the gravel path that cut uphill into oaks and brush. A winding driveway led to a house that looked like many of the concrete block models from the 1970s, with about twenty years of maintenance due. Large, tinted windows gave a good view of the approach, and Haddie pulled up there, though it seemed that to the side there might be a garage.

"I'm going to find the key," Haddie said, jumping out her door.

She had a tight time frame to pick up Andrea's files. *I already botched helping Cathy.* There wouldn't be any time to get Kiana settled in.

An old Ford F150 was parked on the grass in the back, as Dad had promised. The spigot he'd mentioned lay behind overgrown shrubs and a family of spiders that hadn't been disturbed probably since Dad had placed the house key. Wiping off webs, Haddie returned to find Kiana waiting with her duffel bag.

"You're going to have to make yourself at home." Haddie unlocked the door and handed Kiana the key. "I'll call you in a little bit. See if there's anything you need."

"I'll be fine. Thank your father." Kiana slung the bag to her shoulder. Hopefully she'd packed some dry clothes; she was drenched more than Haddie.

Haddie paused, considering the truck. It would be under an alias. The house too, if Kiana looked it up. Dad likely wouldn't want an FBI agent knowing that he had a fake identity. Technically, another fake identity.

"The key for the truck is under the driver's side mat." Haddie would have to talk with Dad about how to explain this.

"I'm just going to settle in and rest. Thanks for being there today." Kiana smiled and headed inside.

Haddie cringed as she strode for the RAV4. Kiana might have been alone during the attack, if they had been tracking her rental car. Would she have survived an ambush without Haddie? It didn't make killing the man any less right, but it did ease some of her guilt.

She had twenty minutes to drive and it was 6:28. Perfect. She hadn't answered Terry. Picking up her phone, she found Aaron had texted.

"Are you going?" He'd texted just a minute ago.

"Where?" Haddie asked. Probably the same seminar Terry mentioned.

"The event, on the forum."

Haddie wiped off a web tickling her cheek. "Haven't had time to login."

"An 'un' seminar." Evidently Aaron didn't want to type Unceasing.

"When?" Haddie needed to leave and get Andrea's files.

"Wednesday, two days from now."

"Maybe. I'll text you after I look at forum." Tapping her foot, she shifted over to Terry's texts and let him know that she'd get with him tonight, apologizing for not responding. She didn't have time for him right now.

She dialed Dad and put the RAV4 into reverse. Even as she navigated down the muddy driveway, someone texted a response. It would have to wait.

"Hey. You got Wilkins settled in?" he asked.

"Just now." Haddie slowed as tires lost traction down the incline. "What do you want to do about your alias here?"

"It's under Tom Carr. Did she ask?" Louis, the puppy, yapped in the background, putting Dad at his garage with Meg.

"No. I didn't want to say anything until I talked with you."

"Good. If she asks, just say that I'm watching the place for a friend who lives out east."

Haddie raised her eyebrows. "And if she pulls up the driver's photo?"

"Then she'll find a clean-shaven man with short brown hair, a ring in his nose, and a tattoo on his neck. The photo's been shopped." Dad shifted to a sterner tone. "Tell me you've both given up on this plan. I've got the report of the body on the police scanner. I'm assuming that was you."

Haddie swallowed, feeling slightly nauseous. "They

won't find the other body. There were two."

"Hell. Tell me this is it. You're done."

He might be right, but she'd committed to Kiana, and it was the right thing to do. These people wouldn't stop hunting her. The woman had likely just lost her career in the FBI, unless they were willing to pursue these people and protect her. It hadn't seemed that way. "I'm doing this." Her jaw tightened. "You've got your own little war going. You can't judge."

He sighed. "No, you're right, but I can worry."

They remained silent for a moment. Louis yapped in the background and Meg said something, likely to her puppy.

"When?" he asked.

Haddie stiffened. Did he plan on joining them? "Tomorrow night. Coos Bay. We can do this. She's been staking out the office for a week."

He snorted. "Not very long. Let me know if you want my help."

Haddie couldn't be sure if she wanted his help or not. More people didn't seem like it would make it any safer, but he'd bailed her out of being tortured by Harold Holmes, and gotten them home from the raves. "Okay. I'll think about it."

Pulling off Oak, she turned right and picked up speed on the larger road. The storm had moved to the east, a blustering wind pushing it along. Wet branches shook under the gusts. Lightning crackled in black clouds ahead of her. She'd arrive with ten minutes to spare.

There had to be some balance between doing the right thing and defending herself. Harold Holmes and Sameedha had killed people before Haddie got involved, and they might have continued. Still, she couldn't just absolve herself of any responsibility. *I made those choices.* She had a choice to stay out of Kiana's investigation, let the woman risk herself even when she'd asked for help, or move forward and chance another confrontation which could lead to someone being killed. Haddie knew her decision, at least in this case. She'd be going to Coos Bay tomorrow night.

She crossed the Willamette River as the sun started to burn through the lingering clouds to the west.

Did she really want to involve Dad? When she'd gone after Liz, he'd been supportive. Breaking into the office he opposed. Would he just grumble the entire time? Kiana had made it clear that she didn't consider this very dangerous.

Haddie pulled into the parking lot beside the address and scrambled out of the RAV4 at 6:49, pleased that she'd made it on time. Someone had painted the back side of the building in a large colorful mural that glistened after the rain. Wet leaves matted the asphalt and the earthy smell of the recent storm lingered.

The law office lay upstairs, according to Grace's directions. Haddie climbed up the steps, swearing at her joints as she reached the office door.

It was locked. Haddie knocked, waited, and tried again a little louder. They had said 7:00. She pulled out her phone and dropped directly into voicemail.

"Damn."

Why would they say 7:00 and leave before that? Andrea never closed early. In fact, Toby often stayed late to accommodate a client.

There were no hours on the door. Haddie's only choice would be to come in the morning and pick up Andrea's files, which meant being late for work. How late depended on what time the office opened.

Sighing, Haddie started down the stairs. She'd be driving back in the morning.

CHAPTER 11

AFTER TURNING OFF THE RAV4, Haddie sat in silence staring at the wall of her apartment building. She was numb, and the day played out in flashes. It had started well with her finishing all of Andrea's tasks. It had quickly gotten worse.

She still wanted to call Kiana. Liz would be over to take some more blood. Maybe not after she learned Haddie had used her power again. First, something to eat.

Grateful that she'd texted Sam to walk Rock earlier, she opened the driver's door and eased out. Her Fat Boy sat in the next space, unused for the past week. Tomorrow she would have Andrea's files; maybe she could ride the day afterward. Hopefully the storm would leave them a few good days to ride.

The air smelled fresh after the rain, maybe a hint of the dumpster and the heat of her engine. Summer left the trees a deep green and some of the shrubs flowering. The clouds that lingered stretched out and let the blue sky through. Sunset hadn't started yet. Farther down the apartments someone spoke, likely on a cell considering the one-sided conversation.

Rock would be happy to see her, and Jisoo would be hungry. *I'll have time to call David and maybe smooth things over.*

"Haddie." Sam jogged across the alley from her apartment.

"Hey, how did Rock handle the rain?" Haddie paused on sidewalk. Happy to see Sam, she'd be even happier to get out of the wet clothes and find something to eat.

"Usual. Quick. All business." Sam studied her, "You look like it's been a rough day."

Haddie swallowed, trying not let the lump in her throat grow to tears. She shrugged. "Yeah, I guess."

Walking along the path to the stairs, Sam joined her heading to the apartment. "What happened?"

"Everything." Haddie couldn't get into the details, certainly not about killing a man. "I was supposed to pick up files for Andrea, and they closed early, though I cut it to the wire and shouldn't have. Grace's cousin is looking for a place, I was supposed to meet her here, missed that." She wasn't willing to discuss Kiana, or any of that.

Sam followed behind as they climbed up the stairs. "You've got red splinters in your hair."

Stroking through with her hand, Haddie didn't find anything. "It's been that kind of day."

They stood silent as Haddie worked keys out of her wet pants. Rock sniffed at the other side of the door. As she stepped in and turned off the alarm, he smelled her over. Sam tried to intervene, but he'd need some attention.

Trying not to wince, Haddie knelt and hugged him. He sniffed through her hair and across her face, squirming as she petted him. "How's my boy? Miss Mum today?" Jisoo cried out from the kitchen.

Haddie just wanted to strip out of the gloves and clothes. Sam had seen her rash plenty of times, and accepted Haddie's lie about it.

Sam joined in petting Rock and his tail beat furiously. "Seriously, you sound like you're ready to cry. What happened?"

Haddie stood, closing her eyes and taking a deep breath. "You ever try to do the right thing, at least what you believe is the right thing, and then someone gets hurt? Not someone you care about, just someone getting in the way?" Her throat thickened as she finished.

"I guess. In my own way. But I don't think in the way that you mean." Sam studied her. "I'm not sure what's going on, but I think you're hurting yourself the most."

Tears welled.

Same stepped forward and hugged her. Haddie let out an involuntary sob and hugged back. How would she feel if she came back from Coos Bay and she'd killed again?

"I'm always here," Sam said. "I don't need to know the details. Just know that I think if you're trying to do the right thing, you have to try. If someone gets hurt getting in your way, that's their choice."

Haddie wiped tears away. "Thank you. I'm afraid that if I don't help, people will get hurt." Rock nuzzled against her leg, jealous that he wasn't part of the hug.

"Then you're doing the right thing. Trust yourself." Sam pulled back to look Haddie in the eye. "I trust you. The greater good wins."

Somehow, Sam's confidence helped. Haddie squeezed her friend another time and then said, "I need to get out of these clothes." The self-loathing didn't disappear, hadn't since the raves, but she could keep moving.

Sam knelt and gave Rock some more attention. "If you're hungry, I could start something cooking. Pasta?"

"I would love you forever." Haddie peeled off a glove and started for the bedroom.

Jisoo howled as Sam entered the kitchen. "Yes, of course you too."

After some food, Haddie had Liz to get ready for and Kiana to check on. Self-pity could wait. She wouldn't be walking away from this without trying. If she'd left Liz at the raves, maybe fewer would have died, but maybe Haddie would have lost a friend.

If she had time, she'd check on the link Terry had sent. Fanatics.

CHAPTER 12

With Rock pulling her up the stairs, Haddie trudged to her apartment. His nails scratched the landing as he took the opportunity to sniff the area.

The house still smelled like Sam's pasta. Sam had gone home after taking a nighttime walk with Haddie and Rock around the neighborhood. Rock seemed to appreciate the extended trip after the rain, and Haddie needed Sam's moral support. Unlike Terry, Sam didn't pry to find out more. She seemed content to know only what affected her, unless it affected Rock and Jisoo.

Haddie texted David after hanging up Rock's leash. "Still up?" He went to bed fairly early.

She dropped in front of her computer and typed the URL that Terry had texted. She made a login, started some water on the stove for tea, and came back to activate her account. The forum looked like one of Terry's usual conspiracy blogs, with thread titles that could have been clickbait for news sites.

The specific thread she found typing in the URL breadcrumbs was a "Greater Glory" discussion where fans of the Unceasing enthusiastically quoted from seminars and other posts. She wondered if they'd read the part where the Unceasing philosophy shunned "the manacles of technology" and they would be without a forum such as this if they truly followed the doctrines. Admittedly, she approached it judging them and the philosophy to be squirrelly since she'd first read it, so she tried to plod through.

Most of the comments confirmed her assumptions. She didn't make it to where they discussed any upcoming event before her tea kettle cried out. Jisoo joined in as Haddie entered the kitchen. She had the tea steeping in a deep mug and the ice ready in her glass when a knock sounded on the door.

Liz. Haddie joined Rock at the door and slid him aside. She peeked through the peephole; Liz wore a light blue blouse with a pair of sunglasses hanging from the neckline.

Haddie opened the door. "Hey."

Liz walked in with a small satchel and glanced at the alarm panel. "I thought you agreed, after Rock, that you'd keep the alarm on when you're home."

Haddie sighed. "I just walked Rock, and knew you were coming." In truth, she forgot more times than not. She led the way into the kitchen and Rock followed, trying to get Liz's attention.

"I'm planning on something bigger for you to push back in time for the next test," Liz said.

Haddie shook her head. "I'm going to need a break. Maybe, just maybe, in two months." She bobbed her teabag in the mug. Earl Grey.

Liz pouted, then her eyebrows furrowed. "Why isn't your purpura fading? It looks worse. How do you feel?"

"Uhmm." Haddie imagined she would have to tell Liz,

but she'd never mentioned anything about Kiana's plan yet. "There was an incident."

Liz's face settled into a distinctly judgmental frown. She gestured for Haddie to continue.

"I was meeting with Kiana. Special Agent Wilkins. She has some information about the people who attacked us outside the hotel during the raves. The man, who I killed, was named Don Mack. She's traced his activities to a place in Coos Bay." Haddie took a breath, still bobbing the tea bag without stop. "When I met with Kiana this afternoon to discuss searching this office, we were attacked when we left. I ended up using my powers again."

"Who attacked you?" Liz asked.

Haddie shrugged. "We're not sure. Kiana wonders if it might be the people she's investigating. I can't imagine they were after me."

"Are you sure?"

"That they weren't after me? Why wait until I'm some-place I never go to — just to ambush me? Since school is out, I'm either here or at work. Pretty easy to find." Haddie squeezed out the tea bag, sniffing at the pungent drink.

Liz flicked a band of hair from her face. "So, did you cancel these plans? Tell me you did."

"No. This could tell me more about those who were running the raves, or Sameedha. Don't you want to know?"

Though slightly tanned from the summer, Liz paled. "No. Not at all."

"I have to do this," Haddie said.

Liz straightened. "Then be careful." She motioned toward Haddie's arm. "I'm still taking blood." She frowned. "Well, this is going to mess up my results. Could you kindly refrain from using your superpowers outside of my testing schedule?"

Haddie chuckled and poured the hot tea over her ice. "I'll do my best. Believe me." She thought of the man today. *I should be able to remember his face.*

With one hand holding her glass, she felt the swirling temperatures against her palm and the condensation forming. Her other arm she laid on the counter for Liz. "I killed this man today. What does that make me? All those people at the rave, they were innocent."

Liz set out her tube and needle. "You did not cause those things. Where would Matt and I be without your help? Dead? You called them suicide raves. I looked them up. California, South America, India. Would that have been me? Us?" She frowned. "Maybe I shouldn't have given you that pep talk. However, did you have a choice today?"

"No, they were firing at us."

"They?" Liz asked.

Haddie nodded. "Kiana shot the other one. Dad said the police found him."

"And still, you're going to Coos Bay?"

"Yes." Haddie had made up her mind. Greater good.

Terry texted as Liz prepared to draw blood. Haddie managed to put down her glass and retrieve her phone without jostling her arm.

"So. Did you login?" he texted.

Haddie typed, "Yes. Wackos."

"You going?"

"Maybe."

"Yaass!" Terry texted. "I'm going in disguise. Something to bring out my Japanese ancestry. How about you, Buckaroo?"

"You're like one quarter Japanese," she typed.

Liz taped Haddie's arm and folded it. "Try to not use your powers — when is this?"

"Tomorrow night." Haddie put down her phone, ignoring Terry's next text. "Don't worry, I'll check in with you when we're heading back so you know I'm okay."

"You say that now." Liz packed up her satchel.

"I will." Haddie sipped her tea.

She still had Kiana to check in on, though the woman might be asleep. Haddie would have to call the law office with Andrea's files until they showed up. Probably better just to go sit outside in case they didn't answer their phones. Hopefully, Andrea would be late tomorrow. Nothing like botching up a simple task to annoy her.

"What are you thinking about? You've got that look like you're running through a list." Liz leaned against the counter.

"Work." It would be difficult to get to sleep with everything on her mind. David hadn't texted back, hopefully because he was asleep and not annoyed at her. If she was going to be up late and alert tomorrow night, then she needed sleep.

CHAPTER 13

KIANA NERVOUSLY RUBBED her ear and checked the time on her laptop. 8:41 a.m. Sitting in a booth with her back to a window gave her a wide view of the restaurant, packed mainly with workers getting ready for their day and elderly retired couples. The smell of eggs and meats had faded to her, now that she'd had breakfast. The cheesy omelet had hardly seemed enough; she hadn't eaten since yesterday's lunch.

The chatter and clatter about the restaurant distracted her, but she needed the Wi-Fi in an unmonitored location. The waitress had tried to have her pay the bill later, after more coffee, but Kiana needed to be ready to leave after she accessed her emails.

The FBI surely weren't the ones who ambushed her after meeting with Haddie, but that didn't mean they weren't involved somehow. She couldn't trust them after Portland. Following the event and the false report, they'd quickly moved her around on minor cases, but pointedly didn't allow her any access to her prior investigations.

Haddie's powers explained Harold Holmes' disappearance. Kiana had determined that quickly; by then though, her supervisors had proven they were part of a conspiracy to hide the mutants' existence. The FBI didn't show any particular interest in Harold Holmes, but they didn't want her continuing her investigation. If Kiana had reported Haddie when asked, she didn't doubt that the woman would have disappeared by now.

Supervisors outside of her department and chain of command had shown up to question her. It smelled of a cover-up, and worse. She had to be very careful. Her leave of absence had surely drawn their notice and suspicion.

Kiana sipped at her coffee, a fresh brew from the taste of it, not wanting to draw the waitress over to refill. Clicking on the Wi-Fi she logged in, connected, and noted the time. 8:43. She'd give herself ten minutes, then she had to leave.

She checked her three disposable email accounts first. Spam and one response from Don Mack's previous employer avoiding her request to send his work sites. She'd hoped that might lead her to the moment when his life altered so drastically.

Wetting her lips, she clicked on her FBI email and logged in. 8:46.

Three emails since yesterday morning. All from the supervisor who had pushed the false report onto her. All occurring after the attempted ambush, the latest sent just twenty minutes ago. They wanted her to report in and answer questions about her previous cases. Urgent. She read each carefully, getting light-headed and nauseous.

Were they planning on finishing the job the attackers had started? She couldn't ignore the timing or the insistence on immediacy. How deep did this corruption in the FBI go? Would they falsify claims against her? Lock her up and then dispose of her?

She couldn't go in.

A chat popped up on her screen. A different agent, not the supervisor, questioned her present activities, demanding a location, and pressing for her to check in. 8:48.

Kiana slammed the lid of the laptop closed. Five minutes. They could easily track the IP to this location.

She left the remains of her coffee and slid out of the booth. The waitress called after with parting pleasantries, but Kiana watched the entrance, expecting any moment for agents to block her exit.

As she stepped outside, she drew a short breath and raced for the truck. It had taken less than ten minutes to get to the café, and she intended to be far down the street in the next couple of minutes. The FBI would send local police first, then follow themselves.

A man dressed in dark suit pants and a light blue long-sleeve shirt stepped out of a silver sedan and hurried toward the restaurant.

Kiana paused at the truck to scan the lot and street. No one noticed her.

The old truck smelled musty, and the dash had splits from the heat and sun. The engine purred into life smoothly though.

She'd passed a grocery store a couple minutes away. Turning left onto the main street, Kiana cut off an annoyed kid in a sports car and joined the rush hour traffic. By 8:52 she pulled behind the grocery store and found an adjoining parking lot at a building supply store. She found a place to park among a number of work trucks. She turned off the engine, shivered, and left her laptop under the seat.

Her life, her career, was over. She couldn't risk going back to the FBI. When she didn't show up they would put out a bulletin; they might have done that already.

Walking through the sand and grass of the median that separated one parking lot from the other, Kiana headed for the grocery store. Her footsteps felt leaden. Since the army, she'd worked for the government. She'd had purpose and direction. Gone.

She'd tell Haddie. The FBI, or whatever internal faction that had been corrupted, might go through her last cases and look up anyone she'd been in contact with.

What am I going to do? Live up in the hills in West Eugene? They'd gotten wind of her investigation. How could she possibly hide from the FBI? Maybe she should just turn herself in.

Kiana shook her head. "No." She'd dig in. Find out what was going on. Perhaps her investigation would expose this element inside the FBI. That was her only chance out of this. Expose the corruption. She needed someone she could start feeding information to, someone outside this jurisdiction, perhaps outside the FBI. A low-level member of the Attorney General's office. Someone hungry to make a name for themselves.

Stopping at the side of the grocery store, she leaned against the wall. She'd start with Coos Bay. Then, see if that led her anywhere.

Haddie would pick her up after 9 p.m. Kiana just needed to lie low for the day.

CHAPTER 14

THE PARKING LOT started to fill around her RAV4 while Haddie leaned against the corner of the building waiting for someone to arrive and head up the stairs. The city had become a dull roar of activity. She'd come at 8:30, when the morning air still felt relatively cool. Now, at 9:00 the sun slanted through the trees, the humidity rose, and the weather warmed toward a summer's day. The air still smelled like rain-soaked earth, but the exhaust had started to overtake it. Not one person had shown up, and the entrance to the stairs was still locked. Toby would be opening Andrea's law firm.

She texted Toby, "Running late."

"You and Josh," Toby replied.

Haddie smiled. "Bet he has a better excuse."

"That's the funny part. No excuse. Just: I'll be late today. Weird, right?"

She'd never heard of Josh calling out without an elaborate excuse. "That is odd," Haddie typed. She squirmed and added, "Andrea yet?"

"Nope. How long you gonna be?" Toby texted.

"I don't know." Gloves on and wearing her business attire with thick makeup to hide the purpura, Haddie considered going back in the car for some AC. "I hope not much longer." She'd looked up the law office's website, but they didn't have hours listed. Who did that?

She watched a woman approach the door, read the list of offices, and move on. Sighing, Haddie pulled back her hair and twisted it into a knot. She should have come here directly with Kiana last night, before dropping her off at Dad's house. Haddie checked her phone again, considering calling David. Their text exchange this morning had been brief, too brief. She imagined he was upset. *I'm making the same mistakes I made in Portland.* Tonight she'd be in Coos Bay, so she couldn't make plans with David at all.

Haddie pulled up the number of Seism Law Office. The law office shouldn't have said they were open until 7:00 p.m. if they were going to leave early. What if they weren't even going to be open today? For the third time that morning, she called their office, but before she got to the voicemail, a man walked up and began unlocking the door.

"Excuse me. Are you with Seism Law Offices?" Haddie asked.

Thick eyebrows furrowed on the man's face as he glanced toward her. "You're the girl? The one supposed to have been here yesterday?"

"Yes, sorry I —"

"I'm not helping you carry them down." He headed inside and dashed up the steps.

Haddie frowned and started slowly behind him. She didn't need him to help. "Thank you."

He wore a sharp cologne, like incense, that left a trail in the hall. Unlocking the door, he motioned for her to wait outside. She stood staring at beige paint that had been scraped and bruised up and down the corridor. A second later he opened the door and gestured to a box sitting on the floor in front of what looked like a steel teacher's desk from a high school.

The banker's box felt half full. "Is this all there is?" she asked.

He nodded and waved her back into the hall.

"Thanks," she said. The door closed behind her. "Lovely."

Lips pursed, she plodded down the stairs. There was still hope that she could make it before Andrea. The office would be cranking with a new case. Juggling the box, she opened the door and headed back into the heat.

There was no sign of Andrea's car when Haddie found a parking spot and retrieved the box. Toby had coffee brewed and the office smelled delicious.

"You made it," Toby said. She had on a light-yellow top with a large collar.

Haddie paused in front of the reception desk. "Andrea coming in?"

Toby tapped a pen against her keyboard. "Yep. She's at the courthouse and will be here in a few minutes."

Relaxing, Haddie leaned her box on the desk. "So, what's up with Josh?"

"I know — strange, right?" Toby gestured in the air. "He's only texted me like twice before. Always a call, always a story."

He'd acted strange in the parking lot as well. Distracted, but that wasn't too unusual. Haddie nodded. "I hope he's okay."

She carried her load out of the waiting room and down the hall, planning to drop it quickly in their back office and grab some fresh coffee.

Grace looked up from her cubicle.

Haddie dropped the files and headed to Grace. "Sorry about missing your niece last night. Something came up." *Like killing a man.* Had Cathy mentioned the gunfire?

Grace shrugged lightly, her expression barely changing. "She's a grown woman. Didn't see me offering to traipse around with her, did you?"

Perhaps Cathy hadn't mentioned the strange phone call she'd had with Haddie. Thankfully. "She's new here. She asked. I don't mind." Haddie wanted to help Cathy, and hopefully, by extension Grace.

Grace gestured to the box that Haddie had dropped in front of Josh's cubicle. "Andrea asked that you scan those files in. Can't be sure if Josh is coming in today or not."

"As much as he's out, I'm surprised she's never replaced him." *Or me.*

Grace continued typing. "It's complicated."

Haddie stopped, box of files in her hands, beside Grace's cubicle. "What's the story?"

Grace stopped typing and looked up with just the slightest hint of a frown. "Andrea went to school with Josh's mother. Friends. His mother is sick, has been since he's been a boy. Part of the reason he's out so much. He takes care of her, pretty much home schooled himself. He does well, considering."

Haddie swallowed. "I never knew."

"He won't talk about any of it. I tried once when I could see he was having a rough time. He just focuses on other things." Grace returned her hands to her keyboard. "Like all of us, he just wants to be accepted for who he is."

Haddie took a deep breath and walked the files into the copy room. She'd never once wondered about Josh's life outside the office. Why had Grace never said anything before? Haddie needed coffee; she slipped into her cubicle and grabbed her anime coffee mug.

By the time Andrea arrived, the files were nearly scanned. Haddie's next list of tasks came via an email, after her boss went directly into her office without a comment to either of them. Andrea never even asked about the files, but some of the to-do list obviously expected them to be in house. *Did I expect a big thank you?*

As Haddie began highlighting the first police report, Terry texted, "Found a solid link between the raves and the Unceasing Foundation."

Haddie glanced up from her cubicle. Grace worked her keyboard, and Andrea had not come out of her office once.

Terry continued, "Anthony Prizer, the billionaire who disappeared after losing most of his money during the raves, his beneficiary is the Unceasing Foundation. What little there is left of it."

Haddie already had Coos Bay on her mind, as much as she tried to ignore it. She didn't really want to focus on anything but work. She'd have all afternoon to obsess during the trip with Kiana. Nevertheless, she didn't want to ignore him or push him away further. "Work's hectic. I'll check on this in the afternoon." Was it possible that the Unceasing did connect with Sameedha and Don Mack?

"Got it, Buckaroo."

She had been a little more distant with Terry. Not just the secrets she kept, but with Livia in the picture, their friendship focused mainly on their weekly game. Haddie couldn't bring herself to drag him into any of her issues — not like she used to. When she'd been digging about the raves, she didn't know they had to do with someone with powers. Even then, she'd kept the demons she'd seen from him.

Right now, she had to focus on work. This evening she could worry about the break-in at Coos Bay. After that, she could focus on the Unceasing seminar with Aaron and Terry. Did she resist the latter because she didn't want Terry dragged into all this?

Andrea walked out of her office just before lunch and spoke with Toby. "Get everyone's orders for Vintage. We're eating in today. I need everything I can get by morning."

Haddie raised her eyebrows. She couldn't see either of them from her cubicle, but she could hear their conversation. Evidently, Andrea had just gotten started on their workload for the new case and didn't want them drifting too far for lunch. Toby pushed her chair back, and Andrea's office door closed. Without Josh, it might end up being a late night.

Toby wandered into their back office with a sticky note and pen. "So you heard. Vintage. What do want?"

Haddie had already pulled up the menu and started to respond, but the office door chimed. Toby rolled her eyes and headed back to her desk.

"Toby, Dear." A familiar voice called out immediately with a hint at a Texan drawl.

"Mr. Palmer, I didn't have you on the schedule for a meeting with Andrea." Toby's tone, though surprised, seemed pleased.

Haddie slid out of her cubicle and started toward the hall.

"No. I wouldn't do that to you, I'd make an appointment if I was here for Ms. Andrea Simmons." Bruce Palmer laughed. "I came here to see if you and Miss Dawson wanted to have lunch. You're the only fair folk I know in this town."

Haddie slipped to the edge of the cutout between the

hall and the waiting room where Toby's desk sat. "Mr. Palmer."

"There she is." He offered her a blue-eyed smile and gestured hopefully toward the door.

Toby shrugged. "Sorry, we can't. Andrea's got a big case so we're all working through lunch."

Bruce looked genuinely disappointed. "Ah, well, welcome as a wet shoe, I see." He glanced at Haddie's gloved hand against the wall. "You feeling alright Miss Dawson?"

She tucked her hands behind her back. "Just a rash that's been springing up. I'm working with a dermatologist. Seems I'm allergic to something."

He frowned and nodded. "Sorry to hear, Miss Dawson." Bruce turned toward the door. "Well, I'll be back around and we'll catch up." As he touched his head preparing to depart, Haddie could imagine him tilting a tall hat. There was something intrinsically charming about the man.

Toby tilted her head and smiled. "Do you think it's the duck?"

"What do you mean?" Haddie asked.

"He always stops by and gets us to go to lunch with him. I think he's got a thing for you."

Heat rose up Haddie's cheeks. "It's the duck." She looked down at the note; she'd forgotten what she wanted for lunch.

Less than an hour later when their food arrived, Haddie got a text from Kiana. "Can you talk?"

Grabbing two fries, Haddie jumped out of her cubicle and snuck down the hall past Andrea's office to head outside.

Humid air tainted with fumes folded in around her. She found some shade on the street side of the building and leaned against the wall there. It wasn't the most private, but even at lunchtime, the heat kept the sidewalk traffic to a minimum.

"Hey, everything okay?" Haddie asked.

Kiana cleared her throat. "Not really. I thought I should let you know that the FBI, one of my superiors, is trying to get me to come in. I don't trust them. It might have something to do with the attack."

Haddie felt a chill rise despite the heat, and her eyes darted around at the people. One Black woman with loose curls leaned against a parking meter, reading a book but faced away. Everyone else looked in a hurry to pass down the street. "What are you going to do?"

"Move forward. If I can find a connection to the FBI and to the people who ran the raves, then I've got a chance to expose them and get my career back. For now, I'm hiding from the FBI as well. I don't know if they'll approach you."

Haddie straightened, away from the wall. If the FBI actively searched for Kiana, how safe would it be to drive out to Coos Bay?

"And tonight?" Haddie wasn't sure if she wanted to bail or dig in and find out what was going on.

"I'm still in," Kiana said. "Up to you if you still feel safe enough."

Haddie grimaced. She hardly felt safe. "I'm in."

"You need to hide that hair."

Haddie had bought a wig that Liz talked her into. "Okay. I got that covered."

CHAPTER 15

THOMAS TURNED onto the exit for Springfield. The midday traffic had been easy enough heading over the bridge. Light wisps of clouds lined a bright blue sky, making for a comfortable ride even with the sun overhead. The storm had cleaned some of the asphalt and left a renewal of green growth and a fresh petrichor in its wake. That illusion persisted as he rumbled onto 126 before the power grid marched across the landscape and the billboards rose over the buildings. The mountains to the east were a blue promise above the concrete and construction.

He'd never particularly liked Springfield, even when he'd come to Eugene in '48 to start a new identity. The people there had seemed to have the singular intention of cutting down every piece of ancient wood within their grasp. It was an act he'd had difficulty forgiving then, and especially when he moved back to the Eugene area in '92; it was part of the reason he'd picked Goshen to the south.

The middle school that Meg would be attending lay just off 126. Instead of I-5, he could have come up Main Street and would test that trip on the way home. Nestled into a residential community, it had a comfortable feel, though many of the homes seemed to crowd the fences and gates of the school.

He rumbled into a nearly empty lot and parked a few spaces away from a cluster of sedans. The woman he'd emailed had been clear with her directions. Leaving his helmet on the bike's seat, he strolled toward a pair of glass doors with his papers in hand.

It had been a first for him, getting a new identity for a school-aged child, or anyone other than himself for that matter. Getting records placed into a school system took more work and money than his usual documents. He already had a backup in the works. Hell, he would need to sell another antique bike at this rate.

The air inside had a cool, antiseptic smell. There were a lot of lights for an empty foyer. Doors around the perimeter had numbers or names imprinted on placards. Toward the back, an open hall gaped, leading to the side hallways.

A young woman working behind the counter lifted a pair of round spectacles as Thomas crossed the foyer. "Can I help you?" she asked.

He held up the manila envelope. "New student forms."

"Dawson or Yentz?" The woman stood, dressed in a short-sleeved blouse.

"Meg Dawson." He handed the envelope to her. "Mrs. Maynard?"

She smiled. "That's me, Mr. Dawson. I've got a few positions this morning. Normally I'm back there." She gestured toward one of the closed office doors. Silently, she began digging through the printouts and copies.

Thomas wiped stray hairs back to the tie of his braid. He planned a campout with Meg. Hopefully Haddie would be past this nonsense and join them with Rock. Perhaps even Sam. The girl acted more an aunt than Haddie. Actually, more like an older sister, which worked. Meg needed women in her life. Haddie never had that opportunity, but they both had lost their mothers: Haddie to a drug addict and thief, Meg — to something worse.

Unfortunately, his lead on Barbara Stevens brought up too many options. Crocus worked on getting more information that might help narrow down the search. Until then, Thomas had a spreadsheet of thirty-four possibilities, and he'd spent nearly a full night digging up drops of information about all of them. Social media worked to his advantage. The low-level soldiers he'd identified had dropped off social media almost immediately prior to joining the campaign. Whoever led this war wanted their operatives hidden.

Thomas, or his previous identity, had lost every blood relation from his immediate family. Why? Now that he'd met Harold Holmes and his brother Dmitry, and heard about Sameedha, he had to wonder if their bloodlines were being culled, or had been.

"You've been very thorough. I appreciate that." She smiled, tapping the papers even on her desk. "I'll begin getting her in the system this week. Would you prefer I call or email if I have questions?"

"Either. Whichever works for you."

She placed the envelope on a small stack. "Very well, I hope to see you at open house. I'll send you the details. It's very helpful for everyone involved."

"I look forward to it." Thomas nodded and headed toward the doors.

Pulling out his cell, he stepped into the heat. He'd already warned Biff to plan on hanging in the office and watching Meg tonight. Thomas opened up his app to make sure that he was still tracking Haddie's RAV4. She planned to continue their fool's plan of a break-in, and he wanted to be close by; she'd refused his direct help.

If she started another mess like the raves, he planned to be ready.

PART 3

We must not squabble, as we have done in the past; it became our undoing.

CHAPTER 16

FROM THE DRIVER'S SEAT, Haddie dug into the back of the RAV4 for her second container of tea. Salt-stung air breezed in from the passenger window. Even with her palms still sweaty from the initial anxiety and the warmth that hung over the Oregon coast at midnight, she couldn't risk the air conditioner running.

The office that Kiana searched lay at the intersection to Haddie's left. She'd parked in front of a gunsmith's shop where a line of empty spots gave her a good view of the office entrance. No streetlamps on the road left a dim, red glow from the traffic signal reflecting on the three cars parked at the bar across the street. Not a soul had moved into her view since Kiana had gone in the main entrance. Haddie had expected some activity, but evidently it stayed open well past two, and those who had come for the long haul had arrived already.

The other cars on the street were parked in front of a two-story apartment building beside the bar. The windows had been dark when Haddie drove up with Kiana. No one on the street seemed to consider lights necessary, leaving her in a comforting darkness. The traffic lights, most often red, kept the office entrance lit so she could watch without worrying that someone snuck past her guard.

Her fully charged phone sat beside her with Kiana's number queued up on text. When they'd arrived, Haddie had been tense enough to appreciate the stop to pee at the gas station. During the wait, her anxiety had lessened to a muted set of nerves. They had no idea how long Kiana would take inside; from the beginning she'd made that clear.

The occasional car sped through the intersection, but only a couple vehicles had turned, both in the opposite direction from where she was parked. The area outside the bar and office on this block seemed mainly residential.

Haddie checked her phone. She didn't do well sitting and waiting. The last text had been from Liz, wanting to come take a blood sample. There hadn't been time after a late day at work and getting ready for Coos Bay. Glancing around to make sure no one had entered the street, Haddie set the phone ready to text Kiana and put it on the console.

Lights from a car behind her lit through the RAV4 as it moved up the street toward her, heading toward the traffic signal. As it passed behind her, Haddie made out in the mirror a woman with a frizz of curly hair driving a new Chevy SS, a nondescript gray sedan that they were supposedly discontinuing. Haddie leaned into her seat, reaching back to find the stiff hair of the wig under her fingers. She took a deep breath as the car's brake lights lit just before the office building. They paused, and Haddie kept the frame of the window covering most of her face. How visible had she been when they'd driven up behind her?

Slowly, the car turned behind the two-story office building where Kiana searched. Haddie's heart raced, her

blood pounding in her ears. The alley led behind other buildings along that block and into some parking. She couldn't
trust herself to imagine what they were doing. The building
had other entrances, but the main door that she watched led
directly to the office where Kiana explored. Haddie picked
up the phone. The agreement had been anything suspicious,
but especially if someone came to the main entrance.

The car stopped at the opening of the alleyway,
blocking it and a back door. Haddie paused. A woman with
loose kinky hair that shifted from her movement got out and
looked right at Haddie.

Turning on her phone, Haddie fought against her
shaking fingers to text Kiana.

The woman stepped around the back of her car, continuing to stare at the RAV4. She had seen Haddie. It could be
a local watch kind of situation, a woman who kept an eye on
the neighborhood. Her eyes didn't glow orange, so she
wasn't a demon. Her face didn't have that yellow haze of the
coerced.

"Go," Haddie sent. The gleam from her phone lit the
steering wheel and likely her face.

She heard the tone first, like hers but a different note.
Sharper. Higher pitched. Instinctively, she felt herself brace
with a grunt that brought out a hint of her own tone, like she
had with Sameedha.

The woman's skin, around her face, ankles, and hands,
glowed softly with blue light.

Red light exploded around the RAV4. It formed into
thin lines of lightning that shifted and repositioned. Two
streams stretched across each side of her hood and down to
the asphalt. A tangle in the center joined them. To each
side, arm-like streams of red lightning caressed her car.

Sharp zaps snapped like a fast rain onto pavement and metal.

Pungent ozone filled the air as Haddie drew in a sharp breath.

Black marks showed on the blue paint where the lightning touched. The windshield darkened in small blotches. Finally, a thin finger found its way in through the open passenger window. Bright and impossible, it darted across her seat and dashboard. The scent of burning fabric drifted inside the car. Stabbing toward Haddie, it stopped just a finger's width from her arm. She jerked into the door and fumbled for the handle.

The woman had created this. She stood there, frozen behind her car, glowing blue light from her exposed skin, framed against the distinct darkness.

Haddie dropped her phone to the floor and managed to get the door open. A second finger reached in as it cracked open, and Haddie was immediately unable to get past whatever barrier she'd put up.

Throwing the door open, Haddie growled. Her tone squelched in the air. The resistance felt like a wave of pressure forcing back against her. Electricity danced around her, but no visions came. No pain prickled across her skin as if her blood shattered.

Like with Sameedha, her power had failed. It seemed that others could block Haddie's abilities, like she blocked theirs.

The large, red-lightning creature stepped back from Haddie and the RAV4, as if stunned. It acted animated, not as if the lightning came from the woman in the way Harold Holmes had produced light, but as an entity of its own, like the demons.

It disappeared, leaving her with a blurry, green image locked in her sight.

Haddie could barely see through the afterimage. The gray sky of the night above the city faded into blackness. She caught a motion as the woman raced back into her car, a faint shape in the dark shadows behind the building.

Stepping out of the RAV4, Haddie considered chasing the woman. *What would I do? Try and kill her again?* Obviously, the woman could protect herself from Haddie's power.

No one had died, and she'd warned Kiana. Shaking, Haddie stood, watching as the lights of the woman's car lit up. She ached to follow, to chase. *No. Don't make this worse.* Maybe she should drive away; they'd set up a second and third meet-up area in case things got ugly. This had been ugly, and perhaps a bit noisy.

A light had gone on inside one of the upper apartments beside the bar.

The woman's Chevy caught gravel or dirt and launched down the alleyway out of sight. *I've lost her.* Haddie could have at least gotten the license plate. However, with the green afterimage following her eyes, that might not have been possible.

She could still smell the ozone of the creature along with burnt paint. How many people were there like her and Dad? It didn't seem possible that people hadn't ever mentioned a twelve foot, red, lightning monster. She couldn't ask Terry. Maybe Aaron could look for her. Maybe the same people who hid the sightings of the demons hid these creatures as well.

She had to make a decision: move the RAV4 or chance waiting for Kiana to evacuate. Peering past the fading afterimage, she searched the street. No one had come out of the bar. The upstairs light remained on in the apartment, but no others. The sounds of electricity probably didn't travel that far.

The electric woman probably had been connected to the office, so Haddie could expect their mission had been blown. *Not really my fault.* She'd been as discreet as possible parked down the street from the office. Others might show up, like they had at the Portland hotel after she'd begun investigating the raves. Best to call it quits. Hopefully, Kiana had found something in the short time she'd been inside.

Haddie could be grateful that she hadn't killed anyone, even though she'd tried.

Kiana had said she would likely take the back way out if they were disturbed. It might take a couple minutes. Sweating under the hot wig, Haddie turned to climb back in to wait inside her car.

The green afterimage swaying in her vision as she turned momentarily confused the silent move of shapes and the color beside her.

A man, face buzzing with a haze of pale yellow lights, slammed into her. The door to the RAV4 snapped shut under his impact.

Haddie flew to the asphalt, the black wig spinning over one of her eyes. She slid for a brief second before rolling up on her shoulder. With a whip of her head, she threw the wig off. Old training came to her as she stood and assumed a fighting stance. Clumsily, he moved forward, and she grabbed both of his forearms and tossed him rolling to the sidewalk.

Standing ready she watched, but she hadn't killed him. She could have used her powers, but hadn't. Gratefully, Taekwondo had come as a reflex this time. Taking deep breaths, she studied the man and thought of Don Mack, an equipment operator who'd been dragged into this against his will. *Thrown into a car, by me.* Were the demons innocent, like him? How many innocent people had she killed?

This man, who could have been cooking at a restaurant the week before, forced himself up to his feet. He wouldn't stop.

But she didn't need to kill him. *No more. Not tonight.*

CHAPTER 17

BEFORE JUMPING OUT THE WINDOW, Kiana watched the car turn out of the alley. The small wooden roof, part of an enclosure for a downstairs back entrance, held under her feet. Taking careful steps down the slant while scanning the back parking lot and alley, she came to the edge just above the dumpster. She knelt and swung off to get her feet quietly onto the outer edge. Crashing through the cheap plastic lid and being trapped inside would not work out well if they had visitors. Besides, it stunk.

She had two choices: follow the gray car and go around the block, or go back the shorter way up the alley directly to the street where the RAV4 was parked. Had Haddie overreacted to the car? Maybe this was a false alarm and Kiana could get back inside. So far, the night hadn't been very fruitful. A handful of papers were stuffed into the back pocket of her jeans; she'd grabbed them at the warning text from Haddie.

Kiana climbed off the dumpster, drew her gun, and stalked around the shadows of the office building toward the street and Haddie's car.

A blue house with a groomer's business in the front blocked her view of the parking spot where Haddie was staking out the building. A chain link fence, the far end reflecting the red traffic light, separated the building from the alley. Across the street, someone in an apartment had turned on one of their lights. Each step beside the office building allowed Kiana to view more of the surrounding area, but she didn't want to risk hurrying and jump into any surprises.

Across from her and beside the apartment building, a figure ran toward her. A short and dark shape, she couldn't make out more than the motion. Taking two quick steps, she slid against the back door, using the inset frame to hide her position.

Kiana's heart beat faster as she saw Haddie, outside the RAV4, circling close with someone in the middle of the street. What had happened? Did this have anything to do with the car that sped down the alleyway?

A quick movement on Haddie's part, and the attacker dropped to the street. She'd lost her wig. Her white hair shone despite the darkness, and red glinted on it from the intersection. So much for the disguise. Or a discreet stakeout.

Kiana looked back across the street. She didn't want to leave Haddie alone in the fight, but didn't want to expose herself until she knew what the person approaching intended. For all she knew, they could be innocent. The apartments bordered one side of the alley, and a warehouse of some sort lay on the other, opposite from where Haddie had parked.

The runner slowed as they reached the end of the warehouse. The red glow of the traffic light exposed a distinctly male face with pale skin and a goatee. He stopped at the corner of the building, partially blocked from Kiana by the telephone pole at the edge of the alley. An ally of the person attacking Haddie, or a curious innocent?

Haddie's sparring partner attempted another close round with her, and she deftly dropped him again.

The man with the goatee raised his hand.

Kiana sprang away from the building to target him around the pole.

Their shots rang out at the same time. The echoes up the alley and street were indistinguishable. He spun with an upper body hit and slammed against the building. Sliding down beside a stack of white pallets, his arms seemed limp.

Kiana turned to find Haddie on the street. Her attacker crouched near the back of the SUV, collecting something off the pavement.

Striding quickly across the alley, Kiana glanced from Haddie's attacker back toward the bar and the intersection as she made her way around the chain link fence of the groomer. A second light had sprung up in the apartment building at the sound of gunfire.

Haddie rolled up to sit. Her attacker approached with something in their hand. A red glint of metal reflected the traffic light.

Kiana shot.

As the attacker's body crumpled to the asphalt, she jogged toward Haddie. A quick glance confirmed that the shooter with the goatee was likely dead or dying. The apartments had all lit up; no one had come out of the bar.

Kiana kept her weapon trained on the person beside Haddie, but there was no movement.

Haddie had one hand on her hip and the other planted on the asphalt to get the opposite knee under her.

"How bad?" Kiana asked.

Haddie shook her head, rising on a knee. "I don't know. Hurts like all hell." Her dark jeans had a small wet spot that spread from under her hand. "I think it ricocheted. I heard it hit the street. What am I going to tell David?"

The man on the pavement had on a light blue T-shirt, turned black across his chest where the bullet had exited.

How long did they have to drive a blue SUV out of town before the police caught up?

Kiana holstered her gun and grabbed Haddie under the armpit, dragging her up. "Keys in the ignition?"

Haddie groaned. "Smart key."

Kiana eased Haddie toward the back of the RAV4. The bullet had grazed a palm's width across the woman's left hip. She wouldn't bleed out. "Which pocket?"

"Right." Haddie dug into her pocket as they limped to her car. "Damn, that hurts." She produced the fob. "I thought you shot me for a moment."

Kiana opened the back hatch and maneuvered Haddie into sitting on a pile of towels, clothing, and a cardboard box lid. "Sorry," she said before lifting Haddie's legs. Kiana rolled the groaning woman into the back and shut the hatch.

Silhouettes marked two of the windows in the apartment building. The music had always been loud inside the bar. No one came onto the street from there. Someone would have called in the shots by now.

Kiana grabbed Haddie's black wig and tossed it onto the floor of the passenger side before she started the SUV. "You okay?" she called back. The windshield had brown marks on it. Burnt paint and ozone hung in the air. "Keep pressure on it. I've got to get us out of town before we can look at it."

"I'm fine." Haddie sounded like she spoke through clenched teeth.

The hood had scorches. What happened?

She drove away from the traffic light. That was where the main street cut through the town and the busiest traffic had been. Kiana turned the east at the corner. She would have to get back to the main street; that highway led east and then north out of Coos Bay. The police department lay on the southeast edge, but there were patrols in the city. It shouldn't take long for them to respond at this time of night.

She jumped when the car dash rang with a phone call. The display read Dad. "It's your father." Thomas Dawson.

"Answer it. Please." Haddie's voice shifted as she spoke, and a seat in the back snapped forward.

Kiana punched the answer button.

"Haddie. You okay?" His voice calm, but insistent, had a background of a police scanner.

"Not really, Dad." Haddie had crawled closer, just behind the driver's seat.

"Get back on Newmark, east to a 7-Eleven. It'll come up on your right. Pull to the far side of the building, you'll see me."

He was in Coos Bay? Did he always shadow his daughter? Where had he been during Portland? Kiana turned left at the next corner, following his directions. They could use any help at this point. He sounded reassuring, like he had a plan.

Haddie snorted. "You followed me?" She sounded indignant, and childish.

In the background, a heavy truck engine started up. "You did say you'd be doing this job in Coos Bay tonight."

"And, that I didn't need your help."

"Are you — hurt?" he asked, ignoring her comment.

Haddie took a moment to respond. "Just a scratch."

Kiana hadn't expected this dynamic between them.

Haddie seemed less mature when confronted by him. Not unexpected, considering her age.

"Agent Wilkins with you?" His tone changed, sharper. Disapproving.

Not an agent anymore. "I'm driving."

"You got those directions?"

"Yes." Kiana stopped herself just short of "Sir." He had a commanding demeanor, despite never having served in the military. At least, not according to his records.

They drove in silence, pulling onto the main road and passing through a quiet, sleeping town. Driving by a gas station, Kiana spotted the sign for the 7-Eleven as a siren whined somewhere. Salt-scented air came in through the open passenger window.

A blue sedan was parked on the right side of the convenience store, and no one was visible on the inside as she pulled into the parking and drove past the windows. On the far side, Thomas stood waving them around the corner. He had two poster-sized, gray squares in a gloved hand. With his long braid and a black T-shirt, he looked the biker part.

A large white tow truck was parked along the side, the towing bar already lowered. He gestured her to drive up on it, straightening her out as she approached with hand signals. He had a tense hard look, and resisted all but the occasional urge to glance inside the SUV for his daughter. Kiana tapped the dash and closed the connection he'd left open.

A tow truck was a good plan. If there were a description, they'd be looking for an SUV, gray, green, blue, and any other number of colors that the witnesses described. They wouldn't look twice at a tow. He stopped her, frowning at what seemed the burns on the hood.

He slapped a magnet on the door, leaning to the

window to peer inside. When he crossed to the back, he opened the hatch. "Let me see."

Kiana stepped out and could see him through the windows.

His brows furrowed as he looked in on Haddie. "Hmm."

Quickly, he walked to Kiana's side and placed an advertisement for Fiora's bakery on the door. "What happened to the car? – Nevermind." Thomas nodded toward the back. "Can you get her into the cab of the truck?"

She nodded. "She can walk. Looks like a graze."

Thomas walked to the back of the tow truck. "There's a kit in the back seat."

Had he planned on someone getting injured? Kiana eased Haddie out. The sirens called out from the west; they wouldn't need to pass by. The side street next to the convenience store was residential and looked asleep. This side of the building smelled like stale beer and piss.

Haddie shifted out, feet first. The stain on her hip had grown, but didn't look too bad. She grimaced at the movement and looked shaken, if not slightly angry.

Haddie walked around the SUV on her own. "What the hell?"

Thomas didn't respond.

Kiana took Haddie's shoulders and moved her toward the cab of the truck.

This was the best way out of the city.

CHAPTER 18

THOMAS relaxed as they crossed the long bridge over Coos Bay. Salt and marsh seeped in through the AC, and the tires settled into a rhythm. Scant traffic, mostly trucks, moved along the highway. At a distance, and lessened by the late hour, lights glimmered from the houses crouched on the shores and dotted the hilltops. Even with the encroaching development, the night's stars shone bright and clear. He could remember when no lights were lit along this bay. He'd nearly moved out here, but knew that population would grow too fast as the coast became popular.

The bridge ended in a small blip of a township, and they passed through the single traffic light on the green. Haddie seemed to have calmed down and rested silently with Kiana in the back seat.

Devil in hell, he couldn't stand her getting hurt. The FBI agent, Kiana Wilkins, had done a good job at dressing the hip. He would look at the wound again when they got back to Eugene. It could use a couple stitches. The one sheriff they'd passed hadn't given them a second glance.

The scanner hadn't mentioned a plate number, so they were likely clear.

Haddie cleared her throat in the back. He looked up, but could only see Kiana in the rearview mirror.

"Why, Dad? Did you imagine you'd have to save me again?" Evidently, Haddie would need to get this off her chest.

"Didn't save you." He sighed and wiped back his hair. "You would've done just fine driving on your own. They never got your plate." He'd had a hard time reconciling his absence in Portland. If he'd stayed, she might not have been hurt so badly. She'd looked a fright coming out of that burning building. He shrugged, more to himself than anyone else. "This is just me being an over-protective dad. I don't believe I'll change any time soon. I worry — about you — and all this."

"Didn't want your help."

She still sounded angry. He couldn't blame her. "I know. Couldn't help myself." He glanced back in the mirror, but only caught Kiana's eyes. "I'll try to be more respectful of your independence." He had been the one to train her this way.

Over the scanner, they said two had died on scene from gunshot wounds. That meant the agent had killed them. Had Haddie used her powers? He'd have to wait until they were alone and she'd cooled down. He still had no idea how much Haddie had told Kiana.

Haddie's tone dropped. "It went bad. Obviously. I came across something new. A woman. She made some kind of lightning creature."

That would explain the SUV. "We can talk about it later." He hadn't wanted to discuss anything in front of the agent. *Too late.*

"What do you mean by lightning creature?" Kiana asked.

Thomas focused on the road, jaw tight. How much had Haddie said to this woman? *Hell, the FBI.*

"When she used her power — a creature made of lightning appeared — red lightning. It attacked me, the car first. It seemed to act on its own, like a demon." Haddie paused. "It stood twice as tall as me."

"How is that possible?" Kiana's tone seemed incredulous. She paused and stammered, "I guess — any of this. How did you survive?"

"I can do this thing. I mean, I've done this thing where I stop them using their powers on me."

"Them?" Kiana asked.

"Haddie." Thomas could only hope that she'd stop. In her mood, she might speak just to spite him. FBI or not, it was bad enough that Liz knew. Secrets were liquid; they always leaked out and the more hands that held them, the worse they spilled.

"Kiana deserves to know what she's up against."

Kiana's tone became more thoughtful. "Are they people like yourself? Someone who can make someone disappear, only different? Is that what happened in Portland? Is that why you were there?"

Haddie grew silent for a moment and Thomas hoped she'd come to her senses.

"Yes," Haddie said tentatively. "But let's ignore Portland. It's over. This lady is alive and driving around. Have you ever heard of strange lightning accidents or burnings? From FBI reports or something?"

"Like the strange burnings around Harold Holmes?"

Kiana seemed to be putting too much of this together. The woman may have put herself on the line committing a break-in with Haddie, but she could still reconcile with the FBI. It could turn everything upside down and force Thomas into a new identity with Meg. It could put Haddie into a spotlight she might not be able to escape.

"What are your plans now, Agent Wilkins?" Thomas asked. "Will you be breaking into this office again? Did you get any information? You're asking a lot of questions. I thought Haddie risked herself tonight to get answers."

"Agreed. Not much in the way of progress tonight. I've got some papers and a few companies to investigate." Kiana watched him through the mirror. "As for going back. Not at this time. They'll likely clear out."

"What next?" Thomas hoped he could kill the conversation, but the agent didn't rise quickly.

Kiana shrugged, holding his eyes. "I'll take a long look at the information, see if there's anything to get a lead on. Nothing stands out at first glance."

"And the FBI? What will you do about them?"

"Hide," she responded.

"You traced Haddie's phone in Portland through the FBI. If you're concerned about them, don't you think they could figure out that you and Haddie were in Coos Bay at the same time? At least use burners."

"All I'm using right now is a burner." Kiana kept a calm tone. "It's not the FBI directly that I'm concerned about. There's a faction inside it. They'll be able to mark me as missing, but hopefully they won't want to use too many resources and draw attention to themselves. I could use help, and already appreciate what you and Haddie have done."

Thomas found himself reluctantly respecting the woman. She held up under fire and didn't let her emotions rise quickly.

"How did Haddie get shot?"

"Shooter came down the opposite alley while your daughter had an attacker under control. I shot him, but too late." Kiana spoke matter of fact, without an apology.

"Dad, stop. Kiana saved me." Her voice had a stressed tone she rarely reached. "I kept trying to not hurt this one guy who attacked me. Stupid. Didn't even think to keep an eye out for a second."

Thomas took a deep breath. The first few times he'd had to defend himself, he'd lived with remorse. He'd had decades between each incident to deal with it. She'd been involved in a lot of death in the past year. He'd seen the effect killing had on soldiers in many different wars. *I should have seen this coming.*

"This is not on you. The agent back there should have done more recon." He wasn't being fair. He'd jumped into situations aplenty.

"Agreed," Kiana said.

Thomas blew out a quiet breath. *This woman keeps her cool.* Perhaps the conversation would drop now. He didn't need her digging into any more about Portland or Harold Holmes, or his own abilities.

He turned west onto 38 and began the long dark stretch down Umpqua Hwy that led to I-5. It was a pleasant ride during the day. Thomas turned the scanner up and raised his voice. "If you plan to go out foraging for more berries, let me know."

He wiped his hair back, eyes lifting to the star-filled sky. "Whether you like it or not, Haddie, I plan on being there."

CHAPTER 19

As THEY TOOK the ramp off I-5 into Goshen, Haddie tried to push away the growing apprehension with a deep breath. Dad's mood had topped an already stressful night, and even the long drive in the dark had done little to calm her.

Kiana had been able to lean against the window and sleep. Or maybe she just didn't want to deal with Dad.

After the confrontation with the lightning and the realization that their investigation exposed yet another person with power, Haddie's mind couldn't stop. How many people like Harold Holmes were out there? How many different abilities? Had they been there all along, and just now she'd become exposed to them?

One car shared the highway leading to Dad's garage, a pair of red lights ahead in the darkness. How late or early was it? She didn't question the time or why Dad went directly to the garage. The last Haddie saw of her phone, she'd dropped it on the floor of the RAV4. Her ass hurt, and she wanted to lie down desperately. She had originally planned on getting no sleep, not being shot. Tomorrow would be hell at work.

They pulled into the garage lot and down to the back beside the Mini Cooper. The motion lights lit Haddie's side of the truck and she winced, looking away.

"My phone's in the car. And some water bottles," she finally said as the truck came to a rocking stop.

Kiana nodded. "I'll get them."

Dad stepped out his side and opened Haddie's door. "How's your bandage doing?"

The familiar scents of oil, metal, and rust came from the garage and the parts piled up on the side. Her hand reached down, but she didn't touch her hip. She'd pulled her jeans back up over the dressing Kiana had done; they helped keep a solid pressure against the wound. It felt more like a burn than anything else.

Haddie winced as she stepped out. "Hurts. Other than that, I can't tell."

Did he plan to take her for stitches? He looked at the blood soaked into the jeans.

"We'll check it at your apartment." He gestured to the Mini Cooper. "Get in the front. I'm going to grab a better kit."

As he headed toward the garage, Kiana stepped out of the RAV4 with the water bottles. "Where's your phone?"

Haddie hobbled over, hoping that it hadn't gotten left on the street somewhere back in Coos Bay. "Should be on the driver's floor."

She took the bottles before Kiana leaned back in, digging under the seat. Haddie imagined her phone with the police in Coos Bay and Eugene police waiting at her apartment.

"Ah." Kiana stepped away, handing Haddie's phone over. "You're father's right. You should get a burner with everything you've got going on."

Haddie felt heat rise along her cheeks as she took the phone. She checked the time: 3:22 a.m. Had she told too much to Kiana, even if she was ex-FBI? Dad had stopped her when she might have been about to say too much. "Where do I get one?" Haddie asked

"Some convenience stores. Ask your father; I get the feeling he'll know."

Juggling the two bottles, Haddie limped toward the Mini Cooper. She'd have to think about how much she'd be willing to let Kiana know about Portland. How would she explain without exposing Liz? And Harold Holmes? That put Dad's abilities out there. How much did she intend to trust this woman?

By the time she'd tossed her water bottles onto the floor and eased herself into the Mini Cooper, Dad had come around the garage with a small satchel.

"Kiana, do you need anything on the way back? Something I can run in and pick up?" he asked. "You probably shouldn't be out much, with your friends looking for you."

"Probably shouldn't," agreed Kiana. "I'm good. Thank you though."

Haddie leaned toward the window, trying to take some of the pressure off her butt cheek in the small car. It had never made sense, and her dad had never given a good explanation why he drove the Mini Cooper. He had a perfectly good Jeep Commander.

The ride across Eugene to the safe house where Kiana stayed proved less comfortable than the longer trip from Coos Bay. The rough drive up to the house from the road was the worst, and Haddie found herself cringing. As Dad parked, she got out and glared at the seat despite his protest.

Kiana looked up at the dark house and then back to Haddie. "Thank you. Sorry things got out of hand."

Haddie shrugged. "Not your fault. I'll call you tomorrow."

"On your burner." Kiana smirked.

"Yes. I'll make that happen." *On two hours sleep.* Reluctantly, she climbed back in and settled down.

Dad put the car in reverse and leaned his arm behind her. "Taking tomorrow off?"

"Can't. New client."

"Won't. You have a choice. That's not going to feel any better tomorrow. What are you going to tell them?" He drove down the hill, jolting her seat.

"Fell down the stairs. Bruised and scraped my hip." Haddie didn't know what excuse she'd make.

He waited until they'd reached the bottom to resume their conversation. "How much are you going to tell Kiana? She's sharp."

Haddie frowned. *I should have had him drop me home first.* "I won't mention you or Liz."

"She might figure it out."

"She probably imagines worse. She fought one of these demons," Haddie said.

"After your description tonight, I'm not sure it could be worse. Be careful what you chase. You might catch it."

Haddie twisted her hair into a knot and stared out the window into the darkness. The lightning creature had been rather terrifying. Was this person new to their powers, or had they been using them all along? She couldn't help being curious. Partially, she wanted to know what she was. Did they know?

Dad took a deep breath. "At least think things through before you jump in."

"In what I tell Kiana, or chasing these people?"

"Both," he said.

Haddie tapped at the window. "Maybe we need her, Dad. She knows what I can do; that's no secret."

"Maybe. Be careful. Think who you're involving when you mention details: me — Liz. You saw how quickly she tied the information directly back to Harold Holmes."

How bad could it be? If Kiana went back to the FBI, it would be disastrous. That didn't seem likely. Haddie wasn't about to out Dad. Even if the FBI found out about Liz's involvement in the raids, they'd just cover it up.

Maybe he's right. *I need to let this go. I'm not made for this.* However, the thought of ignoring the lady who could make electrical monsters made her jaw clench.

Tonight hadn't gone that badly. "I didn't kill tonight."

"People died." He sighed as he said it. "That's not on you. The thing about killing is it can eat you up. Some people turn hard. It's best if you make sure you're involved in the right thing before you risk your life or the lives of others." His tone had a sense of urgency, or pain to it, like he had to let her know. "If you must defend yourself, then accept that. If you put yourself into situations where you might have to defend yourself, then look at that carefully."

How many times had Dad killed, in war and outside of it? Is that what she would do – chase down people like this lightning lady until someone died? He talked as if he had it balanced somehow. How did you do that? *Doing the right thing.* Dad had just said the same thing Sam had said. Haddie couldn't bury her head in the sand if something threatened Liz or someone she cared about.

But maybe she didn't need to chase this down. Don Mack hadn't deserved to die. Neither did that man tonight. They'd been coerced, compelled to attack her. While waiting for Kiana to get out of the office, she had hurt the man on the street badly enough that any typical man would have given up. Still, he'd risked his life knowing that Kiana had a weapon, just for the chance to stab Haddie.

Aaron had told her how he had coerced men who attacked a girl when he was in college. He had done it instinctively to protect, much as she had done with Dmitry. Someone with Aaron's powers controlled the man she encountered earlier. *Not to protect.* Stopping that would be good. Perhaps the leads Kiana came up with could stop that. Wouldn't that be worthy?

They pulled into the back of her apartment, and she imagined how upset Rock would be; he knew when she'd been hurt. And Jisoo would be hungry.

Haddie just wanted to sleep. Andrea would have a new set of tasks once she got back from the courthouse, depending on how it went. She had Aaron coming in for the Unceasing seminar. Maybe she could skip that.

"You want me to drive you to work tomorrow? The bike might be rough on your wound." Dad parked the Mini Cooper where her RAV4 usually went.

Haddie shook her head. She might have, but didn't want any more lectures. "I'll be fine." He couldn't keep leaving Meg alone so much; she'd move in with Sam if she had the choice.

He grabbed the black satchel and pointed upstairs. "Let's get you stitched up."

"You?" Haddie stopped, her hand on the door handle.

"Four stitches — max. I can do that much."

Haddie cringed. "Shouldn't you get back to Meg?"

He chuckled. "I'll be gentle."

A moment before, she'd been ready to fall asleep as soon as she walked in the door. Now, she felt like every nerve stood on end as she got out of his car.

He had to be as tired as she was. Had he left Meg with Biff? He wouldn't have left her alone.

Haddie paused at the bottom of the steps. "Dad, why aren't there more of us? Harold Holmes and all that?"

"You're procrastinating."

A bit. "I'm not."

"I wish I knew."

"Do you think Meg?" She started up the steps when he didn't answer.

CHAPTER 20

HADDIE GROANED at her phone as it buzzed from the dresser. "Hateful thing."

She'd placed it out of reach to make herself get up. Her eyes felt like they had mud in them, and her ass like it had a brick under the skin. She smelled like she needed the shower that she wouldn't be taking.

Rock whined lightly from the other side of the bed.

"Turn it off, Rock. Make it stop."

She imagined Andrea's face and shifted a knee off the bed, unwilling to roll off her stomach. Loose pants today. Skirt? She hadn't worn one since freshman year. *Did any still fit? No, I've got to ride the Fat Boy today.* How long would it take to get the RAV4 fixed? Staggering, she made it to her feet.

Turning the alarm off, she saw the message from Sam. "Let me know when you need Rock walked. T messaged me."

Punching out a message with thick fingers, Haddie replied, "I'm up."

The bandage didn't look bloody, but it looked too small

for the amount of pain she felt. Jisoo, despite his surprise midnight snack, called to her from the kitchen. Haddie limped out of her bedroom. Dad had been right. It hurt worse. She laughed at the thought of riding.

Aaron and the Unceasing seminar would not be happening. The whole burner phone thing, she'd never asked Dad about. Maybe he could just pick one up for her. She shook her head, passing Jisoo on the way to the coffee. Everyone could just forget about today.

Jisoo walked the counter with her and rubbed against her arm. "Give me a sec, love." Rock grunted somewhere behind her and Haddie started the water running into the coffee pot.

By the time Sam arrived, Haddie was enjoying the first pour of a cup of black coffee, Jisoo and Rock had been fed, and she'd thrown on a T-shirt. She could have climbed right back in bed.

Sam's black hair pooched out and up on the left side, as though she'd only been up a short while herself. She scratched Rock's head as she stepped inside. "Hey, T said you scraped your hip, you okay?"

Haddie made an effort not to limp. "Yeah. Clumsy." She gestured to the kitchen. "Coffee? Sorry. I forget. I doubt there's anything in there other than water you might drink."

"I'm good." Sam tucked her hands behind her back. "You better today?"

Haddie snorted. "My existential crisis? I doubt it. I do appreciate you talking with me about it. I think you're correct. Focus on what's right."

"You've got a good heart. Even when you're impulsive and jump in feet first. You'd feel worse if you didn't try." Sam grabbed Rock's leash, sending him into a quick prance. "Better than me. I just want to hide most of the time. You get out there and do things. I still haven't got my license; it terrifies me." Sam shrugged and led Rock out the door.

Haddie didn't know if she would feel worse if she didn't try. Could she let the lightning lady go? Could she be okay with innocent people being coerced by some other person with powers like Sameedha? After Portland, she'd been content just knowing that Liz had survived. Yes, she could let this go, here and now. She'd help Kiana, but not to the point of recklessly chasing down everybody who had powers.

She headed into the bedroom with just over an hour before she had to be at work. Brushing her teeth, she heard the phone buzz at an incoming text and wandered out to grab her phone.

"Aaron today at 4:45 Greyhound 355 S A St. Are you coming?"

Haddie stood with her brush in her mouth, motionless for a moment. "Daw." At the moment, she wanted nothing more than to crawl back into bed.

She typed a response, knowing she might bail with an excuse. "Probably. If I can get out of work early."

"Yaass! Later, Buckaroo."

David. What would she tell him? She still wanted to check in with Kiana before work if there was time. Maybe later, from work. *No, the burner*. After lunch then; Haddie could pick one up during her break, if Andrea allowed them out today.

Haddie leaned forward and spit into the sink, looking at her purpura-marked face. *I just want to sleep*. She shook her head, started tying back her hair, and spoke to the mirror. "Put your face on and get to it, Haddie."

CHAPTER 21

A CLOUDLESS BLUE sky added to the heat rising from the asphalt when Haddie slowed in the office parking lot. The pavement already had a dry hot smell that covered some of the fumes from the street and cars. She pulled her Fat Boy into a parking spot facing the office. Her side hurt but had gone from flaming pain to numbness at the ride. It wasn't as bad as she'd expected it to be.

Haddie pulled off her helmet, sweating under it and the gloves. She'd found a pair of black, high waisted pants that fit loosely around her hips. There were only small front pockets, barely good for keys, so she ended up with a purse. That was probably why she couldn't remember the last time she'd worn them.

Josh hadn't arrived; hopefully, he was okay. That might mean an extra load to her work. She imagined his mother. *What illness did she have?* His absence could be unrelated. Haddie knew so little about him.

As she walked across the waiting room, Toby called out from the kitchen. "Morning, Haddie."

Haddie stopped just inside the archway into the hall,

looking left toward the kitchen. Toby couldn't see her, but had guessed right. "Morning. I'll be back for coffee." She ambled down the corridor, trying not to favor her hip.

Grace watched her limp into the back office and paused her typing. "Get shot?"

So, Cathy, the niece, *had* mentioned the phone call. Haddie tilted her head and shrugged. "Scraped, bruised mostly."

"Hmm." Grace went back to her work. "Andrea said to continue where you left off and she'll re-prioritize when she gets in."

Haddie dropped her helmet under her desk. A thin layer of dried coffee coated the bottom of her mug with Yuno Gasa fading on the outside. She stepped out of her cubicle and looked in at Grace. "Coffee?"

Grace nodded and passed her tumbler. "Thanks." As the paralegal, she got the brunt of the new cases. She'd been there when Haddie had left the evening before.

The smell of brewing coffee wafted down the hall as Haddie worked her way slowly to the kitchen. Toby rinsed mugs in the sink wearing a yellow patterned dress. Beside her, and nearly full, the coffee pot on the counter steamed and gurgled.

"You look like sunshine today," Haddie said.

Toby gave a light swirl. "Felt right for today." She frowned. "You get hurt?"

"Scraped, bruised, clumsy." Haddie grabbed two sugars for Grace's coffee. "No Josh?"

"Same message. I'm worried. It's not like him. Not the missing work part, that's totally like him. The texts are weird." Toby leaned against the wall by the fridge. "It's going to be a busy day."

The front door of the office chimed, and Toby bounced up and skipped to the doorway. "Coffee?"

Andrea entered the hall in a brisk walk, turning opposite them toward her office. "No, I stopped on the way." In one arm, she juggled a cup of coffee along with her satchel and a fat manila envelope. Bright blue hair sticks bobbed in her red bun.

Toby silently motioned Haddie ahead of her toward the coffee pot.

What was she going to tell David? *Another lie, obviously*. She had to say something or avoid him until her wound was healed. She texted him from her cubicle. "Good morning. I love you. How's work?"

"Busy," he replied. "I love you. How are you doing?"

She couldn't tell from his response if he was annoyed or just busy. "Okay. Scratched my hip. Sore." She grimaced. *How much can I avoid lying?*

"How?"

Haddie sighed. She'd worked on a lie all morning. "Someone hit the RAV4 in the parking lot and I didn't notice until I scraped against the bumper."

"Hit and run? Do you need anything?"

I hate lying to him. "No, all good. Didn't sleep much. Can't wait to get off work and crash." That part, at least, was the truth. She managed to finish the conversation without any more lies and without making any plans for the night. He had a long drive from Medford to get back from a client.

The fresh coffee tasted good. The morning turned into a long list of fact checking and proofing that left Haddie fighting to stay awake. Dad checked in, wanting her to come by at lunch to get her dressing changed. She didn't have time. Instead, she found out where she could get a burner. He didn't ask any questions and gave her a couple spots, reminding her to pay with cash. Haddie would have to hit an ATM.

She had the Coos Bay Police blotter up on one of her tabs, but they hadn't mentioned anything yet about the shooting. Would this get swept off the news like the demons in Portland?

In another group of tabs, she had multiple searches going on for lightning deaths. As she proofed, she'd think of another way to search and jump over, but so far nothing but typical strikes showed up. No glowing twelve foot red creatures. Even just a suspicious circumstance would have satisfied her curiosity, but many were witnessed or coincided with storms. Terry would have better luck with something like this, but she wasn't going to involve him in her mess.

While Haddie entered another search term, Andrea walked into the back room. "Haddie. Do you have your truck today?"

Haddie minimized the window and scrambled to bring up the right document. "No. It's uh — at the shop."

Andrea glared in the direction of Josh's cubicle before storming toward the hall. "Come get my keys. The DA has released two boxes that I needed yesterday."

Haddie scurried, grabbing her phone and then turning back for her purse, unused to carrying one. Wincing, she lurched out of her cubicle and raised her eyebrows at Grace.

Andrea drove an E-Class Mercedes-Benz, an AMG 63 D, dark with a light interior. It almost looked new for a 2012. Haddie had to move the seat back, and her hip complained at every twist. She smiled the entire time. She'd driven an A-Class at a dealership once, but that certainly hadn't had a sports package. Dad had gotten her in for a test drive; the salesman rode a Honda Goldwing and Dad had fixed his bike.

The E-Class drove like a dream - for the four blocks to the courthouse. After the second turn, Haddie wanted to take it east to the mountains and forget about work, Kiana, and Aaron's arrival. Instead, she took the corner and pulled into the parking lot. The AC had barely started blowing cool.

Even the door sounded snug as she closed it. Haddie walked around the vehicle before circling toward the courthouse. She strode across the street, slightly sweaty, then slowed to look at her phone when it vibrated.

Aaron texted. "You're going?"

"Maybe." Haddie stopped at the edge of the plaza under the shade of an oak. "Have you heard anything about attacks by lightning? I didn't want to ask Terry."

"I have not heard about lightning attacks. Can you explain? Why not involve Terry?"

"I'm trying to keep him safe." Haddie paused, then sent the text.

"Not sure any of us are safe. What incident with lightning?"

Haddie took a deep breath, glancing around her, but the sidewalk traffic remained quiet in the midday heat. She didn't have time to go into everything. "I'll explain tonight."

"Ok," he texted, "so not maybe, definitely going tonight."

"Yes." Evidently, she was going to the seminar after all.

"Have you talked to Terry about the un headquarters in New York?"

Considering everything else, Haddie didn't want to get too focused on the Unceasing. "No. Last I heard, something about Anthony's beneficiary."

"We can discuss that tonight too."

Haddie typed, "Ok." Driving the Mercedes had given her a false sense of energy. She would regret this.

She managed to carry the two boxes in one trip, encouraged by the opportunity to drive Andrea's Mercedes-Benz E-Class a few more blocks back to the law office. She thought about Terry. How much of her protection, perhaps overprotection, came from the incident with Liz and the raves? Her friend had been in danger from dealing with people like Haddie and her dad. If Liz hadn't gotten into trouble at the raves, then Haddie probably wouldn't be so concerned.

The Mercedes purred into life and Haddie sat for a moment watching the traffic maneuvering slowly down the street that led back to the law office. She imagined driving into Utah and Montana on winding roads, like the trips she'd taken with her Dad early in college. She put the car into drive; everything had become so busy these last few years.

The law office sat inside a two-story, beige building connected in a line of stores that ended mid-block at the parking lot on the corner. As Haddie pulled up the street ready to turn into the entrance, she recognized a figure leaning against the slim remainder of wall next to the last window.

Detective Cooper, in his black uniform, made eye contact and scowled slightly while watching her pull in. His carefully trimmed mustache tightened as he pushed himself off the concrete wall and followed her into the lot. What was he doing here?

Haddie sat in the car for a moment, breathing past a momentary panic, before pulling up the seat as far as she dared without locking her knees under the steering wheel. If this had anything to do with Coos Bay, there would have been patrolmen instead. He stood outside the door as she opened it.

"Ms. Dawson."

"Detective Cooper." She tried not to wince as she pried herself out. Without pausing, she headed past him to the trunk. "What are you doing here?"

"Have you seen Special Agent Wilkins?" he asked.

She shook her head as she opened the trunk. "The FBI lady? Not since last fall. She did call about meeting up with her, but that was a month or so ago and she never returned my call. Why?"

"The FBI is looking for her. Have they contacted you?"

"No." Haddie snorted and reached in for a box trying not to show the pain it caused. "You're trying to tell me the FBI lost one of their agents?"

"She's missing."

Piling the second box on top of the first, she closed the trunk. "Isn't that what they do? Find people?"

His scowl deepened. "She was last identified as being near here — in Lane County. Which is why they contacted me."

Haddie felt a chill rise up her shoulder blades. Once again, it felt like Detective Cooper seemed to be working for the people she avoided. It hadn't been true with Harold Holmes. Still.

"I'll make sure and let you know if they call me." She closed the trunk. "Or, you could tell them you've already spoken with me and save me the hassle."

Smiling, or grimacing, she grabbed both boxes and lifted.

CHAPTER 22

THE ONLY SHADE Haddie could find was under a young maple planted in a median of the parking lot. The mulch smelled musky and wet with a faint hint of the tree itself. She fought with the plastic wrapper, wishing she carried a knife like Dad or that he were here to open the damned burner phone.

Customers hurrying back to their cars gave her wary looks as they returned to their air conditioning. When was her RAV4 going to be ready?

The phone had about a fifty percent charge on it. Kiana needed to know that Detective Cooper was looking for her. Not that it should be that much of a surprise. The FBI would likely try and use local enforcement rather than drive all over the country.

Checking her cell, she typed in Kiana's number and proudly dialed. The phone went immediately to voicemail. Haddie compared the numbers, but they were right. Had Kiana forgotten to charge her phone last night? Maybe the new burner didn't actually work.

Haddie stood in the heat, in the middle of the parking

lot, and called herself. Both phones worked just fine. She considered sitting in the mulch. Her hip would hurt either way, but she'd begun to seriously lag, worse than this morning.

She unwrapped the peanut butter power bar, took a flat-tasting bite with a too thin coating of chocolate, and stared at her phones in her left hand. Kiana must have turned her phone off. Why?

Haddie slipped the burner into her pocket, stuffed the end of the power bar between her lips, and tried calling with her cell. Straight to voicemail. A woman in a canvas dress stared suspiciously as she pushed a cart past with a single gallon of milk in a plastic bag.

"Good morning," Haddie said around the bar before she bit off the end.

The woman scurried on, rattling the wheels across asphalt.

It had been a frustrating morning all around. Andrea wasn't happy with anybody. Haddie had proofread a dozen documents, fact-checked nearly the same amount, scanned in a box from the DA, and still saw no end in sight.

Her wound burned, and the bandage needed to be changed. Considering the failure of the burner phone, she should have gone to the garage and seen Dad.

She'd driven west of the office to get the burner; she could make it out to Dad's property and check on Kiana if she hurried. She'd be late returning from lunch, and Andrea would be even more pissed. Haddie didn't relish the extra mileage, but it would make her feel better.

What if the FBI had tracked down Kiana? Where would that put Dad with the property and truck? Damn. Haddie stuffed a phone in each pocket and stuffed the rest of the bar in her mouth.

It took fifteen minutes and an agonizing ride up the hill to find the truck gone and Kiana not answering the door. The air smelled sweeter in the woods; something flowered nearby. It certainly wasn't any cooler.

Why wouldn't Kiana answer her phone? Other than being held by the FBI? Hadn't she agreed that she wouldn't be out driving around? Maybe they'd caught her in the truck.

Haddie sat at the edge of a planter in the shade and typed her dad's number into the new burner phone.

She sighed as it rang through to voicemail. "It's me," she said and hung up.

He had to recognize her voice. She didn't do well with all the secret code stuff; it was fine on TV, but just annoying in real life.

The burner rang loudly and she jumped. "Hey, Dad. Kiana's missing. Doesn't answer her phone."

"Where are you?" he asked.

"The property. Truck's gone."

"If you think something is wrong, then leave there now. Call me from the — find a gas station and call me back." His tone had a firm urgency.

"Okay," she said.

The line clicked off and she fumbled the phone back into her too shallow pockets.

Haddie looked around at the surrounding pines and vegetation, and the distant hills that rolled dark blue against a lighter sky. Could someone be staking out the property? Could they have taken Kiana, and now waited for some blundering idiot to show up?

The south side of the property had thick woods right up to the driveway. The rest had sparse trees and fields for a good distance from the house before the forest surrounded her. From where she stood on a hill, she could see a good distance out to more trees. It would be easy to keep an eye on this house from any number of locations.

Ignoring the pain, she jogged to the Fat Boy and threw her leg over. Her heart pounded as her bike roared into life. Swallowing, she watched the trail ahead, the woods around, and road below as she rode cautiously down the hill.

CHAPTER 23

KIANA ZOOMED in and took another picture of the parked SUV. The black Explorer sat in front of the first house on the street. The second house was her rented Airbnb. She'd driven past the SUV and turned immediately to find a spot to watch from the church parking lot on the hill.

She felt exposed in the sun. The old Ford had no tinting, and she hadn't worked up much of a disguise except for a pair of sunglasses and a green head wrap. The inside stunk of hot upholstery, and the little breeze that came in through the window couldn't compete. She'd worn a loose top, but the fabric stuck under her arms, and sweat trickled down her sides and stomach. Except for the waver of heat off asphalt, she could clearly see every forest-covered hill and mountain for miles. Spotting her sitting in the parking lot at the top of the hill would be even easier. She'd tried to select a parking space where the trees nearly obscured her.

Hopefully, their focus stayed on the rental car parked in front of the Airbnb down the street. The house had asphalt along the front, hedged in by a brown picket fence. She'd left her rental there rather than in front of the garage hoping that someone would stake it out. They had taken the bait, using the neighbor's house. Odd, considering the elderly couple that had been living there.

She took a risk watching them. A smarter move might have been to drive back to Eugene and forget about it. Even with the plate number, she had no resources to look up the registration. Part of her hoped that Haddie or Thomas might be able to help. Perhaps someone might step out of the SUV, roll down a window, or give her some chance at a picture.

The car rental company had agreed to pick up their vehicle today after hitting the card for extra charges. It didn't matter; she couldn't use that card without flagging the FBI. That left only today for her to come and see if her bait had worked. She sat trying to determine her next move.

The office she'd broken into would likely be cleared, if not already, then soon. Haddie's mystery woman had been an unfortunate disruption. There had been three boards with photos and notated connections. She'd been able to get pictures of all three before she had to escape out a window.

The white board that stood out the most had her own picture, linked along with Haddie to Harold Holmes at the top. Whoever these people were, they searched for Harold Holmes. Haddie had likely killed him, or whatever her power did. Just a suspicion. Whatever happened to Harold Holmes, she guessed he'd never be found. Curiously, other than her own picture, she hadn't seen evidence of cooperation between these people and any segment of the FBI. Did the connection not exist, or were they black boxed in some way?

Her own board had included the family of Harold Holmes, including his birth parents and twin brother who was also missing. Either these people didn't care about the brother or didn't know. Kiana rubbed her ear lobe trying to determine their connection with the FBI group. Did one even exist? Perhaps two competing factions? Doing what?

A red, white, and blue tow truck entered the street and passed the explorer. A large, bearded man smoked out an open window, resting a tattooed arm on the side of the door.

Kiana readied the camera, not following the tow truck, but with eyes pinned on the SUV. She could only hope they got out and talked with the driver.

They didn't.

As the tow truck pulled up to her Airbnb, the SUV's lights came on, and a puff of smoke exited the exhaust as they started the car. Evidently, they took this as confirmation that she didn't intend to return. She waited as they backed onto the street, hoping for a shot, but their tinted windows were rolled up and the windshield pointed away. She wouldn't risk following them. They drove west, disappearing past the curve of the hill.

The explosion jolted her upright in her seat.

Someone had rigged her rental car; it was reduced to a flaming black husk. Flames also covered the lawn of her Airbnb. Segments of burning fence rested against the front of the house. The tow truck had shifted forward, and fire burned across the back and underneath.

She didn't see the driver, or his body.

Kiana let out a breath. Shaking, she fumbled to start the old Ford. *They want me dead*. She'd hoped, somehow, that the FBI calling her in might mean that the first attack had been overzealous. Perhaps, as she'd thought, a different faction.

As she backed up, people came out of the church.

Her tags would be exposed for a moment, but most people never thought to look. She rolled down the hill, careful not to speed away and attract any notice. Besides, she didn't want to catch up to the black Explorer.

As she reached the end of the road, she knew she didn't need to worry about the SUV. Whichever direction they had gone, they were long out of sight.

The bombing of her rental car didn't change much, except the pounding in her ears from her racing heart. She'd known the moment they'd attacked her outside of her meeting with Haddie that her investigation had turned sour. It still hurt to lose so much of her life. The military had been her life while her parents lived, then the FBI had become everything. Now, she had a borrowed, beat-up Ford and a temporary hideout in the hills.

I-5 raced north and south in front of her. North lay Portland, where her life had started to change. South was Eugene, where her life ended.

Driving slowly down the road to the junction for I-5, she dug her phone out of her purse. Her fingers still trembled. Over a decade ago, thousands of miles from here, she'd shot two men after an IED took out the truck in front of hers. *Now look at me*.

She powered up her phone as she entered the on-ramp to I-5. Haddie had called once. A Eugene number had called four other times. No one had her new number. Except Haddie. The woman had finally got her burner. *I'll call when I calm down*. She had learned nothing coming here, and the bombing had gotten to her.

Kiana put the phone beside her and merged into the southbound traffic.

She needed to do something about her weapon. The gun had been clean, but now it had three deaths tied to it. She couldn't get caught with it, but she didn't intend to go around unarmed. Maybe Thomas could pick her up a nine. Anything at this point, though she preferred a Glock.

This would be her last outing for a while. Time to lie low and let them think she'd moved on. If Thomas or Haddie could help with supplies, she could sit out the summer up in the hills. Then what?

She'd pulled out all her savings. Parts of South America weren't very open to US influence, so they'd have a hard time tracking her there. She could set up in some town or move around until her Spanish got better and settle in as an immigrant from a neighboring country.

Maybe I do need to just forget all this. Could she just ignore it all? Probably not. Her best hope rested on Haddie — which put the woman at risk. She seemed pretty good at doing that herself. Perhaps Kiana didn't need to worry. Where to go from here?

She needed to show Haddie the pictures of the other boards. The faces and names might have some connection to Portland. Haddie might have a better understanding of what these people were looking for. The lists Kiana had found might have some relevance. Kiana couldn't do anything with them. She'd grown accustomed to unlimited resources. This new life felt like a cage around her.

She picked up the phone and sighed. Haddie might be her only hope.

CHAPTER 24

HADDIE TAPPED AT HER MOUSE, inserting a comment into the document she could barely keep her eyes on. Already, whatever thought she'd planned to type faded against the sense of dread that hung over her.

Kiana still hadn't called. Dad had been clear that Haddie needed to go back to work and act normal. So, she sat with her tea getting cooler, staring at her computer screen, knowing that she would just piss Andrea off more when her work didn't get done on time. Being late from lunch had earned Haddie a few sharp words, but she'd been warned by Toby via text before she walked in the door.

Grace had take-out, so the back office smelled like Indian spices. No one said much when Haddie finally arrived. The tension felt like classroom finals without a party planned afterward.

Dad hadn't been happy that Kiana decided to travel, and he'd tried to convince Haddie not to worry, but he hadn't been very encouraging. There were reasons that Kiana might have turned off her phone, none of which were safe situations. Why hadn't she stayed at the property and let things cool down? He'd advised against leaving a message or calling again. Supposedly, he'd have someone check the property, though he didn't want to explain his plan.

Both Liz and Terry had tried to text her during lunch, but she'd shut them down by telling them that the new case took up all her time. Terry had been concerned about whether she would make it to pick up Aaron at the bus station. Getting off early wouldn't be happening. She'd promised to text him when Andrea finally released them, and they could all meet up before the seminar. Until she found Kiana, other plans were secondary.

At least, the worry over Kiana overrode the sleeplessness. Haddie's eyes blurred, but she couldn't imagine going to sleep. Selfishly, she imagined Kiana being tortured and some dark cabal of FBI waiting at Haddie's apartment.

The burner in her pocket rang loudly, and Haddie stood up, startled. Her cheeks flushed as she looked at Grace and offered a guilty smile. It let out a second round of loud rings before Haddie flipped it open, answered Kiana's incoming call, and hung up.

Either Kiana was alright, or someone else had her phone. Either way, Haddie didn't intend to have the conversation in the back office — on a burner phone. If Andrea stepped out of her office or Toby rolled back into the hall, they'd hear. Not to mention Grace. The clock on the wall showed 1:52 p.m.

"I'm going to the bathroom," she announced to Grace. *Damn I suck at this.*

"Happy for you." Grace didn't stop typing as she flicked a glance up. "Try not to get shot. Again."

Haddie's blush burned her ears as she headed for the hall. Taking a calming breath, she strolled past Andrea's door. The woman leaned in toward her monitor and didn't show that she noticed. Haddie didn't repeat the announcement.

The bathroom door lay at the end of the hall beside the kitchen. Haddie slipped inside and started the water before calling Kiana.

"Hello?" Kiana answered the phone. It sounded like traffic in the background.

Haddie whispered, "Are you okay?"

Kiana paused. "Better now."

"What happened?" Haddie leaned against the bar by the toilet, watching under the door to see if anyone cast a shadow. She'd had plenty of conversations like this in her first job at the mall. It was possibly why she'd been fired.

"I went by the house I had rented — to see if they were watching it. They were."

"Who?" Haddie asked.

"Don't know. I did get their license plate. Maybe the FBI or whoever tried killing me before. Anyway, they rigged my rental car. The tow truck triggered it. I don't think the driver made it. Whoever was staking out my house drove away. Black Explorer."

"Damn. Did they see you?"

"I don't think so. I'll do a loop through a rest area and see if anyone follows me through."

Haddie stared at the bathroom tile. Someone really wanted Kiana dead. "You should lie low, like Dad said."

"Probably. I see you got a burner."

"Yeah. Freaked me out when you didn't answer. Guess I was partially right; things weren't going well." Haddie twisted her hair into a knot, feeling the weariness settle back in.

"Sorry. Old habit. Turned the phone off."

The sound of traffic filled their silence for a moment; Kiana had to be on I-5.

Haddie changed the topic. "I've been looking through the news and blotters. Not one mention of the people who attacked us that first night, nor anything in Coos Bay. They are covering this up again."

"I did want to talk with you about what I found at the office. It didn't seem like a good time on the drive back with your father."

Haddie stood up straight. "It didn't sound like you found much."

"There were some white boards like we use in investigations. One centered on Harold Holmes. Your picture was there. They wrote in the law office name as well. A photo of me. Others, witnesses, known associates. I took a picture."

Haddie swallowed and raised her eyebrows. They were investigating her. At least, her connection to Harold Holmes. Did they know about Dad? She almost asked. Why would someone connected to the raves care about Harold Holmes? "Can I see the picture?"

"Do you want to come by tonight? I'll show you everything. You might have some input on some of these."

"Yes." Haddie cringed. "I've got a thing tonight. How late will you be up?"

"Anytime. I've got a feeling I'm going to nap when I get home. Try and clear my head from this afternoon. Still tired from last night."

Haddie rolled her eyes toward the ceiling. *Am I really making plans for after the seminar?* When did she intend to sleep? "Okay."

"See you tonight." Kiana disconnected.

Haddie turned the water off. After listening to it running for the past few minutes, she had to actually use the bathroom. Maybe she wouldn't make the seminar. The boys could fill her in afterward. At least, she'd have to text Terry soon to let him know she wouldn't be able to get out early. Kiana's information sounded more important. If only she could ask Terry to research strange lightning.

She took a moment to figure out how to put the burner on vibrate before stepping into the hall. Acting nonchalant, she started toward the back office. Toby glanced up but said nothing.

"Haddie," Andrea stopped her at the office door.

Damn. "Yes," Haddie stepped back to stand in the doorway.

Andrea looked haggard; her bun had loosened at the edges, leaving stray red strands at her cheek, and her eyes looked dark. "I need you to get to the courthouse in Albany before they close. Grace has the motion printed. Leave now, call it a day."

"Okay." Haddie stood there a moment. She'd expected to be working an hour or two past closing.

Andrea turned back to her monitor. "Thank you."

Taking it as a dismissal, Haddie headed into the back office. A yellow manila envelope balanced on the cubicle wall separating her and Grace.

Grace had written the address to the courthouse on the envelope. "Cathy had questions on a location in Springfield. I told her to text you — that you'd be on the road." Grace tilted her head. "Be careful."

"I will." Haddie stood in her cubicle and did a quick braid of her hair, tying it off and tucking it in her collar. She could be in Albany in less than an hour.

After a round trip, she'd make it in time for Aaron's arrival. They could talk, then she could beg out of the seminar and get over to Kiana's. Sam would walk Rock. If she could get Aaron alone, she could go over the incident in Coos Bay. Terry might be a little put off, but after what happened with Kiana today, Haddie had no intention of getting him involved any deeper than he already was. Aaron might be able to dig up something about strange lightning.

She imagined a police white board where her picture, Harold Holmes, and Kiana had little strings tying them together. Would Dad be on there? Dmitry, the brother? She finished the last of her tea, tucked her cell phone into her pocket, and grabbed her helmet and the envelope. She hadn't brought a water bottle for a long ride. Haddie didn't relish two hours on the bike with fresh stitches, but she'd take the chance to get out of the office early and meet Aaron.

Haddie glanced at the clock: 2:22 p.m. She'd be at the bus stop before Aaron arrived.

CHAPTER 25

HADDIE RUMBLED past the bus station, looking for Terry at the little wire tables, but didn't see him. She pulled into the lot on the side opposite from where the buses dropped their passengers. Terry's silver Taurus was parked on the far side of the lot. The growl of her bike echoed off the windows in front of her. She chose a space near the building beside an old Honda Silverwing and killed her Fat Boy, letting the sounds of the city streets back in. The sign painted on the window ahead of her offered tacos.

Hell, I'm starving. She'd eaten a biscuit for breakfast and a power bar for lunch. The vibration of the ride had numbed her hip, but as she climbed off the bike, she felt the sharp nudge of the bullet wound over the dull ache of her joints. The heat made it feel like midday, but the sun already slanted out to the west. She had fifteen minutes to spare before Aaron arrived, assuming the bus came on time.

Helmet in hand, Haddie stepped inside the restaurant that shared the front half of the bus station. The room smelled deliciously spicy. Terry was eating at a booth by the window where he could watch for the bus. A foil-wrapped burrito and a drink waited across from him.

He turned from the window as she stepped up, speaking around a mouthful of burrito. "Black bean burrito, right?"

Haddie smiled. "How did you know?"

"Sounded like you had the day from hell. Besides, who doesn't want a burrito?"

Her stomach gurgling, Haddie slid into the booth and took a gulp of the drink. Sweet tea. She grimaced.

"Sorry," Terry said. "No unsweetened."

She shook her head. "No problem." The burrito tasted delicious, though she barely bothered to chew. They used a phenomenal cheese sauce.

"I was going to grab Aaron a burrito, but he seems *so* paranoid. Might think I was trying to poison him."

Mouth full, Haddie tilted her head and shrugged. The scientist *was* paranoid. Probably for good reason. The day they'd met, two demons were stalking him. The next time, he'd made Haddie do a dozen laps before he finally got in her car. She guessed he wanted to make sure she wasn't being followed.

Sauce spilled onto her gloves, and she felt self-conscious. Another few days, and she could take them off. The bullet wound would heal quickly, if her past experience continued. Everything healed quickly except her joints. Dad said his never stopped aching, even after decades of not using his power.

"Are you going to go in disguise tonight?" Terry asked. He pointed to his head, likely suggesting that she cover her stark white hair.

"If I can stay up that late. I got two hours of sleep last

night." Haddie glanced out the window. She knew Terry would be disappointed.

"You're not going?"

"We'll see. Like you said, rough day."

"We need you on this, Haddie. You're the cowboy in the group; get in there and lasso 'em, pull 'em down and hogtie their feet." Terry smiled, but a hint of sadness crept around his eyes. Did he really miss the chaos of investigating the raves? Or Harold Holmes? He tapped the window. "Me and Aaron, we just read stuff and think."

Haddie sighed. "I guess I'm just thinking more. I don't want anyone to get hurt chasing — whatever it is that cowboys chase."

Terry shrugged. "I get it. We'll let you know what goes on tonight."

Haddie finished her burrito and managed to drink a little more of the syrupy tea.

Cathy texted while they waited, and Haddie gave her what information she could about the location, but she didn't know any students who rented in Springfield. There was a hint that Cathy hoped Haddie would have time to meet there, but it wasn't the day for that. Suggesting that they get check in tomorrow, Haddie let the conversation drop.

Gratefully, Dad hadn't started hounding her yet to get her dressing changed. He'd argued with her over picking up Aaron at the bus station and going to the Unceasing seminar. She hadn't even mentioned going over to Kiana's. He'd start texting and calling once he thought she was out of work.

People waited in the seats under the overhang where the buses pulled up. The pavilion had slanted roofs on each side of a planted median that the buses circled. Even trees grew in the middle. An older woman managed to knit in the shade. A couple with a rolling suitcase lounged a seat apart as if to avoid sharing the heat. Most people likely waited inside the bus station during the summer.

When a bus finally rolled up, Terry sucked down the last of his drink as he slid out of the booth. "Here we go."

Haddie followed a little slower. Weary and sore, she tossed her wrappings and cup into the garbage and stepped into the heat with her helmet in hand. Aaron's paranoia swayed her as she scanned the empty lanes around the pavilion and studied the couple and elderly woman sitting on the benches. Terry led them across the patio where most of the outdoor tables sat empty except for one young woman studying her phone between the planters by the street.

The bus passed them and the bus station, rounded the corner in the back, pulled around to the far side of the pavilion, and opened its doors. People exited, some heading for the station, others walking under the overhang toward the street. Aaron stepped to the edge of the doors. Tall, he took up most of the frame as he leaned out to search the area around the bus, his dirty blond hair obscured with a baseball cap. A black backpack was strapped to his shoulders. Haddie could make out a frustrated face behind him.

Terry waved and skipped ahead of her.

Aaron stepped out and froze, looking toward the street.

Two men ran across traffic toward the pavilion. *Damn.* One had the glowing orange eyes of a demon, the other had the yellow haze of the coerced. Aaron had spotted them as well. They'd found him, just like at the ski lift. How were they able to track him?

Aaron ran toward the back of the bus, away from Haddie and Terry, and away from the two men.

Terry stopped, unsure and unaware of the men.

The coerced man already had a gun out. Haddie couldn't let them chase down Aaron and kill him, but she stood out with her white hair. No one else seemed to notice the men, but she and Aaron could see what they were.

Aaron made for the woods on the opposite side of the pavilion, ducking his tall frame as if to minimize his size. The two men ran down that side toward the bus. Haddie had the seats and people between.

Stuffing the helmet on her head to cover her hair, she yelled at Terry. "Get in your car, get out of here." Running toward one of the walkways between each side of the pavilion, she followed Aaron.

She had no gun. She'd have to use her ability.

The coerced fired as Aaron made the edge of the woods and ducked under the first of the branches. The pavilion instantly turned to chaos as people began screaming.

Haddie managed to dodge a man flailing as he ran opposite her through the walkway.

Aaron had disappeared. His two pursuers had reached the woods. The demon had started to change, its skin sloughing off and leaving red raw flesh underneath.

She could smell the gun powder even as another shot rang out from inside the pines. Thick bramble covered the trunks of the trees. In the dense brush, she lost sight of the man with the gun. The moving red hulk of the demon led her.

Haddie dove into the bramble, feeling it tug against her loose pants.

The demon looked back with its dark pits of eyes, but it continued forward.

She hesitated in using her ability. What if these demons were innocent, like the coerced, twisted by someone's powers?

A third shot rang out. If she didn't do something, they would kill Aaron.

A dull noise sounded in the air around them. A roar like a heavy wind in the mountains, but she barely felt a breeze. The pines thinned out ahead, leaving only the thick bramble. Railroad tracks lay beyond with a signal. She saw buildings.

She'd closed the distance with the demon, and the coerced ran just a few paces ahead.

A river lay to their left, and the hint of a small bridge showed through the bramble ahead. She couldn't see any sign of Aaron. Maybe he'd escaped.

The coerced fired again, stumbling so that he shot into the air.

Aaron's dirty blond hair appeared near where the man had fallen; shooting up to full height, he darted for the bridge. He'd ambushed the coerced somehow.

It had slowed him, though, and the demon let out a ragged shriek as it leaped, easily clearing the thorny bramble. Black talons hung from fists at the ends of meaty arms. It had long back legs that sprang like a rabbit. Arcing through the air, it seemed it would pounce directly onto Aaron before he reached the bridge.

Still running, Haddie yelled.

The tone rang inside her helmet, and she stumbled as pain drove daggers into her skin.

The demon faded like mist in a breeze. In that moment, a vanishing gold medallion that hung about its neck glinted in the sunlight.

The coerced, crawling to his feet just a few steps away, faded into the black of night as the visions hit her.

Bullets whistled in a jungle. A single beam of moonlight made it through an opening in the canopy ahead. Red flashes of gunfire flickered ahead and beside her. She growled and knew that three of the enemy vaporized in the trees ahead.

Water sparkled above her, letting in waves of sunlight. Dark vegetation floated just to her right. She rose with a kick from the mud below her and yelled as her mouth splashed free. The villager in the canoe-like boat vanished as he sprayed the water with bullets.

Haddie gasped, feeling like she drowned, and found the coerced man scrambling to his feet, gun in hand. She could see inside the muzzle. Blue steel and a dark abyss. The man glanced toward his right, where the bridge might be.

Her ears rung with the distorted roar that wasn't wind.

Terry tackled him from the side. The gun fired and Haddie flinched.

The two rolled away from her, and she managed to shove a shaking hand into the crushed brambles below her. Thorns stuck through her glove, but they hardly competed with the burning across her skin. Slowly she rose. Aching knees held her. The strange slow roar continued, as if it came from all around them.

The coerced pushed Terry off. Her friend's heel glanced off her helmet. Yellow haze buzzing about his face, the coerced grimaced and swung his gun toward Terry.

The man might have been a cab driver or coffee server at a local bistro. He had a mustache and thin goatee, brown eyes, and brown hair. He could have been anyone. A father. A brother. A son.

Haddie screamed. The tone rang in her ears.

The flash from the muzzle faded with him. The gunshot's roar froze in the moment as it vaporized with the man's body. She could see the shift, a sudden porous aspect to his body, compounding until there was nothing left.

Pain sizzled across Haddie. Her skin felt like it peeled off her flesh, searing and raw. The visions blackened her sight. One scene after the next happened in the depths of the jungle, both at night, both horrifying and ending with death. Nightmares would be added to her dreams and memory. Her helmet pressed against the ground, she shook while focusing on the bramble curled up against her visor. She'd killed again.

Her arm twitched below her. Crushed between thorns and the weight of her body, it hurt only slightly more than the rest of her.

Haddie rolled so that both elbows rested on the ground, and she dragged her knees up, one at a time. Her hip burned, but she could barely notice it over her skin.

"I — you." Terry spoke, his voice vaguely ahead of her to the right.

Terry had seen everything, or at least her attack on the coerced man. There wasn't time to explain. They needed to move. The police would be here. Where had Aaron gone? The bramble around looked sickeningly slick. The remains of her victims. The stench had become familiar.

The roar she'd been hearing had stopped. She recognized it now. The gunshot, the bullet's explosion, echoing back through time.

"Where's Aaron?" Haddie asked, forcing herself up to her knees.

Terry lay in the bramble on his back, leaned up on his elbows, and eyes wide saucers. "You —"

Haddie managed one foot under her. "Yes. I did. We'll talk later."

Terry would be as bad as Liz once he got over the shock. "I saw a demon."

Haddie stood. "Get up, Terry." She felt nauseous, possibly from the smell. *Or killing a man.*

Aaron waited for them, crouched on the other side of the old bridge, though at his height, he still stood out. The structure looked questionable; painted white and gang tagged, steel girders framed a rotten wood floor. How had Aaron made it across?

"You — they vanished."

Haddie leaned down and grabbed his forearm, pulling him up. Her joints screamed at the motion, but he stood. So many buildings around them. An apartment where she could see the second floor. Railroad tracks. Industrial buildings. Houses and windows beyond a sturdier bridge upriver. "Terry. We'll talk. Not right now. We need to run."

If they could get east and then back across the river, they could circle around to the other side of the bus station where she and Terry had parked. Hopefully, the police would focus on the area where there had been gunshots. Where she stood at the moment.

Haddie pushed him toward the bridge and Aaron. "We need to move."

Terry swiveled under her hand and pointed at her hip. "You're bleeding. Did they shoot you?"

She looked at her hip. Blood spotted through brown cloth where the bandage lay underneath. Dad would be pissed. It looked like she'd ripped out the stitches. "No, that was last night."

CHAPTER 26

HADDIE STEPPED GINGERLY across the boards, feeling them give way in some spots. The lazy river didn't flow far beneath, but she didn't want to get stuck. They were in plain sight of the woods.

The entire area stretched uncomfortably barren around the railroad tracks. To the left, where they needed to go, the tracks ran beside a line of trees. Aaron crouched ahead, watching the bramble and woods behind her. Thick brush grew around the railway, and the slope of a hill ahead gave them some privacy. However, soon people would be coming out or peeking through windows after all the shooting.

Haddie pointed down the tracks and Aaron nodded, leading the way. Her muscles fought the continued movement, and her joints ached at each step.

Terry trailed behind her. "What — what are you?"

I don't know. Haddie didn't reply. The sun played against the edge of her helmet's visor, reflecting a strange white haze just to her left.

"Demon-killer." He stated the name in awe, as if there were some pride to it.

Please, stop. The hint of a rolling ball of light swirled over the river.

"Did you banish them back to hell?" Terry continued, as if to himself.

She felt sick. She couldn't have this conversation now. The haze had become an almost defined mist that spiraled around and into itself.

"An archangel?" Terry suggested.

Haddie turned to focus on the glowing shape, and it disappeared. A trick of the light.

Aaron pointed left where the railroad split, one branch forming a bridge crossing the river. The top of the bus station rose over brush; the small woods no longer hid them. "There, or farther down, at that next bridge. Looks like a street."

Sirens called from the city. North, to her left.

To their right, a street ran alongside the trees and tracks, raised on a ridge. Ahead, it dropped and curved as the track split, and crossed the river back toward the block that the bus station was on.

"Farther," Haddie said. "Better if we get to a street."

"How do you do it?" Terry asked.

Too much. Her throat swelled and her tongue seemed thick. "Please, Terry. Stop. It's horrible enough as it is."

Terry continued, "You saved me. Saved Aaron, how is that horrible?"

"Because an innocent man died."

"Innocent?" Terry's tone pitched high, incredulous.

Haddie glanced back toward the woods, the little bridge, and where the glowing ball had been. "He was coerced."

Aaron led them along the right split of the tracks, and

they passed the railroad bridge. He walked faster than Haddie, drifting out ahead of them.

"How do you know he was — coerced?" Terry's tone drifted back toward frantic.

"Terry, please. We'll talk about all this later. Let's just focus on not getting arrested."

He mumbled in a way that let Haddie know he'd acquiesced. "I saw a demon."

Haddie drew in a long breath, savoring the moment of silence. They had to find somewhere safe for Aaron. That wouldn't be the Unceasing seminar.

Terry was right. If Haddie hadn't been there to pick up Aaron, he'd likely be dead. Terry too, if he'd followed into the woods. This wasn't her fault. She couldn't take the blame for every death. She'd made the right choice.

They left the gravel around the train tracks and walked on the sidewalk, nervously glancing at the cars that passed. Haddie pulled off her helmet. The railroad that had branched over the river now ran along the opposite side. Beyond the river and tracks lay the plaza beside the bus station; between lay the lot where she'd parked. As long as the police focused on the side where all the action had gone on, they might escape.

She didn't feel comfortable putting Aaron up at her apartment, and she couldn't risk Terry and Livia — or Liz. Haddie pulled out her cell phone, dropped it back in her pocket, and pulled out her burner.

Her dad answered immediately. "You coming by?"

She glanced at the splotch of blood on her pants. "Maybe. It depends. I've got a problem."

"Okay."

"I'm at the bus station, picking up Aaron. They tracked

him, somehow." She glanced ahead at the tall scientist. "Ended with some gun shots and a demon. I had to use my powers. We've caused a bit of a disturbance, and need to find someplace to lie low for a bit."

Aaron had stopped at the mention of his name, letting her catch up.

"Devil in hell, Haddie." He sighed audibly and paused. "I'll drop Meg off with Sam. Meet me at Kiana's, all of you. No. Drive by Kiana's, past the open fields to where the road splits. Take the split and pull off to the side. If you're not being followed, then I'll call and have you come back."

And if we are being followed? Haddie swallowed. Wasn't this what she wanted? "Okay. Thanks." They'd have a chance to talk things through, compare notes.

Dad ended the call and Haddie folded the phone back into her pocket.

"Who was that?" asked Aaron, stepping into pace with her.

Odd, looking up to a man. Even a couple inches made a difference. "My dad. He helped me and Liz at the rave. He knows everything." Haddie hadn't considered Aaron's paranoia. "We need someplace to hide you. My dad is already helping me hide an ex-FBI agent. We're going to meet there."

"The FBI are involved? This would have been good information to know." Aaron pushed a finger up the ridge of his nose. "I would rather bring in fewer people than more."

"Where would you *rather* go right now? How did they find you?" Tired and in pain, Haddie found it difficult not to snap. "Kiana is not our enemy. She was trying to find out more information about these people. She saved me after the lightning lady left two goons to take care of me. Now Kiana's on the run from her own people."

Aaron's eyebrows furrowed, but he strode on silently.

"Lightning lady?" Terry asked.

Haddie gestured in the air. "She made some sort of lightning creature. Messed up the RAV4, tried to kill me."

A series of closer sirens quieted her. They crossed the tracks and headed toward the parking lot of the plaza.

Aaron pointed toward the shade of some pines planted between the tracks and a service road that led behind the plaza and down to the bus station. "I don't think I like this party. But I'm curious and don't have a lot of options at the moment. Terry, I'll wait here. Pick me up on your way out."

He strolled into the shade and stood beside a pine.

Haddie could probably go down the service road, but it looked too empty. Crossing it, she led Terry into the parking lot. They'd be able to see from the buildings there if any police were collected on this side of the bus station. Cars scattered around the plaza's parking lot, and a line had formed at the drive-thru coffee. Traffic seemed thick on the main road ahead. Everyone was out of work now. Sirens continued.

Liz called on Haddie's cell. She stared at the screen. Liz would expect to be coming over to check vitals, as they'd planned. Too many plans.

"Hey," Haddie said. "You're going to be pissed."

"What?" Liz coughed. "You did it again? Why? When?"

Haddie passed rancid dumpsters heading toward the corner. She didn't have time to explain. "Write this address down." As Aaron said, it was turning into a party. Everyone who knew about Haddie's powers would be there.

She stuffed the cell back into her pocket. They turned the corner of the plaza, walking along the front of a restaurant where an elderly man held the door for a white-haired woman. Haddie let out a tense breath at the sight of the nearly empty parking lot this side of the bus station. Blue lights flickered off trees and poles from the other side. The police were likely digging in the woods by now.

Terry sounded hurt. "Liz knows?"

Haddie nodded her head. "She was there when I met Aaron at the ski lift."

"She never told me."

"Because I asked." Haddie shrugged. "I didn't want you involved in this."

"And — what is *this*?"

"Hell if I know. Dad thinks it's a war. All I've seen are people with powers trying to make money." They passed a bakery and crossed the lot in front of the phone store.

"By killing Aaron?" Terry asked.

"Yeah, some parts don't make sense, unless they're trying to keep it all quiet."

"I think your dad's right."

"We'll see. We can talk about it in a bit." She gestured toward his car. "I'll meet you up by Aaron. Follow me from there."

Haddie crossed the lot toward her bike. Lights from the cop cars flashed inside the restaurant and bus station. She slipped on her helmet and fished for her keys. She'd been lucky she hadn't lost them out of the ridiculous pockets.

She'd survived another confrontation with the coerced and demons. Killed both of them. Somehow, it didn't weigh on her as heavily as Portland had. Maybe this *was* war, and she'd become a soldier. Is this how they felt? Is this how Dad felt in those wars? She'd done what she'd needed to do to save her friends.

Haddie winced as she climbed on the Fat Boy. She

backed up before she started the engine. Once it was rumbling underneath her, she dropped it into gear and quickly rode back to the parking lot she'd just walked through.

CHAPTER 27

THOMAS STOOD in the shade enjoying the scent of pine and hot grass that drifted across the hill. His presence disturbed a pair of Gray Jays who chided him from a twisting oak across the driveway. He'd parked the Jeep a few feet up the drive where the trees and brush hid it from the road; even he wouldn't be visible to a casual glance. He'd picked this property for the rural set up, the view, and the back road access it gave him in case he had trouble at the front entrance. He'd almost moved Haddie out here once. The air blew in clean from the western hills and off the big lake just a few miles to the northwest.

He'd have to burn his identity and sell the property once he'd gotten rid of the ex-FBI agent. Too much risk in trying to hold on to it.

He'd been holding onto a lot lately. First Haddie, letting her know about his real life, going through a heartache that he'd promised he'd never do again. *But, here I am.* Second, Meg. He hadn't been able to just sit and watch her get killed by whoever slaughtered his old family. Not that he hadn't gotten involved with family members from his past identities; he had. He rarely got in the middle of anything like that personally because it risked his present identity. Maybe the years had caught up with him and he was getting soft.

In the distance, he heard Haddie's Fat Boy rumbling down the main road. Their relationship had changed far beyond what he'd expected. His life had always been back alley negotiations at some level or another, hiding his identity and playing a public face. Something he'd never wanted to teach her.

She passed the entrance to the driveway at a good clip, a silver sedan close on her heels. Terry and Aaron.

Thomas waited. No one followed.

He flipped open his phone and dialed her.

"Hey," she answered.

"All clear."

"Okay." She sounded in a good mood, considering the day's events she'd described.

A black car pulled into the entrance in front of Thomas. "Wait," he said. He pressed back into the grass, watching as it worked up the hill toward him. "We've got company."

"That might be Liz."

Thomas squinted, recognizing the slight build and sunglasses. "This is not a party, Haddie." He hung up with a sigh.

He turned to move the Jeep back to the house and out of Liz's way. Bringing anyone into Haddie's situation risked everyone. However, she hadn't had much of a choice with Liz in Portland. Nor with Aaron and her friend Terry today. *Devil take me.* This whole situation had blown up over the past few days.

He pulled in front of the house as Liz putted beside. Her car sounded like it would die climbing up the hill.

Grabbing his kit off the passenger seat, he worked his way out of the Jeep.

"Hey T." Liz brushed a stray strand out of her mouth. "Summer home?"

"Friend's."

They both turned at the rumble of Haddie's Fat Boy coming down the main road. Thomas stepped down to the drive and waited. The sun still shone over the western hills behind them, but the trees stretched long shadows.

Liz turned as a door opened and Kiana stepped out. "Your friend?" Liz asked with a smile and waved.

Thomas sighed and glared between the two of them. "Haddie's."

The breeze blew uphill carrying the scent of someone's fire. Haddie's bike growled closer, and she pulled around the corner leading the silver car. Thomas waited until she passed and then followed, pointing her friends to a place to park by the oak. Her hip had dried blood on the fabric. She'd probably ripped her damned stitches out. She could have given it one day to begin healing.

He waited until she'd turned off the engine. "Need new stitches?"

She pulled off her helmet. "I'm guessing so." Nodding toward Terry and Aaron, she asked, "What's the plan?"

"You tell me. You've already got one stray, and now you want me to hide another?"

Haddie hooked her helmet on her bike. "Should I put him up on my couch?" The edges of her mouth resisted a smirk. She knew he'd argue against that plan.

"No. Since you've got everyone here," he said, eyes flicking at Liz, "Kiana can play host while I get you stitched back up. Then everyone can chime in on a plan."

"Stitches?" asked Liz.

"It's a long story about a lady you would not have enjoyed meeting," Haddie replied.

Liz tucked her hair back over her ear. "Worse than Sameedha?"

"Who's Sameedha?" asked Terry. Black hair and brown skin a shade off Haddie's, he could have been from the islands or South America. He seemed nervous — uncomfortable — standing still.

The taller, pale man with dirty blond hair waited stiffly on his side of the car. Aaron. His eyes studied Thomas, the house, and the surrounding woods with suspicion.

Thomas pointed Haddie toward the house. "Stitches first." They could talk after he got a look at her wound.

As Terry started to speak, Haddie shook her head and led the way. Thomas followed behind her, letting the men and Liz trail him. Kiana's lips tightened and she went back inside.

Haddie paused at the door, looking past him to the others. "Thanks, Dad. I'm sorry I'm so much trouble. I'm grateful, really."

Her makeup had smeared but still hid much of her skin. Snags puckered threads out of her work clothes. From the look of it, she'd had a tough time at the bus station. He wanted to protect her. His life had evolved into a cycle of protection where he hovered about those he loved to keep a cruel world at bay, then released them when the time grew too long and knowledge about him would become their pain.

He had to learn to release Haddie, but in a new way. She needed the freedom to protect herself, but he didn't have to leave. Haddie knew the worst in him — saw it in her visions.

He just had to be there for her. "No trouble, Haddie. I love you."

"I love you too, Dad."

Thomas gestured to the door. "Let's get you stitched up."

CHAPTER 28

Haddie stepped in Dad's hillside house, surprised to find a huge room stretched out ahead of her with tile flooring leading into a plush carpeted living room. The kitchen on the right had rich wood cabinets and a black fridge.

"This is beautiful." Why hadn't they lived here? The entire living space at Dad's garage would fit in the one room.

She could smell stir fry, but the kitchen looked spotless and unused.

Kiana, with a tight frown, walked ahead of them into the living room. Large windows let in the afternoon light.

Dad gently guided Haddie toward the left where a short hall led to a pair of doors. "We'll use the bedroom."

Furnished with only a large bed, the room had its own bathroom and a walk-in closet only slightly smaller than Haddie's apartment bedroom. Dad had her lie in the middle of the bed while he sat on the edge to work on her wound.

She soaked into the mattress, hands under her chin. "Nice place."

"Good price. Good access and exit."

"We could have lived here." She winced as he pulled off the bandage.

"Yeah. Thought about it."

"But?"

"We did just fine." Dad wiped cooling alcohol across the wound, the fire set in behind it.

"You're thinking of putting Aaron up here?"

"Up to him. I'm not burning any more identities for your friends. This one will have to be it." He tugged at her hip.

Damn. She felt thread glide through flesh. "How many?"

"Properties or identities?"

She tried to shrug as she lay there. "Both."

"Twenty-eight properties, not including this one. Eight identities, not including this one."

"Damn, Dad. Paranoid much?"

"You've got two."

Haddie rolled to her side. "Wait — what?"

He smiled, focused on his work. "Working on a third — considering the messes you like to get into."

"And you didn't ask?"

"Nope." He tugged and grabbed a pair of small scissors off the bed. "If I get us into trouble, I want a plan in place. It's better that way."

When they stepped back into the main room, Terry was gesturing in the air, describing Haddie's latest encounter with the demon and the coerced man. Kiana sat on the couch and Aaron leaned against the kitchen counter, backpack at his feet. The two had picked opposite sides of the room. Liz seemed the most attentive of Terry's audience, but turned as Haddie stepped across the tile.

"Any new symptoms or experiences?" Liz asked.

Haddie shook her head. "Well, I guess I saw some kind of light. Might have been the sun on my visor."

Liz seemed excited. Even Terry, after his initial shock, had returned to his usual exuberant self. Only Kiana and Aaron showed any reservation.

Dad passed Haddie and addressed Kiana. "It seems Haddie found you a roommate. Problem?" He jerked his thumb toward Aaron.

Kiana tilted her head and rubbed her ear. "Don't really have any options."

"Exactly." He pointed to the back of the room where a hall cut behind the living room wall. "You settled in downstairs?"

She seemed surprised. "Yes. How'd you know?"

"Safest. Back entrance. Fewer windows."

Haddie stepped beside her dad. "You said you had some pictures of a white board?" she asked Kiana.

"Three. I'll get them." Kiana nodded and rose from the couch.

Liz had come to stand by Haddie, leaving Aaron by the kitchen and Terry pacing between them and the window looking down the hill.

Dad turned toward Aaron. "This work for you? Plenty of bedrooms to choose from."

Aaron looked at Haddie. "For the night. I'll work up a plan to get out of Eugene." He slid up his sleeve and checked his watch. "Internet?"

"Nope." Dad shrugged. "But I think the neighbor's password is Voyager19. Weak signal."

"Thank you." Aaron looked down, adjusting his cuff over his watch and looking momentarily awkward.

Where would he go from here? He never talked about his personal life, and she'd never asked. If he'd been on the run all this time, where did he stay? Maybe Terry knew.

Kiana arrived with a white board of her own, pasted with photos printed on letter paper and some actual typed lists. She placed it on the couch and immediately Haddie noticed herself in a photo with Harold Holmes and Kiana — and Meg's picture on another photo. She didn't recognize any faces there, but the sketch at the top looked a lot like Dad with a bushy mustache and long sideburns.

"Do you recognize any of the people, other than me, you, Detective Cooper, and Harold Holmes?" Kiana asked Haddie directly, but glanced at Dad as well.

Liz stepped up beside Haddie. "Where did these come from?"

"An office in Coos Bay." Kiana said.

Liz leaned in toward the photo of Meg tied with a string to the sketch of Dad. Haddie rested her hand on Liz's shoulder. Dad might not want that part of his life exposed. If it had to do with Haddie, then she could make that choice for herself to let everyone know.

Glancing to the side, Liz resisted meeting Haddie's eyes, but said nothing.

Aaron spoke up from behind, just a step away from Dad. "These people are organized. Do you have copies?"

Kiana shrugged and nodded.

"Yaass. This is amazing. What are these lists?" Terry swooped down at their feet and sat on the floor in front of the couch. "No. These two are Anthony Prizer's properties. Or were. Some have already been sold. This one. This is where the Unceasing seminar is tonight. That we won't be going to. And here's a list of seminars, some haven't even been announced."

Aaron shifted closer. "How did you find this office?

Through the FBI?" He spoke to Kiana who hovered behind the board and couch.

"No. Despite them. A faction inside the FBI falsified the attackers in Portland."

Aaron interrupted. "The demon encounter beside the Chinese restaurant?"

Kiana nodded. "Along with Don Mack, coerced according to Haddie."

"How can you tell?" asked Terry.

"Shh." Haddie put her glove on his head and pressed down. He squirmed, but patted her hand.

"I tracked him to the building in Coos Bay, took some leave, and staked out the office for a week. Then Haddie watched the entrance while I got these."

Aaron leaned in close to Dad and Terry, studying the images and list. "So from the raves, demons, and coerced to the Unceasing in New York to your investigation into Harold Holmes. Connected. Either one group is studying another, or there is a hierarchy of leadership controlling all of this."

Dad leaned in front of Haddie, scrutinizing the lists. He rubbed his hand over his hair and straightened abruptly. What had he seen? She imagined something to do with Meg.

Kiana leaned her hands on the couch. "There's a group in the FBI working to help cover this up. I'm not sure whether they work to support these people or use them."

"The missing photos on the net. Any picture of a demon is gone within minutes. Seconds," Terry said. "We need to find out what this other list is. Locations and dates." He looked at Haddie's dad. "No internet, really?"

Dad stepped away, and Haddie glanced after him. He'd seen more than just the picture of Meg. She turned back to the lists, but they were meaningless to her. Everything she'd been dealing with, Harold Holmes, the raves, and Meg, were all part of one conspiracy. Dad's war. But what did they want?

Aaron moved into the spot that Dad vacated. "And the demons. My puzzle since the beginning. What are they?"

Haddie touched her braid; the hair had frayed out. It would be a knot. "Could someone be turning people, or animals, into demons? Like the lady who made the lightning at Coos Bay? Like the way Sameedha made people act at the raves?"

"I don't think so, but I don't have any basis. Just the physiology seems too precise. Like gene splicing. Impossible." Aaron looked over at her, touching the bridge of his nose.

"I saw a demon today. I should have got a picture." Terry shook his head.

Liz cleared her throat. "I saw them on the ski trip - thought I was hallucinating. We need to study them."

Aaron nodded his head in agreement. Haddie felt a little knot of guilt rise from what she'd let Liz believe. No more secrets. She glanced at Dad and pursed her lips.

"Hallucinating. I could be tripping right now." Terry raised his hands in the air. "That burrito. All this — food poisoning." He gestured across Kiana's whiteboard.

Haddie ignored Terry. "Have you noticed they wear gold medallions? They're controlled by them. I made one disappear at the rave and the demon went berserk, attacking anyone."

Liz asked, "Can you get us one? I mean, if there's an opportunity, could you just vaporize the demon and leave the medallion?" She smiled sheepishly. "Maybe a little flesh to do some testing on?"

Aaron looked up at that comment. "Yes. Agreed."

"That sounds like fun," Kiana said, "but I don't feel like hunting one of those down is likely. And other than these random properties we could check out, I think New York sounds like the most solid lead. There's a good chance they'd have records and more information inside the Unceasing headquarters." She shrugged. "Maybe you'll find one of your demons there."

Haddie turned sharply. Hadn't she had enough for one day — the past two days? "You want to break into another building? Probably better guarded than Coos Bay?" She shook her head. "I can't. I need to sleep. I'm famished." She couldn't get caught up in another crazy trip. *I need sleep.*

Kiana pointed to the fridge. "I don't have much, but —"

Dad rested his hand on Haddie's shoulder. "Haddie's right. Let's not fly off after the first shiny thing. Let's grab something to eat, talk this over, and sleep on it. Then we can decide."

Terry sprung up. "As they used to say in your day, you buy, I'll fly." He held his hand out toward Dad.

Haddie sighed, grateful for the time to absorb all the information. "Come on Terry. I'll go with you." She had Dad's card.

CHAPTER 29

HADDIE TOSSED her helmet onto her couch and followed it with a groan, lying on her good hip. Not that all of her didn't ache. She nudged some of the discarded clothes under her into a pillow. It felt good to be home. *I'm not sure I'll make it to bed.*

Rock ran between her and Dad, getting random scratches and darting away. Jisoo cried from the kitchen.

"What did you see, Dad?" Haddie asked. "Besides Meg's picture?"

"Will Liz say anything?"

"I doubt it." She waited as he eased into the chair.

He leaned forward and wiped his hair back, staring at the floor. "The people who are looking for Meg - I've had people continuing to investigate them. I've identified quite a few of the foot soldiers. We've been watching them."

"Your private war."

"Yes. You call it that. They're exterminating anyone they fear might have my power. I'm sure of it. That identity spent a lot of time in Southeast Asia during the war. It was a rough time for me. I ended up using my power."

"I've seen." Haddie reached back and began taking the braid out of her hair. Thinking of the nightmares that came with using her ability always made her edgy.

"My people came up with a name: Barbara Stevens. I've searched a lot of Barbara Stevenses, but only one in Boise Idaho who owns a distribution company. That company bought a property on Anthony Prizer's list. I remembered the address because of the price; it was far too good a deal."

Haddie's hand froze, finger entwined in the loosening braid. "You think she's the one behind killing your family — your last family?"

"Maybe not the top, but higher up than the foot soldiers. I'll put someone on her tonight."

She continued untangling her braid. Everything she'd ever believed about her dad had been just the surface. The more she learned about him both impressed and scared her.

"What will you do?" she asked.

He shrugged and focused on Rock. "Whatever is necessary to protect Meg."

If he found that Barbara Stevens was behind the deaths in his previous family, would he kill her? The woman might lead them to whomever created demons or the coerced. She might be creating them, or be the lightning lady. She could be behind the Unceasing. There could be connections with her that could answer the other questions. More than the Unceasing office in New York.

Haddie shook her hair out. "You don't want the others to know?"

He tilted his head and studied her. "And learn about my past? No."

"I could just suggest that we follow this one lead. It's less than a day's ride from here."

Dad's eyebrows furrowed. "Absolutely not. I don't want

anyone taking that risk, especially you. I don't need you and Kiana and this scientist fumbling around with Barbara Stevens. You might drive her out of sight. Then where would I be?"

They could work carefully this time, with Dad's help and resources. Terry and Aaron could see if there were any connections with the Unceasing. They didn't have to know about Meg or Dad's past. Haddie started to argue the point when Rock perked up and ran to the door, putting his nose to the crack. After all that had happened the past two days, Haddie's pulse raced.

Sam opened the door. "Hey, Boy. Did you miss me?"

Rock wiggled and backed up as Meg and Louis followed Sam.

"Hey, T. Haddie. Meg saw a ghost just now." Sam knelt to rub Rock's neck. Her trans pride button dangled off the front of a blue T-shirt. Louis wriggled against her jeans to get to Rock.

Meg wore a similar shirt with her pink backpack strapped over her shoulders. "It was like a gyroscope."

"The ghost?" asked Dad.

"Yep. Then it flew off." Meg smiled and began scratching the top of Rock's head.

Louis wove between the three of them, leash tangling until Sam got it off his collar. She looped it carefully to hang by the door. Sam frowned at the blood stain on Haddie's hip. "You okay?"

Haddie shrugged. "A scratch. It's been a rough couple days."

Sam glanced from Meg to Haddie's dad and then returned to Rock. She'd likely bring it up later. Louis darted under her legs and shot to Dad's legs. The puppy had gotten big over the past few months and easily got his paws up in Dad's lap, nosing at his hands.

Dad tousled the puppy's ears. "Well, we need to be going, Meg. Haddie needs some sleep."

Haddie yawned at the mention and winced trying to sit up.

Meg pouted, focusing on scratching behind Rock's ears. His tongue lolled and he rolled his happy eyes back at Haddie.

"Haddie, we've got camping in a couple of weeks. Offer is still open if you want to take a break," Dad said.

Meg gave Sam a secretive look. Perhaps she didn't look forward to the idea of a campout.

Rock grumbled, pushing past Sam to the door. Haddie stood. It could just be one of the neighbors. Rock tended to note anyone in the hall nowadays. Two crisp raps came on the door. Dad gently pushed Rock aside and opened the door.

Haddie could see an older man in a suit with a short, almost military style, haircut.

"Is Hadhira Dawson home?" a second man asked, hidden by the edge of the doorway. The man she could see searched her out in the room.

Haddie's chest tightened.

"Who's asking?" Dad grumbled.

"Special Agent Sugg of the FBI. Who are you?"

Haddie stepped past Sam, gesturing for her to get a hold of Rock. There could be any number of reasons why the FBI were here, the likeliest being that they were looking for Kiana.

"Her father." Dad glanced over as Haddie stepped up.

"I'm Hadhira," she said. Sliding through the door she

tried to pull it closed behind her, but Dad followed. "What is this about?"

Special Agent Sugg had a thin mustache and slightly longer hair than his companion, but wore the same simple suit. "When was the last time you saw Special Agent Wilkins?"

Haddie leaned against the side jamb of the door relaxing somewhat. "I don't remember exactly, maybe last fall."

"Have you heard from her recently?" asked Sugg.

"Yeah." Haddie nodded. "She called a month or so ago."

Sugg nodded. "And you left her a message?"

They were trying to see if she would lie about anything. Haddie felt her chest tighten again.

"Yes. She wanted me to discuss something with her, I assumed some information on Harold Holmes, but I couldn't make the appointment. I called to reschedule, but she never called back. I didn't really think about it."

"And your relationship with Harold Holmes?" Sugg asked.

"None. He shared an office building with a victim whom our client was being accused of murdering. I met him a couple times when I went to the office to ask questions about the relationship of the victim and our client. Is there something I should be concerned about?" Haddie hoped her tone came off nonchalant, with a bit of worry toward the end.

Suggs ignored her question. "Why did Special Agent Wilkins question you?"

Haddie shrugged. "From what she said, I was one of the last people to see him before he left." She carefully didn't say disappeared.

"And what happened when you met with him that last time?"

Haddie gave the same answer she'd given Kiana. "Nothing. He was in a hurry to go somewhere, and the victim's office was closed. No one was there."

Suggs looked at his partner. "We came by earlier in the evening, but you weren't home."

Haddie didn't offer them an explanation. "Is there something I should be concerned about? Has Harold Holmes returned? Was he the one who killed Sarah and Mark Colman?"

Suggs shook his head. "We'll be back if we have any questions."

The two agents turned and left down the stairs. The FBI wouldn't stop until they found Kiana. The dark cabal within would kill her — after they tortured out the names of Haddie and her friends and family. *I'm becoming paranoid.*

As the agents neared the bottom of the stairs, Haddie turned and whispered, "Dad, we have to tell Kiana about Boise."

He shook his head. "Sleep on it. We'll talk tomorrow." He opened the door into her apartment.

Sam and Meg looked up, holding Rock between them as Louis circled. Both were wide-eyed and Meg bit her lip.

"Asking about an old case from the law firm last year," Haddie said, answering their unasked questions.

Sam nodded, lowering her eyes. She looked worried, but accepted the answer.

Meg stood up and adjusted her backpack. "They didn't look nice."

Dad rubbed his hair back. "People in authority rarely are."

Rock sniffed Haddie. *I've got to do something.* She

looked at Meg and Sam with Louis swimming around their legs. These demons, the coerced, the lightning lady, and any of the others she'd dealt with since the raves did not seem the type to care about any lives. Barbara Stevens' people had been trying to kill Meg. Terry and Liz would mean nothing to them. They wanted Kiana dead. *No.* Haddie wasn't going to sit around and wait for that to happen. Perhaps Dad had it right. *This was a war.*

PART 4

The blood of the Noveilm remains, brought out in our sacrifice and pain.

CHAPTER 30

KIANA STOOD outside the house staring east at the night sky. Specks of Eugene lit the land that sloped away from the building. The stars fought the glare of the city; if she looked north or south, they became clearer. Only a few clouds drifted in the sky, sliding in from the northwest.

The temperature dropped quickly, thinning the heavy fragrance of the woods. Fir, pine, and summer grass mixed with the occasional wildflower. It brought back a memory of Bosnia. An easy nine months of action before base, and then the hell of Afghanistan. *That's where I am, on the threshold again.* She couldn't just sit in the woods while something rotted inside the FBI. After the army, it had become her sanity. Organization and rules. She waved away one of the pestering insects and considered going inside yet again. The window upstairs had stayed dark even after night fully dropped over the hills.

Her new roommate had disappeared into the small bedroom directly above hers after the others left. Somehow, having him right above her was disturbing. An intelligent man, a scientist, Aaron had an emotionless reservation that made her uncomfortable. He'd brought some useful information regarding the Unceasing, and had relevant observations in their discussion, *but . . .*

Kiana opened the door and returned inside to a dark hall where she'd removed the bulb. Retrieving the shovel and garden stakes, she returned them to their places leaned against the outer door. Slipping into her borrowed bedroom, she closed the door before flicking on the light. She'd blocked the windows with a double layer of curtains, borrowing from the second bedroom downstairs. Paranoia felt embarrassing. *What do you call it when they really are after you?*

The white board was on her bed, leaning against the side wall. Her notes about the Unceasing headquarters in New York took up three pages of the legal pad lying in front of it.

Little in the information she'd gotten from Coos Bay helped her make plans for New York. First, she had to get there — with the FBI monitoring transportation. Then, she had to set up a location to stake out the building. She would take longer this time. Her leave had been indefinitely extended.

Again, she leaned in and studied the photo that had caused Thomas concern. The sketch could have been of him, but who were all the other people? Perhaps he'd just been surprised, like her, at the resemblance. His other focus, the one that had pulled him away, she could make no sense of. Down at the bottom of a list, a random business in Boise Idaho sold by the deceased billionaire. She'd had to look up Boise just to get a sense of where it lay on the US map.

What part did Haddie's father play exactly? Obviously, he wanted to protect his daughter. That Kiana could respect.

Her phone rang lightly from atop the pillow, and she flipped it open. Haddie's burner.

"Hello," Kiana answered.

"Hey, my dad just left. Everybody left. The FBI were at my apartment. Like you warned."

Kiana breathed down the tension that threatened to rise. How close were they? "Looking for me." She made the statement to give herself a moment without becoming silent.

"Yes. I kept to the basic story. You set up an appointment, I missed, I left you a message and never heard back."

Had they really sent out someone just for that? "Did you see — the thing that lets you know if they are coerced?" Could she get Haddie close enough to some of the superiors that Kiana suspected? *And if I could — what would I do?*

"No. Damn. I would have freaked. I would have started with that."

Kiana looked at her boards. "I need to go to New York anyway. Better sooner than later, if they're snooping around here."

"How? I don't know if Dad cares about the Ford, but won't they spot you at some point? FBI stuff?"

The Ford might work, if she could come up with a decent disguise. An eye patch or asymmetrical haircut helped avoid facial recognition, but that would be awkward close up. "You think your father would be okay if I took the truck?"

"Maybe. Let me look into some options before you jump on a plan."

Haddie obviously didn't want Kiana leaving. That could be for any number of reasons, but she couldn't help feeling it had to do with Haddie's father. However, if they could come up with a plan to get to New York safely, Kiana would take it. Staying low might be the safe move, but it symbolized a death of its own. A failure. She had to act if she wanted to fix this.

"Call me tomorrow?" Kiana asked.

"Yes. We'll talk then." Haddie sounded relieved and hung up quickly.

A day wouldn't hurt. There were plans to make anyway.

Kiana pulled out her laptop and began searching for the neighbor's Wi-Fi.

CHAPTER 31

HADDIE STOOD in front of the mirror naked. Dark rings hung around the eyes that stared back. Purpura marked her face, neck, and hands in dense rashes. Singular random spots marked her shoulder, chest, and stomach. She still wouldn't get the wound wet, but it looked well on its way to healing, pink rather than angry red at the edges of the bandage. She could smell the alcohol and antibiotic ointment. Her activity hadn't done much except help enlarge the impending scar. Dad said most of his scars were gone a decade after the initial wounds. Running the water in the sink, she tried to drown her thoughts. She needed to get to work. She desperately wanted to wash her hair, but she only had time for a sponge bath in the sink. A loofah bath to be precise.

Rock had been restless all night, and she'd awakened multiple times with nightmares, perhaps because of his activity. Usually he crashed beside her through the night, but he'd been gone a couple times when she woke.

She assumed work would still be hectic. Andrea had been pushing everyone. Maybe she could talk David into lunch; he seemed distant, but she hadn't had time to even text him yesterday.

Images from Kiana's whiteboard crept into her thoughts. So much had happened in the past few days, exhausting and exhilarating.

Of course, Dad called as soon as the water warmed up and she had lathered her arms and pits. She wiped her hands on a towel and traded it for the burner phone on her nightstand.

"You headed to work?"

Fragrant lather dripped down her forearm. "Soon." Why would he call to see if she was going to work? Did he think she was halfway to Boise with Kiana?

"The RAV4 will be finished today. I can get it to you tonight. They needed to repaint two panels. Match is good. You'll never notice." She could hear Meg talking in the background. "Lunch? I can change the dressing."

"In a restaurant bathroom?" Haddie snorted. A glob of lather dripped off her elbow and landed on her foot.

"Lunch?"

He didn't normally press to do lunch. It might be the dressing, or he really did think she'd be going to Boise. "I'm going to work, Dad. Not Boise." They *should* go to Boise — get ahead of this.

"Never said you were."

"We should go. I'll call out of work." *Maybe lose my job.* "These people are dangerous. What if they get hold of Kiana or Aaron? Torture our names out of them? Track them to us?"

"This is why I don't involve others." He spoke sharply. "Sorry. I know you're trying to help them. You didn't mean for all this to happen."

But I caused it. Dad wouldn't even know about Boise if

it weren't for Kiana searching that office. Bringing that up wouldn't sway him. He could be stubborn. Kiana would be heading for New York. *Should I ask about the truck?* Maybe at lunch.

"You send your people out to Boise?" she asked.

"Yeah. I've got them watching the distribution center and the house. Both are going to be difficult. Boise has a lot of open space without cover."

Two places? There had only been one address. "Both owned by Barbara Stevens?"

"Her company. They own other empty properties and some land. I'll have someone else search those." Dad's tone shifted, harsher. "I have three more people mobilized. I'm confident I can get one inside."

"The distribution center?"

"Yes," he answered.

He has this worked out. This sounded like a long plan. Infiltration and surveillance. Probably the better way. *I would just climb in through a window and end up with dead people.* Haddie slumped, suddenly tired. Better that she just let it be for now. Focus on work.

"I got to get ready for work. I'll call you about lunch."

"Okay." Dad dropped the connection.

She tossed the phone down and headed back to the bathroom. The water had just gotten warm again when she heard her phone buzz. A text. Terry or Liz? Probably Terry, but she didn't have the energy or time.

She pushed the door to the bathroom closed with her foot and ignored her phone.

CHAPTER 32

HADDIE WINCED and swore trying to move quickly to her regular cell as it buzzed for a second round. She'd gotten as clean as she could in a sink. Makeup would take the rest of the time before she had to leave. Smelling like soap, she found her cell.

Terry had texted, "Been working with Aaron all night. We found something interesting."

He'd waited a couple of minutes and added, "Might tie into your Lady of Lightning."

Haddie wiped a random drop off her eyebrow with the back of her hand. *Just tell me, Terry.* He knew she couldn't resist any information on that woman. "What?" she typed.

He followed with a series of texts, a sign of his excitement, hitting the send button.

"Boise.

"There were a number of strange deaths from lightning there.

"One whole family.

"Same happened in Michigan 12 years ago. Anthony

sold properties in Boise at a ridiculous price. Aaron's going to Boise to check."

Dad wouldn't like that. He should have expected it though. Maybe he didn't know Terry well enough. *I should have expected it.*

"When does Aaron leave?" she typed.

"Aaron's having breakfast with Kiana first. Then he'll get a cash deal with uber to Brownsville or Sweet Home. Says he gets truckers to carry him long haul if he has the time."

Haddie raised her eyebrows, staring at Terry's text.

"I'd take him if I could. Livia would freak." Terry texted immediately.

"Damn," she swore. Dad had to do something now. If he worried about her and Kiana messing up his stakeout, then he'd need to be there to make sure. Is Kiana planning to go as well? After she heard all this, she just might forget her New York trip. *Isn't that what I wanted?*

"Not that I told Livia anything." He typed.

Haddie blinked at Terry's text. She needed to call Dad back. She typed quickly, "Tell him not to do anything yet. I'll get in touch with him in a minute."

Haddie started to dial her dad, tossed the cell onto the bed, and spun to look for her burner. She was horrible with all the secretive stuff.

Rock had come in to stare at her.

"Don't judge, Rock."

She grabbed the burner and dialed Dad. "Listen. I didn't do this, but Terry and Aaron, and probably now Kiana, all know."

"Know what?"

"About Barbara Stevens. Well, Terry didn't mention

her, but the properties in Boise. Aaron is going out to check on them. He's talking with Kiana about it now."

"Why? What do they know?" He sounded calm but stern.

"They started looking for strange lightning deaths, I guess. They found some. In Boise. They tied that to the properties sold in Boise. So, Aaron will be looking at the same places you have people looking into." She paused, staring back at Rock.

"Devil take me, Haddie. We've got to deal with this."

Am I supposed to tell Aaron where he can go? How would she argue against him going?

"How?" she asked.

"I don't know. Hell."

Why do I feel guilty? She took a deep breath trying to calm herself. This had been what she wanted. Storm down to Boise and dig around. What could she tell Kiana and Aaron? Dad already has a crew there investigating. They'd want to know why. She didn't have an answer that didn't point out something suspicious about Dad.

"Call them. Tell them we need to meet this morning. I'll bring Meg up to stay with Sam again. At least they'll be happy."

"What are you going to say?" she asked.

"As little as possible. We need to get this under control before it all falls apart. I need this information from Barbara Stevens. I can't have everyone muck it up."

"I don't know that Aaron and Kiana are going to listen unless they're given a very good reason." She doubted Dad would be willing to tell them the truth.

"I'm thinking the same thing. Please, call them and convince them to talk first. I'll pick you up."

Haddie dialed Kiana.

"Haddie, we were just talking about you. Did you ask your Dad about the Ford?" Kiana sounded excited, almost cheerful.

"He wanted to talk first. This morning?" asked Haddie.

"Okay. Terry and Aaron dug up some information. We should get together. Does he have something new?"

I have no idea what he's going to say. "Maybe. See you in an hour or so."

She dropped the burner by the cell on the bed and swirled toward the bathroom. Makeup. Her head spun, but she couldn't say she was entirely disappointed. Dad's original plan had been better, though she hated the idea of sitting around waiting for news.

Damn. Haddie twisted and picked up the cell to text Toby. Andrea would be so pissed.

CHAPTER 33

THOMAS PULLED the Jeep into the driveway with Haddie in the passenger seat. She'd complained about him turning off the AC, but he enjoyed the scents of pine and fir that came with the country air. What could have been the same pair of Gray Jays flew up into one of the young oaks with alternating squawks. The morning sun lit the house and hill above. He would miss this property. It was getting close to time for him to move on; he felt it in his bones. Meg would miss Sam, but she'd adjust in time. His connection with Haddie would have to adjust.

The old Ford sat out front, but there was no movement from the windows. Kiana and Aaron would be impatient, expecting to move quickly on their new information.

People had lost the subtle art of waiting. He'd spent the Kalmar War as a scout and learned the value of intelligence gathering. Vietnam had been the brutal proof of either failed intelligence or wanton disregard of it. Kiana, military and FBI, should have better sense. Perhaps he could persuade her. Haddie was too young, too impetuous. She seemed to hear the reasoning of careful investigation, but her emotions got in the way. He could hope to direct them, but the likelihood remained slim while he kept his secrets. *And I intend to keep them.*

He parked the Jeep beside the Ford and squinted at the house. "Do you think they'll listen?" he asked Haddie.

"Maybe." She shrugged and opened her door. "You can be pretty convincing, or intimidating."

Thomas snorted. Intimidation wouldn't work with either Kiana or Aaron; he could be sure of that. Kiana might be convinced. He climbed out of his door slowly. "What's your view on this?" He'd rather know honestly what he was up against.

Haddie strode toward the door. "I want to know — now — but I don't want a mess like the raves with a bunch of dead people on my conscience."

He nodded. That would do.

Kiana sat on the couch while Aaron stood at the kitchen counter with his laptop. They watched as Thomas followed Haddie into the house. Someone had cooked sausage and eggs. He should have asked if they needed supplies on the way in.

He leaned on the edge of the kitchen counter near Aaron, but spoke across the room to Kiana. "Haddie's bent on seeing what facts we can get from the Boise properties. I'd rather this didn't devolve in action, like Coos Bay, so I've hired some private investigators to begin getting us some preliminary information."

Kiana's eyes widened slightly, and she nodded slowly. Aaron looked back at his laptop while Haddie crossed the room to sit on the couch beside Kiana.

"The two occupied properties, one business and one residential, are on the outskirts of the city with arid, open country around them. Not the best situation for surveillance." Thomas rubbed his hair back. "I've got some help coming to the initial investigators."

Neither interrupted, but Kiana looked down.

He continued, "I'd say we should have a better idea of the situation by this weekend."

"What's your interest in this?" asked Aaron, without looking up.

Thomas shrugged. "Trying to be helpful. Haddie's all I've got. I'd appreciate no more reckless leaps where she might get hurt."

Haddie frowned, but stayed silent. She wouldn't like being coddled, but Kiana looked as though she appreciated the motivation, perhaps even believed the half-truth. Aaron remained aloof. Had he gleaned that this conversation would happen? His tendency toward suspicion was obvious.

"How long do you want to have these investigators there before we do anything?" Kiana asked.

"Give it a couple weeks, see what they come up with. We'll likely have a better idea of expectations this weekend." There would be more people coming over the next two days. Terry's revelation to the group had accelerated the time frame. People would have to be tailed to see if there were more players in Boise. Wiretaps took time and planning. Rushing added too many risks. If they were alerted, he could lose everything. He needed to know who hunted Meg.

Aaron spoke quietly. "I've got no reason not to do my own investigation at the same time. We can share information."

Thomas felt his jaw tighten, and consciously unclenched. "I'm working on getting us a house near the residence. We can all use that location." In fact, he'd rented three already through a realtor. One was for the woman working on infiltrating the distribution plant.

Kiana tilted her head, almost apologetically. "I have to agree with Aaron. I'd rather not sit here and wait. I appreciate the resources, but there's nothing for me here except the FBI looking for me. I doubt they're focused on Boise. I didn't even know where it was." She glanced at Haddie. "There wouldn't be any reason for Haddie to be there at all."

Thomas blinked slowly as Haddie frowned and fumed. *Those were the wrong words.* Now she'll want to go for sure.

Surprisingly, she remained silent. It didn't matter. He couldn't let these two bumble around in the middle of his operation and risk Meg. He'd have to go out there, and Haddie wouldn't let that happen without her.

Thomas nodded. "So, what's your plan?"

Aaron finally looked up from his laptop. "I'm still not convinced that your motive is just about Haddie's safety."

"How many kids?"

Aaron frowned. "Me? None."

"Me? One. I intend to keep it that way. I don't give much of a damn what you believe." Thomas shrugged. "Getting yourself killed won't shade my day." He looked to Kiana. "So, no plan?"

Kiana swallowed. "We hoped we could borrow that Ford."

"Not mine to lend," he lied, "but I got some friends who do car sharing. They'll provide a document that will pass most questions, and they'll confirm that you didn't steal it if they're called by the authorities. Insurance will be a cash deposit. Not the finest cars, but they'll get you eight hours across the mountains."

She nodded. "Understood. Thank you."

"Then what?" he asked.

"We'll stake out the properties and get their routines."

Thomas fished in his pocket. "You gonna camp, or you got somewhere to stay?" He didn't bother waiting for an answer, tossing a thumb drive down the counter to rattle against Aaron's laptop. "I mentioned arid and barren, right? These are initial drone photos around the two occupied locations from this morning. Not a lot of places to stakeout from. You park a car on one of these roads, and someone will be coming by to check on you real soon."

He turned to the kitchen cabinets and moved to the one over the fridge where he kept the coffee. Kiana stood from her seat on the couch and Haddie followed. Aaron glanced at Thomas before he put the thumb drive into his laptop. *He trusts me that much.*

Thomas made coffee while they watched the videos. They were long-distance shots, but they showed how little cover would be available. The morning sun had broken through clouds, and sparse vegetation sprouted from dry soil. The only trees were either planted around the residence or far off on the horizon. Without decent resources, they would have little chance avoiding detection; Kiana at least would have to recognize that. She returned to her couch, and Haddie followed.

He poured himself a cup of coffee and waved the pot toward them, but got no takers. "Tonight they'll have cameras up and live feeds going. Might even be able to get a cable technician into the residence if all goes well."

Aaron's head jerked up at the last comment, a hungry look on his face. As Thomas blew on his coffee, the scientist's face hardened.

"I'll take your help getting a car. I'm heading out there.

Whatever information you're willing to feed me will help, but I'm not sitting here," Aaron said.

Crowned idiot. Kiana would follow from the expression on her face, and they'd muck the whole operation. He'd hoped that he could sway at least Kiana to limit their interference. He'd even considered sabotaging Aaron somehow. Now he'd have to babysit all of them. Hopefully he could keep them from doing something foolish, risking Haddie, and losing his lead.

Thomas sighed and strolled across the room to face Kiana. "Haddie will follow, you realize."

Haddie didn't argue the point. Instead, she twisted her hair nervously. She'd probably been thinking the same thing.

Kiana glanced at Haddie and drew in a breath. "I can't stop her — and — her ability to see these coerced and demons would be helpful."

Thomas followed Haddie's glance to Aaron. She knew something she hadn't told him or anyone about Aaron. Interesting. Could the man see the same glowing she'd mentioned? Did that mean he had powers? If so, what were they?

"So, you'd risk her? Or are you willing to play this safe and use the intelligence resources I'm providing?" he asked Kiana.

"Dad." Haddie looked close to exploding.

"Coos Bay was my fault. However, I didn't have any resources. I think you know that I would handle this differently. Cautiously," Kiana said.

He did. In fact, he gambled on that. They were about to stumble into his operation, and Aaron certainly couldn't be trusted to care about anything other than his own interests.

The man would not respect any concerns. Haddie could be impulsive to the point of rash. She might bristle at any suggestion from Thomas, but she'd worked with Kiana. He counted on Kiana's military and FBI organizational reliance.

"Someone needs to lead this motley crew if you don't want it to fall apart." He locked eyes with Aaron.

The man's lips twisted to the side. Aaron would resist any direction from Thomas.

"Kiana's experience should serve us best in that regard," Thomas spoke, judging Aaron's surprise. "I'll drive the Jeep."

CHAPTER 34

HADDIE'S JAW DROPPED. Dad stalked across the room and picked up his coffee, seeming to enjoy the stunned silence.

Aaron's eyes were narrowed, glancing between Kiana and Dad. He still had the frozen video on his laptop.

Had Dad planned this all along? He'd seemed adamant that his investigators work alone. *Certainly without us.*

Kiana seemed as stunned, but she leaned forward. "When?"

He'd just implied Kiana would be leading them, and still they looked to him for direction. It had always been that way. As a child, he'd prompt her to decide on her own, but she'd look for his approval.

Dad finished his coffee and walked to the sink. "Give us an hour to get Haddie packed, and we'll meet you any time after that at my garage." His eyes flicked from Aaron to Kiana as he rinsed his mug. "I'm sure you've figured out where that is by now."

Kiana blushed. Had she been stalking Dad?

Aaron just nodded, closing his laptop and offering the thumb drive.

Dad shook his head. "Keep it."

"These investigators of yours, can we meet them?" Kiana asked.

Leaning on the counter, Dad shrugged. "Don't see why not. They'll be doing most of their work tonight. Is there a reason?"

Kiana nodded. "If you're asking us to rely on these people rather than our own efforts, I'd like to know the kind of people you've hired."

"Fair enough. I'll set up a meet with one this evening. We can discuss the rest in the morning. Does that work?"

"It does."

"Ready, Haddie?" To Kiana, he gestured toward the coffee pot. "There's a thermos over the sink."

Before Haddie could reach the kitchen, he'd slipped out the door. The house smelled like his coffee, but breakfast hung in the background. She'd managed a power bar. *I'm starving.* The smell of breakfast killed her; hopefully she could grab some food before they got on the road.

"See you in a bit," she said, passing the kitchen counter.

Aaron bit the inside of his lip, watching her with a wrinkled brow.

She shrugged as if to say, "I wasn't part of this."

Outside, Dad strode toward the Jeep Commander. He'd bought it used when she'd been in high school, and they'd done a dozen camping trips with it. The Hemi in it made it a power horse that he'd kept from under her foot. She'd driven the Mini Cooper for her learner's permit. The Jeep worked well for road trips.

She climbed in the passenger side as he started the engine. "What are you going to do about Meg?"

He leaned his arm back behind the seats and put it into

reverse. "I already talked this over with Sam. Biff will help with supplies."

Dad planned for this to happen? He'd argued against it.

She belted herself in. "At Sam's apartment? How long?"

He studied her face for a moment. "If this goes my way - weeks."

They started down the drive. *I didn't really think this through.* She swallowed. What would David think? *What lie am I going to tell him now?*

What was Andrea going to say? The job at the law firm had been so important a year ago; now she risked losing it and couldn't bring herself to be too concerned. She would lie. Make up some excuse and hope that Andrea didn't fire her. Would she be that upset if she lost the job? *Yes, I'd miss it.*

As they drove out of the hills and aimed east toward the city, Dad closed his window and hit the AC.

Rock and Jisoo would be okay with Sam and Meg's attention, though Haddie would miss them. She'd have to pack, something she was horrible at. The open-ended time suddenly felt daunting.

"What about the RAV4?" she asked.

"When it's fixed, they'll bring it to the garage; it'll be there when we get back. I can have Biff drop it off at your apartment if you prefer." His tone matter of fact, he had to know she wouldn't be comfortable without her car.

Did he think this would stop her from going? Have her change her mind? Haddie stiffened in her seat. She'd have to depend on him, or Kiana, for everything during their trip. Her cell vibrated, and she pulled it out of her pocket, happy for the distraction.

Terry texted, "Did I miss the invite?"

Did he mean the meeting this morning, or the trip to Boise? "Sorry," she texted.

"No prob. Did Aaron show you the links?"

"??" Haddie texted. She hadn't even talked to Aaron this morning.

"The lightning deaths."

Did he know their plan? Surely at some point, Aaron would mention it if he hadn't already. "Not yet. I'll have time." She'd almost typed "in Boise" but somehow it felt dangerous on the cell. Later she could text him on the burner.

"I'm tracking that other list. I haven't found anything yet, maybe I'm looking in the wrong places."

Haddie tried to remember the list. It had some major cities on it. She had been more concerned about Meg's picture. Hopefully, this trip wouldn't risk Dad losing any information about her pursuers. "Where are you looking?"

"Events in those cities on those dates. Community calendars, forums. I've also got some facial recognition going on with the pictures on the white boards. Difficult with picture of picture. Some have come up, so I got a list going. So far, all are dead."

This tied into Dad's war. "Can you send me the names?"

"Will do. Be careful. Have fun, Buckaroo."

So, Terry did know. "Thanks," she texted.

Haddie turned to Dad. "Terry's been doing facial recognition on some of the photos Kiana took. The ones on the white boards. Probably coming up with names of Meg's relatives."

He nodded with a light frown. "Suspected he would."

They were near her apartment. What would she say to Liz? Pulling out her burner, Haddie entered Liz's number.

"Yes?" Liz would be at work already.

"It's me."

"Lose your phone?" Liz asked.

"No. A burner."

"Neat. Are we meeting tonight? I assume you've made it through the night without using your power."

"Yeah, but I'm heading to Boise. Me, Dad, Kiana, and Aaron."

"I feel left out," Liz said.

"You and Terry. I don't know how long we'll be gone."

"I can assume that with your father along, you won't get into crazy trouble. Right?"

"Yeah, should be pretty boring." Haddie glanced at her dad, but he seemed focused on the road. "I'll check in with you on this phone."

"Okay. We're not going to get to test any time soon, right?" Liz sounded bummed.

"Not if I can help it."

"Ha ha. What about David?"

Haddie drew in a tight breath. "Yeah, I don't know what to tell him." She twisted her lips, not wanting to say more in front of Dad. *What* am *I going to say to David?*

"You'll think of something. Watch yourself out there. I'm getting back to work."

"Wait, Liz?"

"Yes?" In the background there were other voices, as if a door had opened.

"Something strange I never got to mention about the attack on Aaron." Haddie waited for a second as the background noise faded. "There was one of the coerced and he had fired a gun — just as I used my power. Now, the whole time leading up to it, I had heard this noise, like a wave crashing in the background. I didn't think about it at the time. If an explosion, like the bullet, were sent backward in time, would it stretch out and have less effect? Like, instead of a loud explosion, a slower, duller one?"

"I love it. We'll add it to our list to test."

"In your little shed?" Haddie asked.

"Maybe that one we'll do outside. Your father's place up on the hill is good."

Did I just agree to a new test? I'm an idiot. "I'm hanging up before I come up with more stupid ideas."

She held the phone in her lap, her smile slowly fading as she looked across the hood of the Jeep.

Taking a deep breath in and out, she dialed David. It was late enough in the morning that he'd be out of the gym and on the road to work. Maybe even with a client if he was in Eugene today.

"Hey," he answered. From the background noise of traffic, his cell had picked up the call in his car.

"Morning. I'm with Dad and we're driving out east." She glanced at her dad, unsure if she should mention Boise. "I'll be gone a couple of days. I can call, I just wanted you to know before I left Eugene."

There was an awkward moment of silence before he spoke. "Like Portland?"

"Yeah, no. Dad is checking up on some properties and asked me to help." She winced. Lame.

The silence stretched out longer this time. Haddie fought not to fill it.

"Okay."

Her heart dropped at his reply. *I'm killing this relationship.* "Listen, I'll call tonight." *Promises.* "I love you."

"I love you, Haddie." David dropped the connection.

She held the phone, shaking slightly. What am I doing? They'd be in Boise sometime today, creeping around, trying to find lightning lady, who could be this Barbara Stevens Dad was looking for. This wouldn't end well. People would end up dead. *That's what happens when I get involved.* At least some good might come from it if they could protect Meg. Sam would agree that it was the right thing to do. What would David think, if he knew the truth?

"This is the right thing to do, Dad, isn't it?" she asked.

He frowned. "You know my thoughts on this. However, second best considering your friends."

Haddie nodded. She'd be careful and not jump in — think things through and not be rash.

CHAPTER 35

KIANA PULLED off a rural highway in Goshen far busier than the one near the hillside house. Businesses and residences clustered together along the flat road while there seemed to be little depth to the side roads, especially those that ended at the edge of the interstate. Farms or fields broke out between and behind the buildings.

The white auto garage had an open bay where a motorcycle waited, surrounded by walls of parts and benches littered with tools. It seemed to fit Thomas.

The Jeep was parked inside the lot at the grass swale next to the road, a large white tow truck was parked along the back, and a Mini Cooper sat along the side of the garage. A bearded young mechanic stepped out of the darkness of the bay wiping his hands. His hair rose from his forehead and swept back. The smile on his face grew cheerful and gregarious as he tossed the towel to a bench. Waving, he gestured her to the back beside the garage, rather than in the lot.

Aaron shifted and stiffened, though his expression never changed. They'd drifted into a conversation about demons during the ride, and his theories aligned with hers on some accounts. Mainly, that they were of government design, a super-soldier experiment. He'd silenced abruptly when they'd turned into the street beside the garage.

She parked where the man directed and shut the engine off, unsure what to do with the keys. The bearded man approached as she opened the door. "What should I do with the keys?" The smell of grease and gasoline hung in the air.

"Under the mat's fine." As she stepped out, he extended his hand. "Name's Biff. You don't look like FBI."

Kiana wore her head wrap and a black sleeveless shirt. She'd tucked her gun and holster in her duffel. "What do I look like?"

He rubbed his chin, looking delighted at the challenge. "A lawyer on vacation, or maybe an Olympic swimmer."

She chuckled and pulled her duffel bag from behind the seat. "I do like a few laps in a pool. But that might be a stretch. Name's Kiana."

"That's what T said." Biff nodded his head toward the Jeep. "Also said to stow your stuff in the back."

"T — for Thomas?"

"That's him." Biff offered his hand to Aaron as they reached the back of the Ford. "You must be the scientist. Tall for a scientist, aren't you?"

Aaron shook Biff's hand, but didn't respond.

"Okay, then." Biff gave Kiana a look, eyes widening comically.

He strode to the back of the Jeep and opened the hatch. Three suitcases of varying shapes, colors, and styles were packed on one side, a cooler sat in the middle, and a card-board box of food sat on the right.

"Toss your stuff on Haddie's." Biff motioned to the suitcases.

Kiana placed her duffel on the pile, but Aaron slipped his backpack over his shoulder.

Biff shrugged and shut the back. "They're inside the office waiting on you." He gestured toward the front of the building at the road, and then to the open bay. "I'm packing bearings if you need me."

The office had a small tree planted on the street and a door facing a sidewalk along the front of the garage. Through a large glass panel in the door, she could see dim light inside; Thomas sat at a desk watching her approach with his phone in hand. He had a grim expression but nodded toward her.

Haddie stepped up wearing a rough black wig and opened the door. "He's almost ready. There's a bathroom if you need it." She motioned them in.

The small office had little more than a desk and a fat blue couch. There were two doors off to the side; one was marked restroom and the second employees only, where she guessed he lived. She couldn't find any other residence under his name.

Thomas sat at a plain, wooden desk with a stained calendar blotter taking up most of it. He typed on his phone silently and then looked them over when Aaron stepped in beside her. "We put water bottles in the back of the Jeep. No thermos?"

Kiana shook her head. "I'd been up for a while before you two came by."

"Bathroom?"

She shook her head. A brief memory flashed of her own family going on a road trip. That's what he reminded her of.

He tapped his phone and grimaced, standing. "Let's do this."

"Everything okay?" she asked.

Thomas shrugged, gesturing toward the door. "Just checking in with my people. We've got a place for us to land once we get there."

Aaron led the way, and Kiana followed into the sun. Haddie trailed behind, and Thomas closed the door carrying a small backpack. *Haddie will be in the front with him.* Despite his inference that she would be in charge, he still held command, and something bothered him. Had he gotten disturbing news? *How much can I trust him?*

Thomas walked around the back of Jeep. "I'll take 58 out, work over to 97, and get on 20. Give me a heads-up well before you need to stop. There are some long stretches between stops, but I know the route pretty well."

Kiana slid in behind the passenger seat and closed the door. Despite a wide back seat, she suddenly felt trapped — locked into a path she had little control over.

They were just heading to Boise. *Isn't that what I want?*

CHAPTER 36

WITH HER HEAD itching from the wig and a badly needed shower, Haddie leaned the side of her forehead against the window and looked out at the Boise River. A red bridge crossed over the greenish water, parallel to the highway. Young boys climbed along metal girders vying for places to jump into the river. As they passed, a boy leaped into the air; she never saw him land.

Hills had started to rise ahead of them, tan with green life tinting the tops. The city spread all around her, rooftops sprouted above the trees, and taller buildings formed a line ahead of them.

She'd offered to map the route with her cell, but Dad seemed to have the directions locked in his head. He'd rattle them off and they faded in her mind. They drove into the city late in the day, with the sun dipping far behind them and the smell of fried food lingering from dinner eaten in the Jeep.

Oddly, Dad had spent each stop checking his phone. He'd said he'd been coordinating his five investigators. A likely reason, but she rarely saw him on his phone under usual circumstances. This whole trip felt strange, tightly organized with no clear sense of a plan.

Aaron had remained quiet most of the trip. Haddie had texted with Sam, Liz, and Terry just to burn some of the time. She'd sent a quick text to David, and his reply had been briefer. Kiana and Dad had done most of the talking, and that hadn't been much. From the sounds of it, most of the activity would happen in the evening when investigators would set up cameras. A cable line was to be dug up and cut. Hardly anything too exciting.

"We're going to the rental house first?" Haddie asked.

Dad glanced into the mirror, probably at Kiana. "I want to change your dressing. We'll contact Robinson from there. He knows we plan to meet up this evening."

They'd gone back and forth, but Kiana had agreed that they could change at the rental property. She seemed adamant that they meet at least one of his people. Dad used changing Haddie's dressing as an excuse, and they all knew it.

"It'll be sunset by the time we can meet your investigator," Kiana said.

"We'll be quick. Almost there."

Traffic slowed as their highway merged into the city, stoplights and intersections crossed their path, and pedestrians scattered across sidewalks and crossings. They were through the city in minutes, and after one turn they entered a residential neighborhood with the sun shining through the windshield. How Dad kept all this in his head, she couldn't imagine. Cars pulled in and out of side streets and trees thickened along the one-lane roadside. The hills to the southeast grew close.

He slowed and pointed through the windshield before

he turned down a side street. "Up there, that's their residence."

A cluster of green trees sprouted around a square shape nestled in a brown, dry hillside. The hill continued to rise above it.

"What?" Haddie asked. "That house on the hill?" She didn't recognize it from the drone video. The hill had seemed like a plateau. There had been a golf course nearby.

"Mm-hmm."

She leaned her head down to see past him to the house, but buildings and trees blocked her view as they wound into a community of closely packed residences. Nice two-story houses had garages in the front and manicured lawns. This didn't seem like the kind of place Dad would like to stay.

He turned into one of the driveways, and the lull of their drive ended in front of a two-story house with a wide garage that took up most of the front. Grunting as he climbed out, he grabbed his pack and water bottle.

"Should we grab the bags?" Haddie scrambled to collect her phones and chargers.

"Ask Kiana," he said, closing his door. He headed for the front door.

Kiana already stood outside, stretching. "Now I'm in charge?" She nodded toward the back. "I'll help."

Aaron followed Dad inside with his backpack, leaving Kiana and Haddie with their luggage.

Like the other residences in the neighborhood, trees and bushes were planted in mulch-filled gardens carved in the short grass. She stowed her belongings in her jacket pocket and lugged two suitcases up concrete pavers. The house smelled like bleach and flowers. A stairway faced the front door, and Haddie left her bags at the bottom. The living room stretched to a pair of sliding doors that overlooked a golf course, possibly the one in the video. She could some-what begin to place the setting in her head.

Kiana walked directly to the window in the back. Aaron unpacked his laptop in the kitchen behind the stairs. He checked a sheet hanging on the fridge there. Dad had disappeared.

Haddie wandered toward Aaron. "Dad upstairs?"

"Yes. I would guess he is checking the view of the residence." He'd begun powering up his laptop. The note on the fridge had helpful house information, including the Wi-Fi connection.

"What are you hoping to get out of this, Aaron?"

He paused, pushing his finger up the bridge of his nose. "Answers. Like all of us. I am overwhelmed with the complexity of the apparent connections. Demons, the Unceasing, coercion, and people with abilities. Even with Terry's enthusiasm for the interrelations of the Unceasing and demons, I had reserved some skepticism. The more data we produce, the links become increasingly probable." He studied Haddie for a moment. "However, I do not believe we have the full story in all of the situations. Your father, for example. His interest in your situation seems unusual. Considering his nature, I would assume he would separate you from any contact with these circumstances."

"I think he knows that would be impossible." Haddie shrugged.

Aaron continued quietly so that Kiana could not hear, "You once asked me if anyone in my family exhibited my ability. Why did you ask that?"

Haddie swallowed. "Curious about the origins. There seems to be different powers. I've been looking for the answer to . . . why me?"

"I can understand that question. Since I have learned of

more people with abilities, I wonder why now? If it were genetic, then our ancestors might have had similar experiences. Why is there no suggestion of that in history?" Aaron glanced over as Kiana entered the kitchen. "I believe there is some answer other than genetics."

Kiana frowned. "Your theory is that the government has been selectively altering DNA in the population and is monitoring a national experiment. With demons as the result."

"Hypothesis. It is an explanation without any substantiation," Aaron corrected.

"I only partly agree with it." Kiana turned at the footsteps thudding down the stairs.

Haddie turned into the living room as Dad walked down to her bags. "Kiana?" He grabbed their two suitcases as Kiana left Aaron in the kitchen. "Do you care if I put Haddie in the master bedroom? It's got the best view of the residence." Dad nodded toward the living room. "I'll sleep on the couch. That leaves the other two rooms for you and Aaron."

Kiana gestured up the stairs. "Sounds fine. I'd like a clear view of this house before we head off. What do you have?"

Dad began climbing the steps. "A pair of 25x70 binos."

Her stomach fluttering, Haddie scrambled over to grab her remaining bag. In seventh grade, she'd used Dad's binoculars standing on the roof of the garage in Goshen, most of the time peeking into windows of the neighborhood or watching cars on the interstate. Finally, she felt the excitement of the investigation. Video drones and binoculars.

The bedroom was little more than a wide bed, a padded chair, and a dresser.

She got a turn peering at the house after Dad changed her dressing. Surrounded by an oasis of trees against the dusty hills, it looked like a castle. A square, flat-topped building rose two stories off a beige pedestal sunken into the hillside. A huge rock looked as though it sprouted out of the ground and protruded toward the building, threatening it. Lower roofs spread from the sides, but she could clearly see the rows of windows along the front facing. The drone had circled higher up and from a distance, so that it seemed more of a complex than a single building. Dirt roads wound back and forth behind the residence, leading to the plateau above.

"Ready?" Dad asked.

The sunlight had already turned the front of the building golden. It would be dark soon. The hills behind the residence were where they would meet one of Dad's investigators. Dad had said there were public trails there, but she couldn't see them from her lower elevation.

Haddie placed the binoculars on the dresser. "Let's go."

PART 5

I myself have used it wantonly, without purpose or mercy, and regret those harms but not what it has taught me.

CHAPTER 37

Haddie drank from her water bottle trying to clear the dryness of her throat. Silence filled the Jeep. They'd pulled onto the same residential street and continued south along the bottom of the hill. This close along the base, she could only see the tops of some trees surrounding the castle-like residence — little more than that. The golf course spread along the right, a verdant green that seemed unnatural in Boise.

One of the investigators, a man named Robinson, waited on the public hiking trail behind the house on the hill. They were going to meet him there and despite a long day, Haddie found the intrigue exhilarating. She wasn't sneaking into some building herself, for once; that was someone else's job. Liz wasn't inside waiting to be rescued. Haddie could just sit on the outer edge and be a part of an investigation. Dad had been right; taking time for preparation was a safer way to get results.

They parked in the golf course lot; it was scattered with cars, and she was surprised people played until dark. The air coming off the greens had an earthy moist smell.

Dad pointed across the single-lane highway. "That's the trailhead. About fifteen minutes to get to the top. We'll need flashlights to get back down."

He'd warned Haddie, so she patted her jacket pocket to make sure she hadn't lost hers.

Kiana did the same; she had thrown on a hip-length jacket and was wearing her holster under it. She fastened one of the buttons as they started walking.

The trail he pointed to could have been leading into someone's back yard, as two houses bordered each side of it. The hill rose quickly, and the trail curved along the slope behind the house on the right. It led away from the direction of the castle house she wanted to see, but likely wound back at some point.

Kiana stepped up to join Dad. "This Robinson, he's planting trail cameras?"

"He's got the east and north side of the residence." Dad gestured up toward the crest as he spoke.

"We'll all have access?"

Dad nodded, leading them into the dust with long strides that forced Kiana to keep up. "I'll have the links for us when we get back. The other cameras too. We'll have full coverage of the residence and the distribution center."

The hill seemed small now that she hiked it, but the trail wound close to the slopes, so she only saw part of it. The sweet smell of plants and dusty earth filled the air as they walked. The brush that had looked so sparse and dry on the video seemed lush and vibrant up close. Still, the tallest trees were barely her height and thinly spread. Anyone climbing through would be visible.

Down the slope to her right, a residential neighborhood tucked in as close as it could against the hills. Kids played in a couple of the green yards, and Haddie could smell barbecue drifting up from somewhere.

A silver glint played along the trail ahead. Metal flakes dusted the grass and sand. She could smell grease and oil, as if someone had tried to repair an engine on the slope. They traipsed through the patch and continued up the hill.

The trail split. Ahead, on the path that continued straight, she could make out a couple. The woman looked east through a camera on a tripod. The man, younger with a topknot, waved at them. Dad led them left, north up a harder climb along a steep switchback that left the houses behind. As they turned back and forth along a rocky ridge, she could see the city. They'd climbed surprisingly high.

Her cell buzzed, and she almost left it in her pocket.

Liz texted, "I found it!"

Haddie sighed, glancing at Dad ahead. "Found what?"

"The brick. I put a picture on marketplace saying I was looking for it. A woman responded. Over seventy years ago it showed up here. Some farmer kept it back in 1947. Story was, they thought it was a military mine of some sort. Local police drilled a hole in it."

Haddie raised her eyebrows. *It had worked.* Somewhat. It must have kept its shape if they thought it was a bomb. She started to question why someone thought to drill into a mine, but left it. *I've got enough going on.*

"Cool," she texted.

"More than cool, but you're busy. How's it going?"

"Hiking," replied Haddie.

Dad called out at the sound of a pair of bikes skidding down from above. "It's tight here, they won't see us until the last minute."

Haddie shoved her phone in her pocket, and with the

others, pressed to the edge of the trail. A young couple on mountain bikes veered around the curve, kicking dust as they tried to slow, narrowly shooting past. Dad's gaze followed them with a frown. He'd never enjoyed biking; too fast, missed everything, he'd claimed.

When the trail abruptly flattened at the top of a broad plateau, the view disappointed Haddie. Neither the house nor the trees surrounding it were visible from the trails, just distant rising hills and dry brush. The sun still lit the hilltops and mountain peaks beyond. It lay golden orange in the west, still fierce. Except for a tall building or two, Boise might not even exist from up here.

"Where's the house?" Kiana asked.

Dad pointed ahead and to the right. Their trail led straight along the edge of the plateau. If they continued on it, they'd pass behind the castle house from his gesture. "It's up there. There are trails that lead down to it from the top of the ridge. Private property, we won't be going down them."

Twenty or thirty paces ahead of them, a small man stood looking north, away from them, not realizing that they had crested the trail behind him. The wind blew in from the east where a line of clouds darkened the horizon. He didn't turn until they were almost on him.

He was dressed in a loose T-shirt and cargo pants, and he had short black hair, light brown skin, and small eyes. Startled, he moved to pass them along the path with the slightest greeting.

"Evening," Haddie said, but he'd already moved behind her toward Aaron.

The plateau stretched ahead, seemingly flat in comparison to their earlier climb, but in fact, bumpy.

A heavier figure with a large backpack walked slowly, further up the trail to the north. At Dad's pace, they gained on him quickly. A large gray backpack bobbed with each step, and he used a tall walking stick.

"That's him," Dad said, motioning toward the big man.

In a moment, the man had noted them and casually paused to tie a boot. He had thinning gray hair, large ears, and a full white beard and mustache. He smiled broadly and waved. As he gathered his walking stick and stood, he faced them and sniffed the air as if enjoying his hike.

A large, round area the size of Dad's jeep looked as though someone had dug it up and sifted through it. Where the sand clumped and plants grew in the earth and trail around it, the splotch wisped fine dust from the wind and their passing.

"Robinson?" asked Dad.

Haddie turned, raising her eyebrows. He'd just identified the man to her, but it sounded as though they'd never met.

"Tempest?" The man's smile faded, and he squinted, studying Haddie and the others.

"Yes," Dad said.

Haddie smirked. "What?"

"Gaming name." He glanced at Haddie, then Kiana, speaking quietly. "Keep your own names out of it."

Kiana whispered, "You don't trust him?"

"I don't trust anybody." He raised his voice and jerked a thumb at Kiana. "This is the boss. She's got questions."

Kiana darkened with a blush. She'd asked a couple questions of Dad, none that he hadn't answered. Haddie imagined that the only reason she'd asked to meet the investigators was to get a sense of what kind of people he had doing the work. Haddie herself had imagined one of his biker friends. This man looked professional. *For all I know.*

"Any activity from the targets today?" She nodded in the general direction, only the crest of the plateau from where they stood.

Robinson smoothed out his beard, tugging at the bottom. "From up here? Nothing. I didn't get here 'til a couple hours after sunrise, but I've seen nothing on that ridge. Bikes and hikers on the trails, but they're all along the same path you just came from."

"What's the scope of your assignment?" Kiana asked.

He tilted his head slightly, but rattled off instructions as if reading from bullet points. "Trail cameras installed at the north and east boundaries of the residence to capture traffic. Report any potential burn. No engagement. Withdraw, then monitor and maintain cameras. Await further instructions." Robinson shrugged. "Simple, easy money. Your rules."

Dad looked at Kiana. "All good?"

She nodded.

Robinson tapped his walking stick into the sand. "I better get at it then."

Haddie turned with a sigh. She'd expected something more from the meeting, or from this hike above the castle house. Dad had everything under control; they just had to sit and wait while Dad's plans unfolded. They'd return to the rental house, and she could sleep.

Aaron, who'd been standing back behind them, turned to lead their return as Dad started along the trail. The sun had just dropped behind the mountains to coat their plateau with darkness, though the summer's evening sky still lit the ground.

Haddie had only taken a step when she paused. Kiana passed her with a quizzical look and Haddie pointed.

A diminutive, glowing figure was positioned down the trail, close to where it dropped out of sight. The little man they'd passed. Wisps of blue light rose from his face and arms and trailed off his legs.

CHAPTER 38

HADDIE OPENED her mouth to speak, and a tone rang deep in the air around her. The ground shook under her feet, and she stumbled, crouching and reaching out.

Kiana dropped to a knee as she pulled out her revolver. Aaron, who stood farther down the trail, looked at them and began running away.

Dad turned toward her, his eyes widening. "Haddie!" he yelled.

Haddie spun to find stone climbing out of the sand around Robinson. Like fingers reaching from underground, several long rocks pinched up and in against the man. With his feet trapped, he pushed against the closest stone in front of him.

Impossibly, they seemed to shift and shape themselves. One seemed a conglomeration of earth and rock packed together. It rose up against Robinson's back. His pack tore. Small, mottled-black boxes and cameras tumbled out.

Robinson screamed. Stone grated against stone. Crushing. Haddie imagined she heard his legs breaking. Five fingers of rock lifted him up and squeezed. Robinson silenced and bones snapped. She could hear him burst with a pop. Blood squirted from the cracks.

Haddie felt the warm spray against her face. He rained onto her wig.

The rich, metallic taint of blood stunk around her.

Still the stone fingers crushed until just the ragged remainder of the pack pushed up and over them. Black camouflage cameras clattered onto the sand.

Haddie staggered back. The little man had done this. Nearly falling, she spun back to where she'd seen him at the edge of the trail. Barely visible, light blue wisps trailed off his skin. His tone reverberated again.

Aaron had veered off toward the edge of the plateau, heading nearly west. Kiana knelt, staring at the remains of Robinson, her gun pointed at the stone pillar that had replaced him.

The earth around Dad began to mound. The soil below his feet opened into a hole.

"Dad!" Haddie yelled.

Rock sprung up around him. He tried to leap away, but his footing slipped against loose dirt. The ground dropped out from under him. In a moment, stone fingers reached as high as his hips. Grinding and shifting, they moved to pinch in on him.

"Fight it, Dad! Use your song!" Haddie yelled.

He doesn't know how. When she first protected herself against Sameedha, she'd used her song instinctively.

She tried to protect him now. The tone inside her rose, but she was too far away. Stumbling, she took several steps closer.

The rock lurched.

"No," Haddie growled. Her tone rang out. The earth and stone pillars blew away to nowhere and nothing. Dad stood in a waist-high, twelve-foot-round bowl.

Needles of pain ripped across her skin. Nightmare visions blacked out Dad, Kiana, and the little man who attacked them. She dropped into Dad's past. Still in the jungle. Forever the jungle. As the evening sky of Boise rolled in around her, she blinked away the image of four dead villagers lying tangled in grass. One boy younger than Meg had cold, dead eyes.

The evening sky of Boise returned, dark blue with a haze in the west toward the city.

Dad slipped, trying to climb out of the pit she created. Not noticing the little man, Dad scanned around them. He still didn't know where the attacks came from.

She wanted to speak. Trembling, she recognized the circle around her dad. It had been the odd spot she'd noticed.

Kiana had spun toward Dad when the rocks started reaching out; now she crouched, staring at Haddie.

Swearing, Dad lunged out of the hole.

The small man's tone restarted.

The ground around Haddie shook. She stepped out, widening her stance. Hips and knees complained at every move.

The hum rose from her. A distinctive note, different from her usual tone. She fought his power, and it had that same feeling she'd experienced with the Lightning Lady and Sameedha. The tones collided, squelching. Sand and stone vibrated in growing patterns around her. The tremors shook Kiana and Dad. In seconds, the little man stopped.

Her skin still prickled so that she barely wanted to

move. At least fighting another's power didn't cause the same damage.

He stood at the far end of the trail, light blue in the darkness of the landscape. The sky behind him had darkened as the sun set. A cloud far to the south flamed orange. *I could kill him.*

His tone started again. It was a deeper note than hers. Deeper perhaps than any of the others she'd heard. She felt weary, but braced herself and scanned the ground around them. Somewhere behind her, a dull roar burst out.

Kiana dove for the ground. "Watch out!"

Haddie never had a chance to react. The first stone to pass her had an oblong shape. Easily the size of her head, it zipped to the right of Dad.

The second rock caught Haddie's left side. Elbow screaming on impact, her left arm flew out in front of her as she spun. It felt huge. The boulder scraped along her jacket and tugged her into a spin. The sky and sand swirled around as she flailed.

Slamming onto the ground, she landed on the side that had just been hit. Pain flashed from shoulder to stomach. Rolling, she sucked in air and stared at a dark blue sky. Gray rocks danced around them, thudding into the ground. Her left arm throbbed, and she didn't dare move it. Her only sense of direction came from where the rocks had flown.

The little man's tone had been short, and she cringed at the thought of it starting again. Had anyone else been hit?

"Dad?" She pushed up on her right elbow.

"Hell, Haddie." He spoke from behind her. "You okay?"

She'd been twisted from where she'd been facing. The pain in her side hurt worse than her skin. Haddie turned her head, trying to get her bearings — and find Dad and Kiana. Aaron had run away.

Kiana lay nearby, her gun in her hand and her eyes searching from where the stones had come.

The little man's tone began once again, and Haddie jerked up. Twisting up onto her right wrist and hip, she found him, pale blue tendrils in the darkness.

He seemed smaller. Kneeling, he likely suffered the same consequences she did when she used her power.

Haddie screamed, and her tone rang in the air around her. The blue threads at the far end of the trail evaporated.

With her skin feeling like it had been shredded off her, she cried out. Her right elbow couldn't hold her weight, and she fell flat on her back as the visions came.

Bright morning sun beamed across a steaming rice paddy. The soldier beside her grunted from a bullet. The crack of the gun came a moment later. Rising from the nearly still water, three enemy soldiers opened fire. Her shoulder burned. She growled, and they faded away, leaving only ripples.

The sky turned dark except for the fire raging from a barn. It shed orange light across her yard. Her horses were trapped inside; she knew it. Bullets crashed into the door she had just opened, and she heard her wife cry out from the kitchen. A window smashed as the bullets thudded into the side of her house. The two men sat on their horses, firing but missing her. Haddie turned to find her wife on the floor. A dark shiny pool of blood seeped from under her. Haddie screamed, silencing the bullets. The horses behind her snorted before they scampered off, riderless.

The nightmares ended, and Haddie sobbed. She didn't just see, hear, and smell them. The horror of losing her wife, Dad's wife, would live in her dreams.

She couldn't move. She didn't want to. Her hands felt like they had no flesh, stuffed in stiff gloves. Where the wig bit into her scalp, it burned as if the hair had been ripped out.

"Haddie?" Her dad's voice.

She cried for his loss. For a woman long gone. Her body shook, and she flinched as Kiana reached her, touching her shoulder.

"I can't," Haddie said. There had been such emptiness in that vision. *I don't want this.*

The emotions of the visions eased as Kiana knelt beside her. Reality — a sense of now — settled in. The little man and his stone. Then Dad arrived, eyes darting across the plateau before he reached for Haddie's left arm. Pain sent lights dancing in her eyes. The sky had gotten dark, grayish behind her and purple-black at her feet.

She thought she might have screamed as he moved her arm, but her mouth just hung open.

"Let's get her out of here." Dad moved around to get behind her and reached under her shoulders.

I can do this. The week had taken its toll. She wanted to just lie there. Instead, she reached down with her right hand and found the ground, pushing up as he leveraged her into a sitting position. "I can stand," she said. She curled her legs under her and let him push for leverage while Kiana steadied her right arm.

"Where did our lanky friend go?" Dad asked.

Kiana grunted. "He's the smart one, remember? He ran. Last I saw, he'd made the ridge."

Haddie got onto a knee. A light rumble, not the earth moving, sounded in the air. "What's that?" She got a foot on the ground, almost surprised she didn't topple.

The sound increased, and she felt Dad pause. "Hell," Dad swore. "We've got company."

Haddie swiveled, steadied by both Kiana and her dad.

She could see lights playing across the ridge down where she expected the house to be. Distinct two-stroke engines, perhaps three or four, sounded from below. One might have been a four-stroke.

It didn't matter.

They had to run.

CHAPTER 39

HADDIE SHUFFLED MORE THAN RAN. Dad started off quicker, slowing as he realized she still limped. Kiana, with her gun drawn, ran between them and the four-wheelers.

Light from the sky still lit the ground, though the sun had long since abandoned them.

Behind them, following a path that led from the other side of the castle house, light beams danced along the edges of the ridge as the headlights pitched and engines whined up the slope. For the moment, the lights only lit the stone and brush, yet to crest and begin across the plateau toward them.

We have to go back. The path they'd taken up to the ridge above the castle house was still a good distance away. Aaron likely had already reached it. As the ATVs raced behind, they'd be exposed on the plateau for a while before they could get out of sight.

Her side slowed her the most. Bruised along her back, she wondered if her ribs might be cracked, as pain shot through them with each step. Her left arm seemed numb, but she held it tightly to her chest with her right hand.

A beam of light bounced off the brush to their left. The engine's whine echoed clearly across the plateau — a two-stroke that just dropped into gear. The next time, a swath of light swept across the ground at their feet as the driver must have turned. Light lit the side of Dad's grim face as he jogged beside her. His fingers tightened on her arm.

Their silhouettes stretched ahead of them, shifting in an eerie dance of prey and predator.

A second ATV crested the ridge behind them, joining the whine of the first.

Somewhere ahead lay the edge where the little man had attacked them. Close to there would be the path down the slope and ridges. Surely it would help to get off the flat, open plateau. How many riders? How many guns?

Haddie winced as Kiana fired two shots at their pursuers. Two of the lights trailing them veered off, lighting up the shrubs to the left.

The ground ahead of Haddie became too dark — her footing was unsure. Dad didn't slow, but she couldn't bring herself to move any faster.

Kiana sprinted up the trail to rejoin them. "I don't dare waste too many shots keeping them back. Will you be able to stop them?"

She means with my power. Haddie couldn't imagine trying to use it again. Her hands and face still felt burned and raw. *Would Dad expose himself to Kiana?*

Haddie's eyes had readjusted to the darkness, and she swore the ridge disappeared just ahead. She glanced back. Four pairs of headlights spread out behind. The closest rode deeper in the plateau off the trail, bouncing and dipping as it raced to come alongside them. The sky looked deep blue behind it, ready to turn to stars and the black of night. The ATV would catch up with them long before that.

The rattle of automatic gunfire echoed from that direction. Dust bloomed between the plants to her right.

The headlights turned toward them again. Haddie caught the shine from her left first, then from behind. The ATVs had all turned toward them, bearing down for the kill.

Kiana fired from close behind, then swore. Returning bullets dusted the path around them.

The headlights lit the trail ahead clearly. The bushes parted, and then the path disappeared. They were almost to the ridge. Two guns fired from behind.

Aaron stood up out of the brush, suddenly looming like a pale stick in the light. He held a gun in both hands and aimed toward them.

Haddie flinched as his muzzle flashed. She knew he didn't shoot at them, but the ATVs that followed.

In slow, even timing he squeezed out shots, leaving flashes of light in her eyes. At the last click of an empty chamber, he dove out of sight again.

Haddie had gotten her legs under her, ignoring the twinges in her side.

At the edge of the trail, Dad spun and yelled, "Get to the Jeep. I'll be right behind."

Haddie heard his growl and his tone in the air before two more shots from Kiana pierced the night. As Haddie shuffled down the sandy incline, suddenly blinded in the darkness, one of the whining engines behind them abruptly disappeared. Dad had used his power — in front of Kiana.

Lights from the valley below winked between brush. Behind, she could hear footsteps along the trail, following her. Before the next turn in the switchbacks, her eyes had adjusted to the dim light. Dad and Kiana scrambled behind.

Headlights from the remaining ATVs lit the brush at the top of the ridge.

"Go," Dad yelled. His voice was hoarse, and he likely would be feeling the effects of using his power, but it didn't slow him.

Haddie grimaced, nearly teetering at the next turn. Her right arm reached for balance as she swung left, and pain raced up and down from the elbow. Righted, she clasped her left hand back to her torso and aimed downhill. With her heart racing, she drew deep breaths into a tight chest. Streetlights had turned on below. Night crept closer.

Thinking she'd found Aaron ahead, near the edge where families barbecued, she instead saw the man's topknot and the woman with the tripod. They were little more than silhouettes. They should be running. Surely, they heard the gunfire.

The first ATV reached the ridge above and began maneuvering down the trail. Headlights splashed one area of the path, then moved quickly off. Gunfire rattled, and Haddie could hear bullets striking the brush around her. She cringed as they seemed to pelt everywhere. Escape seemed nothing more than random chance.

Kiana sent out two more shots, and the ATV's engine above wound high. It crashed against brush above, calling Haddie to look up.

A satisfaction flickered as she saw it bounce wildly. *Kiana hit it.* Haddie swallowed. *It's going to end up down here.*

Uncontrolled, the ATV dove through the brush above where the switchback turned. In a slow roll, the four-wheeler shot off the edge. The engine whined. The driver flopped in his seat, about to fall out. The passenger held onto a rollbar in one hand and an automatic gun with the other.

Both had yellow haze in their faces.

Her heart pounding, Haddie dove out of their way.

She burst through dry, brittle brush into open air. Flailing, she tried to find ground below her. She caught a glimpse of residential lights, brush, and shadows. Her jacket bunched up at her shoulders as she hit a slope of sandstone and rock. Dragging her right hand to slow her progress, she slid sideways to the trail below and bounced to a stop on her injured left side.

Gasping, she looked up.

The ATV crunched, back wheels first, into the path only an arms-length from her. The passenger lost hold of his gun and rollbar. He flew up, while the four-wheeler continued to bound down toward the houses below.

Haddie stumbled to her feet as the passenger rolled down the trail ahead of her. Dad and Kiana were somewhere above. A second four-wheeler had begun driving down the trail from the plateau. Gunfire echoed from above, and bullets whispered in the brush around her.

They didn't even care if they shot one of their own.

The thrown passenger, an older man with flabby cheeks, rose to his feet, ignoring bleeding scrapes down the side of his face. He spotted her immediately and began trudging toward her.

She took a single step, turned, and planted a heel-kick firmly into his chest. He let out a surprised grunt as he flew off the trail. The slope dropped so sharply that she couldn't see it from the middle of the path. He let out cries as he tumbled out of sight.

We need to get out of here. Where had Aaron gone?

He'd shown up for a moment, fired his gun, and disappeared.

Haddie stumbled into a run toward topknot and the woman with the camera. They were hurrying, trying to get the camera detached. *Just leave it.*

Dad's investigator, Robinson, was dead; the whole stakeout was botched. The little man had been the cause. Had he called the house and had them send the ATVs?

The couple ahead left the camera attached and started running with the tripod over the woman's shoulder. They ran east along the trail, opposite the direction Haddie would follow to get to the Jeep.

She could hear Kiana and Dad scrambling behind her. The ATV grumbled slower as it maneuvered the switchbacks. In spurts, an automatic rifle fired downhill. She could see the headlights bobbing and weaving, but little else.

The last turn gave her a bright view of the neighborhood below. The couple with the camera were running silhouettes up the straight trail along the slope. Night nearly covered them.

She heard Dad's tone ring out and another ATV disappeared. Still the fourth and last fired down the slope, but bullets no longer rustled the brush around her.

She jogged along the path that led back toward the trailhead by the road. The lights she could see there were likely the golf course or the houses along the road. To her left, the neighborhood residences were close enough she could see inside lit windows and into back yards.

Haddie looked over her shoulder toward the ridge where Dad and Kiana still ran from the last ATV. She couldn't leave them, but she was hardly in any shape to help.

She turned at the sound of brush crunching and sand

scraping ahead of her.

Flabby cheeks and a scraped face lunged toward her. The haze looked like minuscule fireflies racing in and out of the man's skin. Solid and heavy, his bulk hit her square in the stomach.

Together they flew off the trail.

Haddie sucked in a breath as they dropped past where she expected ground to be. She pushed her right forearm under his chin while they rolled in the air. He held on with both arms around her waist and back.

The houses below drifted into view. Brush. Fence. Sand. The man's face locked in a grimace, with the haze winding through it. Wide-eyed, he barely seemed to realize they were falling.

She stiffened, leveraging all her strength between her arm and shoulders.

When they hit, most of the impact went to his head and back. His arms slacked as they began rolling. The world spun around her, and her left arm slapped the ground.

The man drifted away during their spin.

Haddie brought her right arm up, trying to protect her face. Before she could see it, she slammed against a wooden fence and heard it crack.

Staggering and groaning, she managed to stand. The man lay still against the fence a few steps away. Above, the gunfire continued.

Dad. Kiana.

The sparse brush that held onto the side of the incline grew at a sharp angle trying to reach the sun. She had to get back up there. *Not up this slope.* Stumbling, she headed west along the fence toward the growing glare in the evening sky above Boise. She'd have to go back to the trail-head and start up again.

CHAPTER 40

Kiana leaned against the stone, tugging at her head wrap.

"Through and through," said Thomas. His hands staunched the blood on the front and back of her leg.

The gunfire above continued. The people on the trail had lost them and were raking the slopes with bullets, perhaps hoping to spook them out or catch a random hit.

Too late. They'd already managed to get a shot through her right thigh. She hid with Thomas in a rocky crevice just off the path. Hopefully, Haddie had escaped. There was little reason to worry about Aaron; he seemed perfectly capable of keeping himself out of harm's way.

Between bursts of gunfire, another vehicle roared across the hill above, heading in their direction. There would be more soon. They'd search for bodies at least. Haddie wouldn't leave her father here. She'd come back. Kiana couldn't be the cause of their death.

She handed the head wrap to Thomas. He wadded it up and forced her to hold it on the larger wound at the back of her leg.

"You need to leave me here," she said.

He started taking off his belt. "Maybe." His face looked dark, mottled. Purple spots were visible against his pale skin.

What were he and Haddie?

He fished a bandana from one of his pockets, folded it, and strapped it under her belt to press against the wound on the front of her leg. He then looped her head wrap under her leg, pinned it, and tightened the belt.

"Now, before they start looking." Kiana laid her hand on his shoulder. "Go."

"Police will be here soon. All those houses below. The FBI will find you."

"If these goons don't kill me." She nodded uphill.

He looked weary, and it hadn't just been the rock hitting Haddie that had slowed her down. Whatever power their family had, it took a lot out of them to use it. Thomas had stumbled downhill after his last usage. She couldn't expect him to do it again, and he couldn't get her off this hill in the shape he was in.

"Take my gun," she said. "There are three rounds left."

He rubbed his hair back, glancing uphill as they let out another round of shots. "No. I'd rather you keep it." He took out his phone and held it low to avoid lighting them up. "I'm going to leave a message for my people to come up here and assess whether they can help you. If it's clear, they'll be calling out for their pet Fluffy. Just yell out that you saw her."

Kiana chuckled, then winced. "Go, Thomas. Before Haddie comes up here." There would be no rescue. But, it was nice he cared enough to try.

He nodded. "Let's see how this plays out." He patted her knee and began crawling down the ravine.

The sky had almost turned to night. The haze out of Boise had risen on her right. Her sweat and blood mixed with the scent of dry, spicy brush. Once he was gone, she'd start working her way down behind him. *A good way to bleed out.* What choice did she have?

The gunfire had stopped. Engines idled above. Two vehicles. When the wind shifted, she could hear voices up there. They likely realized that she and Thomas were hiding on the slopes. Or had been killed. They'd have to decide whether to search or retreat. Perhaps they'd called in and awaited instructions.

Her heart had calmed. Perhaps too much. *How much blood have I lost?* She couldn't see Thomas anymore. The headlights from the vehicles pointed down on the ridge below, just above the neighborhood.

Dirt filtered into her hair, but she moved too slowly.

A flashlight flicked onto her head, the gun she'd just started to lift from her lap and her wounded leg. "Just hold right there," a husky voice said. "Got one!" he yelled back.

CHAPTER 41

THOMAS RAN through the underbrush in a crouch. Pungent scents shifted and lingered on his jacket. Just down the slope, he could see the trail. Still no sign of Haddie.

Above, three ATVs sat on the ridge, visible only by their headlights. They didn't venture down the trail any closer to the neighborhood below. Would they find Kiana or withdraw? If they withdrew and he confirmed Haddie was secure, he'd head back. His fingers and neck still felt raw, but he could bring back the kit from the Jeep and work up a sled to get Kiana off the hill. If they didn't find her.

He reached the trail with a clear view of the neighborhood below. Streetlights had come on, and the houses were lit from nearly every window; some were blue from televisions and others warm yellow. With all the gunfire, he expected everyone to be outside, staring up at the vehicles on the ridge. Perhaps the sound didn't carry that well, or carried over the residences.

Jogging, he quickly lost sight of the headlights above. The golf course lay close to the Boise River. Houses lit up the opposite bank, leaving a swath of darkness between.

He'd be able to see the parking lot soon. In this light he wouldn't be able to know whether Haddie waited there.

Aaron had surprised him. He'd been sure the man had escaped. For that brief moment, Thomas had wondered if they'd been betrayed. Still, he didn't trust the man.

Kiana had been the biggest revelation. She'd resisted his every attempt to disrupt her or get a rise. He finally believed her. Who would have thought he'd ever trust an FBI agent, even an ex-FBI agent? He hadn't wanted to leave her, but Haddie was his focus.

The ATVs whined into movement, and he slowed to glance back. Their lights flickered against the edges of brush along the trails. The hill had darkened so that he could barely make out the path he'd just run down. The lights from the neighborhood were too bright.

Thomas focused ahead. He couldn't use his flashlight. Carved into the edge of the slope, the path grew tight. He would have few options if the ATVs drove this way.

He'd seen the glow that Haddie had described on the people who drove the ATVs. So many centuries he'd considered himself the only one with powers. Never had he thought that his children or ancestors would have his abilities, at least he'd rarely considered it. This year had brought him facts that he didn't want to accept. Haddie, the coerced, the demons, and these others with abilities hadn't fit into his perception of the world before Harold Holmes. He'd have to adjust.

The golf course came clearly into view. Lights lit the clubhouse and surrounding grounds. A car in the parking lot started up, turning on its headlights and swinging toward him. The road lay between, and a few cars whizzed past.

For a moment, he thought he saw a moving silhouette

on the trail ahead. Haddie? Aaron? He paused for a quick check of his surroundings.

One of the ATVs seemed to move in his direction. He could see headlights for a moment, then the curve of the slope swallowed them. He could run forward or watch from behind, but not both on the narrow trail. Sparsely dotted with brush, the incline offered little place to hide up or down.

Again, the hint of a shape on the trail ahead, between the distant lights of the neighborhood beyond the golf course. It had to be one of their team. Any random hiker would have a flashlight, and the coerced would have a yellow glow. They weren't very far away, but he'd have to make a choice soon.

"Dad?" Haddie called out. She climbed the trail with a steady gait. He'd seen the stone that had winged her; she likely had cracked ribs. She should have gone to the Jeep and waited.

"Haddie," he called back.

She stopped, silhouetted against the lights of the golf course. As he grew closer, she asked, "Where's Kiana?" She held her left arm against her chest.

Thomas swallowed, unsure if he could get her back to the Jeep. "Took a bullet in the leg." He slowed to a stop in front of her.

Haddie raised her eyebrows, seeming stunned. "You left her? We need to get Kiana."

"We will." He nodded toward her arm. "Broken?"

"Feels like it. I don't know." She shook her head and her jaw tightened. "We can't leave."

"I've got people coming." He turned back to check the hill. The lights from one of the ATVs lit the brush on the slope, following the trail he'd just run down. They moved slowly, searching. "She's hidden, and we've bound it to reduce bleeding. She can't walk on it though, not without help."

Haddie frowned and her eyes hardened.

She's not going to let this go. He could understand. The thought of leaving Kiana behind tore at him too, but he couldn't risk Haddie. "If you go back to the Jeep with me, I'll get the kit and head back in. You've got to stay with the truck, though. You are in no condition to help."

Haddie opened her mouth to argue. Robinson's blood speckled her thick makeup and stood out as headlights lit her face. Quickly her eyebrows furrowed in anger.

Thomas turned as gunfire sprayed out from behind him.

The ATV whined as it sped up, bouncing down the thin trail. Muzzle fire flickered above the bright beams.

The headlights winked out as Haddie yelled.

Thomas heard her tone, and he caught his own growl in his throat.

Another ATV, high on the ridge, continued to whine, but its headlights lit brush on the trail far up the hill. They would have heard the gunfire and know the hunt was still on. Thomas had to get Haddie off the trail. He might have time.

Haddie had dropped to one knee. He reached out to her right shoulder and steadied her. What experience of his did she just relive? She'd stopped asking questions about them. It hurt them both.

Her eyes focused on him as she returned from the visions.

"We have to go," he said.

She shivered, moistened her lips, and spoke. "Kiana." Her voice weak, she rose. Her right hand shook as she grasped her left to her chest.

"I'll go back, once you're safe in the car."

He reached over to her left hand and found the button-hole on her cuff. She held her gloved hand loosely and winced as he moved her arm to button the sleeve to her jacket high near her neck. It would work until he could make her a sling. Her eyes drooped and she swallowed slowly. He didn't dare test her ribs, but she would have reacted to a punctured lung long ago.

High above, the ATV grumbled, moving at a slow speed in a low gear. Perhaps they searched the surrounding slopes, or had become careful after the disappearance of their companions.

She let him turn her down the trail, away from Kiana and toward the Jeep. He'd left people behind before, some to die. Leaving Kiana bothered him more than he would have guessed. More than anyone had in a long time.

He kept them at a steady gait, gratefully downhill, considering Haddie's condition. Stars shone behind them above the hill as they reached the trailhead. The ATV still motored above, but they hadn't followed far enough down the trail.

Hopefully, he still had people planting some cameras near the driveway entrance and across the street where he could monitor the surrounding hill. He could capture plate numbers coming and going, if his targets didn't all bug out tonight. The entire mission could be moot by daybreak.

Aaron was squatting at the trailhead and rose as they approached. "Kiana?" he asked.

"Wounded. We'll have to go back for her. I want Haddie safe in the Jeep." Thomas watched Aaron's expression. They could all hear the ATV on the ridge. The man had little interest in a rescue mission, but he might not outright refuse. Thomas could use an extra hand getting Kiana down.

Haddie started to speak, but Thomas marched them toward the road. Most of the cars had left the golf course parking lot. Nothing seemed unusual around the Jeep. Robinson had likely been the target, and they'd just shown up at the wrong time.

His phone vibrated and he pulled it out, pausing at the side of the road. His game app had a new message. It would be one of his investigators. Tempted for a moment to wait until he got to the Jeep, he opened the app and message.

It came from the woman he had setting up cameras along the driveway. "Activity on high ridge over residence. Multiple units have left on vehicles and gunfire noted. One unit returned with possible prisoner."

"Kiana," he said absently.

"She messaged you?" Haddie asked, a hopeful tone in her question.

He shook his head. "No." He typed a message to his investigator, "Monitor and advise of any change."

If he told Haddie, she'd want to barge in and save Kiana. Not that he didn't, but he hardly had the firepower, even if the attack on Robinson had siphoned off the bulk of their guards up the hill. He had no idea what waited inside the residence. If he didn't tell Haddie, he risked their relationship and he dismissed her independence, yet again.

"Kiana might have been taken captive. Transported to the house."

"We have to get her." Haddie spoke without a thought. As usual, she was ready to charge in without a plan.

He motioned to the street as traffic thinned. "We need a strategy." He could count on one of the investigators for some dangerous activity. The remaining three were picked for their technical abilities, not storming a hostile building.

"And what's that plan?" Haddie asked.

Crossing the road, he looked north to where it led to the residence he'd hoped to monitor.

Two pairs of orange dots bobbed down the road toward him, like bicycle reflectors, but too high. As they passed in front of lights, he realized they were two men and the glow came from their eyes. *Demons.* Haddie had described it, in detail. He'd just never seen it before.

"Demons." His tone conveyed surprise, rather than urgency. "Devil in hell." He dug in his pocket for the key. "Get to the car. I'll lead them off. Leave if you have to."

Tossing the key to Aaron, Thomas raced to the golf course.

Haddie yelled after him, but he needed her out of the way. He'd use his power again, if he had to, but he wanted the demons away from Haddie.

They took the bait and veered from the side of the road as they spotted him. Their clothes seemed to fall off as they ran. One loped as its knuckles hit the manicured green. More than clothes had fallen off; the skin went with it leaving red, raw flesh and muscle. It was the size of a large ape and moved like one. The mouth seemed too wide, open with bared teeth. The eyes sloped back, and long fleshy ears flopped like a donkey's.

The other demon seemed almost human in form, except it seemed to have no mouth and barely any nose. Black shining eyes dominated the face, a mass of sinew and muscles that stretched from where there had once been hair. Dark red spines grew out of its forearms and aimed toward its too long fingers.

Thomas raced toward a ridge ahead, where trees and

flowering bushes grew in a barrier. The demons would reach him before he could make it. He would have to use his power anyway. At least he'd made it a good distance from the Jeep.

Lights flashed across the grass to his left, and Thomas made out the whir of an electric cart coming from behind.

"Off the course," a man yelled. Some idiot, possibly working for the golf course, had spotted him and drove out without seeing the demons.

The cart bounced behind Thomas, coming up on the wrong side. Headlights from the golf cart played over the demons.

"What the hell." The man still had not realized the danger, and let the cart get between Thomas and the demons.

The loping demon reached the cart first. It leaped, slamming into the man. The pair tumbled from the golf cart, and it flipped onto its side. Blood sprayed out before they completed a single roll across the ground. The man, dressed in a dark green shirt, had a gaping hole torn out of his neck and shoulder. The demon shook the detached flesh in its jaw like a dog worrying a rat.

The second demon, spines bristling from its arms, leaped over the two of them and bounded for Thomas.

He yelled. His tone rang. The two demons and the man's flesh disappeared. Thomas staggered under the pain. Using his power too frequently increased the pain, made it feel as if he'd been flayed. He fell to the ground and propped himself up with burning palms.

His world turned to day and the golf course to a mud daub village. The woman he saw had been beaten. He'd never realized until Haddie that the visions he saw were those of an ancestor. The clothing and housing seemed ancient; all of his visions had been like this, steeped in cruelty. He sang, and the woman vanished.

Next came a young boy, innocent in his pleading, wearing little more than a sackcloth for clothing.

Night returned around him again. Thomas knelt, arms stiff to keep from falling to the green. The fresh grass mixed with some foul scent that he imagined were the demons.

The golf cart lay ahead of him. The dead man stared at the stars while blood trickled from the gaping remains of his neck and shoulder.

Panting rasping breaths, Thomas shifted to look back toward the parking lot. A light had turned on with the fall of night. He could make out a silhouette in the driver's side of the Jeep, hopefully Aaron. Thomas would be in no shape to drive. Through a decorative copse of older trees, Haddie moved toward him from the edge of the pavement.

A black SUV pulled in from the road, its lights off.

Thomas, his voice rasping and dry, swore as he pushed himself up. "Devil take me."

CHAPTER 42

HADDIE TURNED at the sound of tires on pavement, and a chill raced up her neck. The black Explorer reminded her of Harold Holmes for a brief, terrifying moment. Behind tinted windows she could clearly see the yellow haze glowing around their faces.

Aaron sat in the driver's seat of their Jeep watching her, a silhouette from the light that shone. She had just started onto the grass surrounded by well-spaced oaks and fragrant pines. Calf-high boulders interspersed with flowers and brush to protect the golf course from the parking lot. Shades of green grass, clusters of dark trees, and white sand pits stretched ahead. Cars still sped down the road between the course and the hill on the other side. Dad lay beside the overturned golf cart where he'd just killed two demons.

She'd been fuming to go after Kiana, and still intended to, but after the two demons and this SUV, she'd lost confidence. Dad had been right about firepower. She was in no shape to help, and Aaron clearly would retreat the moment things got heated.

The SUV rolled down the lane leading from the road,

easing behind Dad's Jeep. Aaron had disappeared, possibly lying down in the front seat. Haddie stood frozen, hoping the trees gave her some cover. She'd gotten better at keeping her wig on and stood facing away so her blood-spattered white top wouldn't be seen from their angle. Above the sharp scent of pine, she could smell Robinson's blood and her own sweat.

The SUV passed the Jeep and crept toward the next car in the row, a white Toyota Camry that faced away from her.

Far back at the clubhouse a door opened, and raucous conversation emerged. Two men, laughing and perhaps a bit drunk, talked too loudly as they headed toward the lot.

The Explorer made a turn at the building and circled up the other lane in the parking lot. Nine cars, including Dad's Jeep, were left parked. Perhaps if she stood still, they wouldn't notice and leave without an incident. She wanted to turn and check on Dad, or on the voices of the men who approached, but she remained motionless. *Just wait — patience.*

After checking all the cars, the SUV rolled toward the exit. Then it pulled in front of the driveway and blocked them in. Haddie swallowed. *If I run, they'll know we're here.*

She felt exposed. Just under the branches of an oak, she stood maybe ten steps away from the front of the Jeep. The light from the pole across the lot speckled down her legs through the leaves.

The passenger door opened on the opposite side of the Explorer, and one of the coerced stepped out.

The man had light hair cut into a mullet and carried a short, automatic rifle at his waist. He either hadn't heard the voices of the men coming toward the parking lot or didn't care. Walking quickly, he moved for the Jeep, which put him in a direct line toward Haddie. Either he suspected something or was just checking the closest vehicle.

Her heart raced. *I could make him disappear*. She drew a sharp breath, recoiling. *I can't*. Her body — her skin still felt raw. Besides, it left the Explorer and at least the driver to retaliate. *Dad is right, we don't have the firepower*.

Still, she held her breath as the man walked close by the window of the Jeep's passenger door, looking inside.

He continued, rounding the front of the SUV, peering inside.

Aaron must have slid into the back.

Haddie relaxed. If they never found Aaron and didn't spot her, then surely they'd leave. Only the loud gregarious men walking toward the lot would be in danger. Would the coerced shoot anyone in their search?

The man lowered his gun to his leg and looked at the clubhouse as if hearing the voices for the first time. His back was to Haddie, but she could see his glance in their direction. Would the activity scare the coerced off?

Their approach didn't stop his search.

He stepped to the driver's side of the Jeep, then lurched back and raised his rifle toward the driver's door. "Out!" he yelled. He must have spotted Aaron in the Jeep.

Haddie felt a chill run through her. Would Aaron surrender? She had to do something.

The driver of the Explorer rolled down his window. A heavy brown beard with wide rounded cheeks might have been a jovial face once, but now it wore a snarl. He swore, clumsily maneuvering his weapon into position while remaining seated.

Dad raced by her, and Haddie jumped. Her heart stopped. How long had he been near her?

As large as he was, Dad managed five strides across the

pavement before the light-haired man reacted to him. The coerced looked back, alerted at the sounds of boots against asphalt.

Dad gained two more steps as the man hesitated.

The coerced turned as her dad took two final steps. The muzzle flashed, aimed at the asphalt in front of the Jeep, as Dad lunged. He tackled the man at the hips as bullets sprayed into the ground.

"What the —" One of the golfers wearing a lime green, short-sleeved shirt yelled from the edge of the parking lot beside the building. Brush hid his companion from Haddie, but she could see a white cap through the leaves.

The driver of the Explorer seemed unsure, pausing with his gun aimed at his windshield. He glanced at Dad's Jeep blocking his view, then back toward the golfers. What kind of instructions had he been given? The first man had wanted Aaron alive, otherwise he would have shot into the Jeep.

Dad rolled free of the coerced and stumbled back with the weapon in his hand. It wasn't pointed for firing, just torn free of its owner. Dad couldn't see the driver from where he stood.

Dad. Haddie stepped forward, gesturing silently toward the Explorer. The driver might just decide to shoot everyone, including his companion. Dad didn't see her, focused on the light-haired man rising from the pavement.

Instead, the driver saw her and finally brought the muzzle of his gun to the window.

Damn. She dove through the bushes at the edge of the parking lot. Pain ripped through her left elbow as she slapped to the asphalt. Gunfire spit from the Explorer as she flinched and rolled. Bullets thudded behind her and ricocheted off the large boulders. She instinctively moved to use the Jeep for cover, even yards away.

Aaron. He'd take the brunt of the attack, hidden in the Jeep. She hadn't thought it out.

Bullets thudded into the front of the Jeep with crunching, metallic twangs. Headlights and blinkers shattered.

The two golfers stood, dazed or drunk. *Run, you idiots.* They stared at Dad and the man firing from the Explorer. Haddie couldn't see the driver anymore, but his muzzle flash flickered off cars.

Dad crouched, aiming the gun at the passenger who scrambled away toward the front of the Jeep. Surprisingly, the driver paused his gunfire for a second. Haddie used the silence to drag herself across the asphalt toward the white Camry. Her left arm and side raged against the movement.

Dad used the lull to run toward the back of the Jeep. He fired first and then disappeared against the back of the truck. Gunfire rattled from both guns. Windows in the Jeep shattered, the rear driver's side window collapsing.

Haddie couldn't see the coerced or Dad. *Aaron.*

One of the golfers moved. The man in the green shirt dove for the Camry and stuck his head under it, his feet stretched into the parking lot. His companion lay crumpled on the sidewalk, and blood marked the walls of the building.

The Jeep tilted. The rear driver's door opened and Aaron's backpack rolled out. *He's alive.* Haddie panted out a breath — almost a sob. She remembered Kiana, captured and wounded. *We can't leave her there.*

Dad's tone rang out, and the gunfire ended with the echo of a deafening silence. Haddie scrambled to her feet. The Explorer was gone. Aaron slid out the back door, seemingly uninjured. She couldn't see Dad.

A sedan had stopped on the road, and a pick-up truck

blared its horn as it came up behind, having missed all the action.

Haddie got her feet working under her and ran past Aaron toward the back of the Jeep. Had Dad been hit? Antifreeze hung in the air; she could see the puddle under the front. Bullets had torn their way through the driver's door and the back panel.

Squatting, Dad leaned back against the bumper. Relief crossed his face when he saw her, erasing the pained expression. His voice a mere whisper, he spoke. "We've got to get out of here."

Haddie knelt down and he shook his head, sliding up against the back of the Jeep. The crumbling window looked ready to fold onto him. "Are you okay?" she asked.

"No. But I didn't get hit." He handed her the automatic rifle. "I'm realizing — from your conversation about this Don Mack — that these are not professionals."

Haddie frowned. Did he mean that they were innocent? Forced? Or that they weren't professional soldiers? Probably the latter.

Aaron came up alongside Haddie. "We should go."

Dad looked him over. "I'm impressed. Not a scratch."

A small smirk teased at the edge of Aaron's lips. "We should go."

Nodding, Dad stood up squarely with a wince. "There's no coming back from this," he said to Haddie, nodding toward the Jeep. "We need to leave it here." He started limping toward the golf course.

Haddie followed. The Jeep, registered in his name, and the witnesses would have the police, or worse, hunting for Dad. He'd leave her. Get a new identity. He wouldn't leave her, just hide. *I can't focus on that now.*

The golfer didn't move, though he'd wedged more of his body under the Camry.

They passed under the trees into the grass. Haddie carried the still warm rifle in her good hand. "Dad. Kiana. We have to get her." Guilt flushed up her neck. He likely could barely walk, and she wanted to storm the castle house. *I can't leave Kiana.* They might all end up prisoners, or dead.

"Yeah."

Did that mean he had a plan? "So, what do we do?"

He gestured to the toppled golf cart. "Flip that over. Not sure how much farther I can walk."

Aaron nodded and jogged ahead. "Couldn't have left a bit to analyze?" Large swaths of red smeared the grass. Pulling something from his pocket, he wiped it across the grass.

Haddie stared. Were they going to attack the house in a golf cart?

PART 6

I have recalled my original purpose and will not sway from it again.

CHAPTER 43

KIANA LAY ON MARBLE, the hearth of a fireplace in a room two stories tall. At least that high, two rows of windows rose up the walls. They had faced her toward the inside of the house, where a second floor hung over the kitchen. Interior windows in the upper room overlooked the elegantly furnished great room. The maniacal woman, possibly Barbara Stevens, spent most of her time on the second-floor pacing past the windows. The woman berated her assistant, waving her hands as she complained or gave orders. Then she would wander down the stairs at Kiana's feet, still screaming at her mousy assistant who followed every step.

So tired. The bleeding had slowed in Kiana's leg wound since she'd been able to tighten the belt after the jostling ride from the hill. Zip-tie cuffs had made it difficult, but they hadn't stopped her from tending to her wound. She didn't have the strength to even consider running. *I've lost too much blood.*

The smell of burnt flesh still haunted her nostrils. On the way in, they'd passed a reeking corpse beside the pool.

Kiana supposed she would end up beside the burnt body, once this woman got around to her. The house stunk of electricity, so she couldn't be sure if she'd be interrogated inside or out. Neither seemed like a pleasant option. She was fairly certain that this was Haddie's Lightning Lady.

A single guard watched Kiana from his position leaning against the kitchen counter. He had a dour expression and handled his weapon badly enough that she hoped he might shoot himself. Perhaps then she'd work up enough energy to make a run for it. His partner had been sent to the roof. *How far would I get?*

Footsteps thumped down the stairs as the woman returned. "Tell them to do another sweep. Araki must be hiding up there. Why, I don't know."

The woman appeared around the corner and gave Kiana a curt glance with pursed lips. She had dark brown hair that frizzed out, possibly styled rather than naturally curly. Her purpura dotted the pale skin of her face and neck, leaving her looking sickly. Taller than Haddie, she had a thick solid frame that complemented her high cheekbones and strong features.

The attendant, a young woman with straight blonde hair, followed, speaking quietly into a headset as she cupped her hand over the microphone. She moved her fingers to her ear. "Paul's team is down to just the two of them. They are searching."

"Get the other team —" The tall woman gestured in the air. "Whatever their damn names are." She paced across the room tugging her pale blue dress around her hips.

"Michael isn't responding."

The woman smacked a pillow off the closest couch. "Since when?" Her hair bobbed as she swung around.

The diminutive attendant cringed. "Just now."

"What was their latest report?"

"Searching the golf course. Paul's team had reported the intruders were headed that way." The attendant took a step back, as if trying to predict where the woman would pace next.

"I shouldn't have sent those — things. Who knows who they'll kill?" She shook her head, bobbing her hair about. "This Tempest — I hadn't expected — I should have been more careful. Do we have all three of his private investigators?" The woman glared at Kiana, "Four?"

The attendant swallowed, shaking her head. "Michael hadn't found the third at the distribution center when you recalled them."

The woman paced toward the stairs, started to pull up her dress for the first step, and turned toward Kiana. "Who is this Tempest?"

Kiana took a deep breath. "I don't know. He just hired me on." She'd considered mentioning the FBI, but that would likely get her either killed quicker or in the hands of the cabal buried within the agency.

"Shit," the woman swore, "did you kill Araki?"

"I didn't kill anyone," Kiana lied. "I don't know who that is." Likely the small man up on the hill.

Snorting, the woman tugged at her dress, starting up the stairs. "He's going to be furious about Araki."

A door opened from beyond the kitchen, and the second guard who had escorted Kiana to the residence ran in. "We've got company."

The woman swiveled and stepped back to the main floor. "How many?"

He flushed, his teeth biting into the top of his goatee. "I

didn't see. Maybe four. They're in a golf cart. They parked across the road, and I —" Tugging at the rifle strapped over his shoulder, he looked down and waited as if expecting her ire.

Kiana's hope rose. There were so few guarding the house. If Haddie — or Thomas — used their powers, she might have a chance. She had expected a tight organization after their trip to Coos Bay, but this woman had no leadership or organizational skills. Perhaps that had been Araki, or the other male the woman seemed nervous about. Somehow though, they'd discovered the investigators that Thomas had put into place. At least three of them.

"Do you want me to call him?" asked the attendant.

"No," the woman snapped. "I've got to handle these interlopers first. He's too far away to do anything." She spread her hands in front of her and frowned. "Bring in everyone from the distribution center." She tripped on her hem on the way back up the stairs and swore.

Kiana swallowed. Perhaps the real operation was out of the facility, rather than the residence. She had hoped to learn more about their organization, and she had. It seemed that she dug into a bottomless pit. This woman reported to some man, perhaps the leader that Sameedha reported to? Answers — and more questions. *I'll die before I get to the bottom of this.*

Thomas had his own agenda. Whatever Thomas had expected to find, he might be disappointed. Either way, Haddie and Thomas were going to get trapped if this woman brought in reinforcements.

She wanted to be rescued, but didn't want Haddie or Thomas to die trying. Kiana rolled her head to the side. She wouldn't be able to see them approach. Night draped the sky. A few treetops broke the black. A large rock, where the mountain seemed to cradle the building, rose high enough that she could see gray pressed close to the house. It would be a good place for a sniper to hide — with a clear shot into the upper room where the woman paced. Perhaps too close.

CHAPTER 44

HADDIE COULD SMELL the burnt flesh before they found the corpse. It didn't look like those that Harold Holmes had left. This man had sections blackened in vine-like designs across reddened flesh. Someone had left the body beside a glass pool enclosure stretching out from the main house into a garden that they crept through.

They'd been careful to keep out of sight from a coerced high on the roof; inside, she could make out a stationary one on the lower floor and a third tracking back and forth on the upper floor. No demons. Somewhere in there, Haddie could expect the Lightning Lady, Barbara Stevens. *I'm sure she's here.*

Dad had the automatic rifle — with few bullets — strapped over his shoulder. He dragged at every climb and sagged each time they stopped. She was in little better shape. Yet, with so few guarding the house, the situation was better than she expected. That didn't mean they'd survive or find Kiana alive. *Focus on what's right.* Trying to save Kiana was the right thing to do. Even Dad hadn't argued the point, too much.

Aaron, of course, considered it too dangerous. He'd stayed back at the entrance, supposedly to brief Dad's other man, Crow.

Dad knelt by the corpse. "So, this is what she does?"

The burnt lines on the man's face, neck, and shoulder looked like a growth — a tree. "I guess. Not her directly, like Harold Holmes. She created a creature of lightning. I didn't let it touch me."

"With this blocking that you do." He frowned. "How do you do it?"

Haddie shrugged. "I just do. It's like pushing my tone against theirs. It isn't followed with the pain or visions."

"If I have to use it, I'll try." He nodded toward the main house. "First, I'd like to go for the single coerced that's not moving. Likely a guard. Possibly Kiana's."

Three dots of yellow haze layered above each other in the central square building that rose the highest. The house extended east to the pool they crept next to, and again south on the opposite side of the garden.

Haddie pointed across the garden to a doorway of the south building, close to where it joined the higher square. "There's a door there."

He pointed ahead. "I'd rather go in farthest from that cluster of coerced. We might have to make noise getting inside."

She nodded and followed as they entered a covered patio area with wide dark windows. Her chest tightened and she tried to breathe deeply, exhaling the smell of charred flesh.

Dad managed to pry the cover off an electronic lock and manually turn the dead bolt. *I really need to learn how to pick locks.*

The room beyond, a game or entertainment room of

some sort, had large windows that left it dark but not pitch black. Haddie touched the bulge of her flashlight inside her jacket pocket, but refrained from pulling it out. Starlight would have to do. The room had been used recently. Empty cans and plates had been left on tables.

At one end, light showed under the door that led in the direction of the coerced, people who would likely end up dead before Haddie rescued Kiana — if she rescued Kiana. *I'm doing the right thing.*

Dad opened the door silently and light streamed in. The lights in the ceiling in the next room were on. A long couch sat in front of a large TV placed in front of the windows. A woman spoke nearby, muffled and perhaps above them. Footsteps sounded in time with the motion of the coerced pacing on the middle floor.

He leaned out, peering in both directions, then motioned to the left. He raised one finger. Did that mean he saw one of them? Haddie could see the haze, closer and more distinct. Directly above that coerced, the second patrolled. Still, the third waited on the roof.

She followed him out and paused.

A man leaned on a kitchen counter in the next room, much closer than she'd imagined. What was Dad's plan? Would he kill the man? Just try and knock him unconscious? No, that would bring everyone running.

Her boot heel squeaked as she turned on polished wood flooring. She swallowed and stopped, staring at the man. The noise from the footsteps directly above seemed to cover her sound.

Dad had gained a step ahead of her. He shifted the automatic rifle to his back, strap over his shoulder, and drew his blade from his belt.

He's going to kill him. The man could be a librarian or a teacher for all they knew. Coerced into a soldier.

What had she thought? They could just sneak in and out, without anyone getting hurt? Most likely, she and Dad would end up dead, which was why Dad was willing to kill. To do the right thing.

Haddie felt tired and empty suddenly. They'd pushed Dad into hurrying his surveillance, perhaps causing his investigators to get caught. Robinson and the man outside the pool were dead. Now, they had come to free Kiana, and more people would die. What had Haddie expected?

A huge island with brown marble dominated most of the kitchen. The man leaned against the counter, facing the room beyond. The sink lay just behind him, embedded in the center at his end. Dad stepped into the kitchen to the back edge of the island. In another step or two the guard would see him.

To Haddie's left, a set of stairs led to a landing before switching to climb above her, perhaps eventually to the roof. She had another step to enter the kitchen behind Dad.

Beyond the kitchen, in the two-story room with windows up to the ceiling, Kiana lay on the hearth of a fireplace, watching Dad. *Alive.* White zip-ties bound her wrists. Haddie imagined Harold Holmes' chair. Kiana's slacks were soaked under a tight belt; she'd been bleeding.

Haddie's heart raced, enraged, and terrified.

Footsteps stomped across the kitchen ceiling. A woman's voice asked something, too muffled to understand. *Barbara Stevens.* It had to be. Was she talking on a phone?

Dad strode with two quick steps to the corner of the counter, alerting the guard. The man flinched as Dad moved around the corner of the island. Dad's left hand darted to the gun, entwining fingers at the trigger.

The man, too shocked at the sudden movement, tried to step back as he tugged at the weapon.

Haddie flinched as Dad drove his right fist up and under the man's chin, then backhanded him across the temple.

Dad shook the gun free as the man collapsed. The yellow haze still clung to his face; Haddie could see it through the counter. Dad hadn't killed him.

She started toward Kiana. Dad shook his head motioning to the ceiling with the muzzle.

He made a gesture to Kiana, one finger, then pointed at the room above.

She shook her head, showing two fingers.

There were two there. Barbara Stevens, the Lightning Lady, and a coerced guard. It had to be. Two sets of footsteps, one loud from a heavy step, and a lighter pace following it.

I need to be careful. Haddie might be able to free Kiana silently and help her to the kitchen, then out the back. A second set of stairs ended near the fireplace, likely up to the room. They couldn't wait there until the woman decided to check on her prisoner or the guard woke up. She put her hand out for Dad's knife, nodding toward Kiana.

He paused for a second and then flipped the handle of the knife toward her. With both hands on the rifle, he followed the footsteps above.

The stairs to her left climbed and turned. A hallway led between the landing and the marble hearth where Kiana lay. Blood had pooled by her leg and dribbled down to the wood floor. The two ornate couches stuffed with pillows would have been a more comfortable place to leave her, but she would have bled on cushions and the carpet.

Kiana didn't watch Haddie, her eyes focused on the room above.

Haddie turned as she reached the outer lip and looked up, expecting a balcony. Instead, someone had built windows in the wall, looking down on the large two-story room.

Drawing in a deep breath, she crouched and hurried toward Kiana. They'd either make it out without being seen, or Dad would start firing. Either way, they needed to get out.

Haddie slid the blade between the ties and started sawing.

"She's got reinforcements coming," Kiana whispered.

Haddie stopped as a tone filled the air. She recognized the note from Coos Bay.

The air snapped around her. Leaving the knife wedged between the ties, Haddie cried out and spun. She felt her tone press against the other.

Standing nearly to the ceiling, the creature slammed a streaming hand of red lightning down at Haddie. Sizzling, it stopped just inches from her skin.

Its legs danced along wood, carpet, and the delicate couches. Smoke rose where it touched. A knot of tangled lightning seemed to form a head. Empty air shaped eyes. The torso swirled, feeding the outer legs and arms. The other hand, or stream of lighting, trailed up the chandelier in the center of the room. Pillows smoldered. The glass pane of a coffee table shattered as a finger of red lightning trailed across it. A random ornament flew off the mantle by Haddie's head.

The room exploded and echoed with gunshots as Dad began firing.

Some of the kitchen ceiling lights popped in showers of

glass. Bullets cracked the white ceiling above him.

On the second floor, blood and bullets sprayed onto the ceiling. For a brief second Haddie spotted the dark mass of bobbing hair that she recognized from the woman at Coos Bay.

With a snap, the creature above Haddie vanished.

Dad stopped shooting and swore, tossing the gun aside to grab the one off his back.

The remaining lights in the kitchen had sputtered out, leaving only the light in the main room and upstairs. Bullet holes trailed along the ceiling above Dad, and nothing seemed to move upstairs.

Barbara Stevens is dead. The innocent coerced had died as well. No glow showed where there had been one a minute ago.

The yellow haze from the roof wound down the stair-well. "Dad." Haddie pointed. "The coerced from the roof."

Nodding, he stepped back from the kitchen, just under the lip of the floor above. With his gun pointed at the open-ing, he waited. Blood had started to seep around one of the bullet holes in the ceiling.

Haddie swiveled back to Kiana. She leaned down and resumed cutting the zip-ties.

"She has reinforcements coming," Kiana said.

"How many?" Haddie winced as her left hand shifted, wanting to help with the troublesome plastic.

She sucked in a breath as Barbara Stevens' tone rang in the air again. *She's alive.*

Spinning, Haddie found the lightning creature forming again in the large room. The pillows still smoldered, and one exploded as a red, streaming leg pressed down on a couch. A flame popped up on the edge of the carpet.

Haddie's tone reflexively sounded to fight off the creature, but it had adjusted its focus. *Dad.*

He turned as a red streaming arm reached under the second-floor overhang. His tone sounded with a growl. He'd attempted to banish the creature, not block it.

Red lightning flashed, connecting with the gun and his arm. The weapon spun into the kitchen. Yanked by the strap, Dad flipped over the edge of the counter and slammed to the floor, out of sight.

Bobbing dark frizz moved by one of the windows.

Haddie screamed at Barbara Stevens, but her tone died in squelch.

Barbara Stevens could resist, like Sameedha. Haddie couldn't stop her, but she might be able to protect Dad. Or disrupt the creature.

Frantic, Haddie resumed her blocking tone, racing for the creature.

It crouched at the edge of the kitchen, reaching for Dad. Long tendrils of red lightning stretched between the cabinets, shifting as though searching for their target.

With the couch in her way, she had to slide around the corner and run into the legs of the creature.

A squelch sounded and streams flicked off, reforming away from her. The lightning did react. She'd buckled it backward. The arm it shoved at Dad had been blocked. How long could she do that, before the reinforcements arrived?

Bullets tore through the creature and into the windows behind. Threads of lightning seemed to follow them.

Damn. The coerced from the roof had arrived. Haddie dropped without looking behind her. She turned as bullets ricocheted off marble and clanked into the sink. Focused on the yellow haze, she growled, dropping her defensive tone. It left her exposed. *A mistake.*

Pain scalded her skin. She trembled and a shock lashed across her heel. Haddie couldn't move. The visions took her even as she opened her mouth to protect herself.

Bright daylight. A large bear sank its teeth into her neck before it vanished at her cry.

Dark smoky night. Two rough men, in a camp of dead or dying, raised their rifles in unison. They faded at her scream.

Fire raced across Haddie's skin as she stared up at red lighting slamming into her. *No.* The holes in the ceiling disappeared as her body arched and her vision turned a bright red.

Her song, belated, rang from her strangled scream.

The grip on her released. Her muscles spasmed and melted to the floor. The smell of burnt flesh and clothes drifted on the lungful of air she sucked in. *I can't fight this — and save them both.*

The creature, acting annoyed, pulled back. Then a quick, streaming arm tried to move past to Dad, lying behind her. It failed, reforming as it came too close to Haddie.

Kiana's feet shifted on the marble hearth. If she could escape, they could all retreat, if Dad hadn't been hurt too badly — or if Kiana could kill Barbara Stevens with the knife.

Red lightning straightened up to the full height of the room again and reached a hand toward Kiana, taunting, but not touching yet. Did Barbara Stevens control it, or just create it?

It didn't matter. Haddie had to protect Kiana. She groaned, pushing up with one hand that trembled and legs that wobbled. Somewhere, she heard an ATV. "Dad?" She didn't dare take her eyes off the creature to turn around.

Kiana was trying to work the knife against her bonds.

Barbara Stevens had been able to maintain her defenses and the creature. Could Haddie? The tones were different. *I don't know how.*

Red lines coalesced at the end of the creature's arm. Lightning dropped on Kiana and the woman stretched in pain. Haddie stumbled forward.

A cackle sounded from above. "Which one?" Barbara Stevens laughed.

Lighting pressed from the creature's other hand, searching for Dad. Haddie stopped it. *I can't block both.* Maybe she could push Kiana or Dad back in time. Like Liz's block. Or spread them into a thin gel across the room if she did it wrong.

An ATV sounded closer, whining toward the back where they'd broken in. Possibly the men from the hill were returning.

If she pushed Kiana, that would open Haddie up for attack. She could only hope that Dad regained his gun soon and killed Barbara Stevens this time.

Stepping to the side, she repelled the arm of lightning reaching for Dad. It reformed closer to the creature. The carpet had started to burn at its feet. Smoke was hazing the room.

Kiana's body arched from the back of her forehead to her heels. Her clothes smoked. Burning flesh crackled on her shoulder and chest.

Haddie yelled, "Dad!"

Intent. Push, but not too hard. Her tone rang.

Kiana disappeared.

The visions darkened Haddie's world. *Did I kill her or save her?*

CHAPTER 45

Thomas smelled burnt flesh. His own — guessing from the pain that raged along his right arm. Haddie screamed close to him, and he could hear her song, weak and wavering. If only he could learn what she did to block other powers.

His right shoulder had been twisted, a secondary pain to the electrical burns. He'd had a close call with lightning a century or so before. This creature didn't pack quite that punch. Luckily. His cheek lay on cool flooring, and dark wood cabinets walled up beside him. His right arm crossed in front of his face, the leather smoldering wisps of smoke. *I need to get up.*

A two-stroke engine whined outside. That wouldn't be Aaron; perhaps Crow had found a vehicle, or there were still enemy about.

Blinking, he caught flashes of lightning against the wood. Thomas managed to lift his head. The cabinets and fridge made a corridor with a view to the main room.

Angry red lines flickered and formed, snapping, and

popping as the creature stood in the middle of the room. *Attacking Haddie.*

Thomas pushed up.

The guard lay unconscious at his feet. His clothing had been singed as well. The lightning didn't seem to discriminate.

A fire flickered along the rug, trailing smoke toward the high ceiling.

Haddie lay on her back, screaming through gritted teeth just behind the couch.

The creature pressed a streaming, pulsing mass of writhing electricity down at her. Her tone didn't keep all of it at bay. Lines snapped past and caused puffs of smoke along her jacket.

Groaning, Thomas pushed up onto his knees. He had to kill Barbara Stevens.

He'd come here to find the people who hunted for Meg. Perhaps he had. He didn't have time to search. *I need to get Haddie out of here.*

Kiana was gone.

CHAPTER 46

KIANA SCRAMBLED up the side of the rock, slowing as she came within sight of the top of the building. The night smelled like pine. She'd practiced this maneuver a dozen times. The angle wasn't the best. She relied on Barbara Stevens pacing to make the shot. From the top of the rock, she had a clear view of at least half the woman's room. There were contingency plans, but none as neat as this.

The creature glowed through the windows, just as fearsome from a distance. She shivered. Streaming red lightning had Haddie pressed against the floor. Kiana remembered the sensation. She'd never forget.

She couldn't help but glance at the hearth where she'd been lying moments, or months, ago. For the first time in a long while, she felt back in place. Still on the run, still waiting for the FBI to find her, but back in her own time.

An ATV crawled down the hill, winding through the trail. The headlights disappeared as it turned at one of the switchbacks.

She'd chosen a Remington 700. Taking a deep breath, she pulled it off her back.

Upstairs, just behind the square shape of the building, three windows lined the room above the kitchen. The dark frizz of Barbara Stevens' hair bobbed past two of the windows.

Kiana didn't bother lying down. Standing exposed her, but until the reinforcements arrived, that wouldn't be an issue. Barbara Stevens would be the only person who could see her, but that would only be for a moment.

The woman's ball of frizz stepped into view. She was laughing.

Kiana fired, ready for a second shot. Spiderweb cracks circled the hole in the window.

Barbara Stevens' head exploded in a burst of red spray, and the woman dropped out of sight. The red lightning extinguished.

Rifle in hand, Kiana started her climb down toward the driveway. Deep breaths eased the slight trembling in her hands.

Inside, Thomas wobbled, stepping over the guard. He didn't look in good shape. He couldn't see Kiana, his face turned toward Haddie lying on the floor gulping in breaths of air. Smoke rose in tendrils from her jacket and pants.

Headlights splashed closer on the hill behind Kiana. Swearing at the ATV, she scrambled down. She jumped into the garden and ran for the stairs that led to the patio. They would have to move quickly. She had some idea when those other reinforcements would arrive. Over the past several months, she'd timed the drive at fifteen to twenty minutes from the distribution center to the residence. That left five to ten minutes from now, if the men left the moment Barbara Stevens had made the call. There had to be some buffer getting everyone into vehicles.

Thomas knelt by Haddie. She moved but wasn't getting

up. Kiana lived because of Haddie. She had the scars to remind her of this night. Not to say the experience hadn't been disturbing. Every day since that moment had been spent planning for tonight.

Kiana rapped on the window with the butt of her rifle.

Thomas jerked up and spun.

Kiana sucked in a breath. He would recognize her, wouldn't he? She smiled. *Please don't vaporize me.* That would be a bad end to the night.

He relaxed, and his eyes widened. Had she changed that much over the months? No. To him, she'd been lying on the hearth, wounded, just moments age. Then he'd found her gone. Now, here she was, healed and dressed in black long sleeves and a cap for her night ops. Her hair had grown out, and she'd braided it on her left side.

Kiana drew back the rifle and smashed the butt into the window. Safety glass crumbled in a wide spread. Her boot cleared a hole, and a second slam of her rifle expanded the lower portion.

The room smelled like fire, electricity, and burnt flesh. She stepped through, ignoring the awkwardness between them. They could deal with that later. "We've got the team from the hill returning. The other reinforcements should be here soon."

"How?" Thomas asked.

To him, she'd just vanished. Had he seen what Haddie had done? Probably not.

"Your daughter, evidently." Kiana winced as she looked over to Haddie. "Whom we need to get out of here."

Thomas took in a deep breath then nodded.

Haddie lay gasping behind the couch. Her wig smoldered in spots. She had a burn on her cheek, a flower-like pattern.

The carpet had started to catch fire, smoke climbing up toward the ceiling.

Thomas grabbed Haddie under her right arm and lifted.

Haddie sobbed, but got her feet positioned. Her left arm dangled at her stomach. She blinked twice, seeing Kiana, then her eyebrows furrowed.

He glanced up at the windows on the second floor. "Barbara Stevens?"

Kiana raised her rifle. "Easy shot from that rock outside." She gestured toward the back and then waved over her eyes. "Can you — uhm — see if we have visitors? And how close they are?"

"Hell. I forgot." He frowned but looked toward the back, cocking his head. "Too close. Help me get her out."

Kiana stepped through the broken window and reached back to take Haddie's right arm. Haddie's hand trembled, and her leg resisted rising high enough to get over the sill. With her mouth hung open, Haddie studied Kiana.

Kiana swallowed. Haddie hadn't known if it would work. She might have been splattered over time. That thought hadn't occurred to her in all these months.

Once Thomas climbed onto the outer patio, he took Haddie, and Kiana led them to stairs outside the kitchen. The lower garden and driveway waited below.

"They're in the house." Thomas pointed up. Balconies blocked their view of the windows, but he could likely see their haze clearly.

Kiana planned to take them down the drive a bit, then abandon the road and curve around the slope of the hill, heading straight west toward the road. From there, she could get them across the golf course to the townhouse Thomas had rented.

Haddie's voice cracked, hoarse and dry. "More, a lot

more — down there. Demons too." She gestured downhill, through the rock.

Thomas squinted. "I can see them. Tight clusters moving quickly, passing — maybe on the road. Vehicles filled with coerced and maybe demons. A couple dozen at least."

Kiana kept them moving on the driveway. It directed them away from the house where the two closest threats were. "There's a gully up here where we can get off the driveway; if they're in cars, they might go directly to the house."

Haddie's steps landed more surely. She still reeked of electricity and burning. She blinked too often, as if trying to wash away an image. Thomas kept a hand on her right arm, steadying any missteps.

"I want to get hold of Crow. See if he can cover our backs." He gestured toward Haddie's arm. "You're thinking a straight line to the house?"

Kiana nodded and switched with him.

Haddie frowned. "I can walk." Still, she let Kiana move up beside her. "You're okay? I didn't know what to do. I worried — After I —"

Kiana smirked. "After you sent me back in time? Yeah. Luckily, nobody lived in that house last February. That would have been a surprise." Barbara Stevens had moved in three months later.

Haddie slowly smiled. "Lucky it wasn't seventy years ago," She murmured.

"There's that." Five months ago, seemed more than enough.

Thomas glanced back with furrowed brows. He seemed to study Kiana with concern. Did he worry about her?

There had been a time he'd given her no thought except suspicion.

Gesturing downslope, he spoke. "Crow will be across from the house just west of here. Says there are three vans headed up here. He'll cover if we pick up any pursuit." He smoothed back his hair.

"Crow?"

"An — investigator — that I've worked with before."

Good. Someone who could handle themselves, from the sound of it. Kiana pointed to a dip off the side of the driveway. "Here. It's rough." She could see the vans to the north, headlights off but winding up the slope quickly.

Thomas followed. "We'll need to lie low when they come up this last leg."

Kiana smiled. "Plenty of cover." She'd been hidden up here since before sunset and had walked the path a dozen times months ago when she first started to plan.

He chuckled, seeming to understand. "Thank you."

"Don't thank me until you try the coffee, it's a few hours old."

Thomas furrowed his eyebrows, quizzical.

"I stowed provisions and weapons down here. Just in case things got hot." Kiana glanced back toward the vans. They hadn't made it to the last curve yet. Unless the coerced stopped and began searching the hill, they'd make it out safely. "I brought a thermos for you. Tea for Haddie."

CHAPTER 47

HADDIE STEPPED out of the shower, feeling less than clean, but better. Dad rumbled around in her bedroom. One of her bags thudded, probably dropped in the hall.

She stood at the mirror. Purpura covered much of her face. The burn on her cheek spread an inch wide like an intricate cluster of flowers. Would that heal? How would she explain it to David? *What will be my lie?*

Her left arm hung gingerly across her waist. He seemed sure she'd fractured the elbow. Of course, he had someone who would look at it.

The bullet wound on her hip looked like a zipper, but pink. In all, she'd gone through worse. She held out her hands to look at the scars left from Harold Holmes, visible only if someone knew where to look.

"Ten minutes," he called from the bedroom. The hallway door thumped behind him.

She wanted to sleep, but the knowledge that dozens of coerced and some demons searched the hills just a short distance away wouldn't let her relax. Getting on the road seemed like the best idea.

Dad had left her some loose clothes on the bed. She began dressing as best as she could with one good arm. Outside the window she could see lights where the castle house stood. They'd come to find answers and failed. Dad had gotten no closer to learning who hunted Meg. Kiana and Aaron had gotten no answers. Worse, Dad talked about disappearing and starting over. *Can I deal with that?*

She stood holding her left arm, staring out the window, when he knocked. "Ready?" he asked.

Haddie jumped. "Yes. Can you help me with the sling?"

He'd cut one of his T-shirts into a tube. She imagined it was her dry sling for the ride.

Dad entered. He still looked worn from the night, partly from using his power, but he also favored his right arm. She imagined the lightning had done more damage than he admitted. "Better?" he asked.

"I don't smell like a shorted capacitor, if that's what you mean."

He slipped the cut T-shirt over her neck and carefully slid her elbow in. Each move, no matter how gentle, still hurt like she'd broken it. "We were lucky."

"Doesn't seem like it." Haddie drew in a deep breath. "You're going to leave."

"The police will be looking for me. Worse than them, I'm guessing. You should come with me." He frowned at her silence. "We'll meet up regularly. Just have to be careful."

He'd take Meg with him. She swallowed, driving away tears. A new life. A new family. He started for the door, and Haddie followed.

"The garage?" she asked.

"Been selling it to Biff every month since Harold Holmes. We just don't file anything. Today, he will."

She paused a step. "Biff?"

"Always been the plan."

"Jerk Automotive?"

Dad stopped at the top of the stairs and lowered his voice. "See if Liz will do you a favor. When the warrant comes out, see what the charges are."

A deep voice bellowed from below. "Ride's here, T." Dad's investigator, Crow, had escorted them back to the house. He'd continue her dad's operation, from the conversation she'd heard on the golf course.

Haddie winced as she followed Dad down the stairs.

Aaron waited in the foyer by the door, backpack on and ready to go. He'd seemed surprised that they survived and not the slightest bit awkward about abandoning them. In fact, he'd chided Dad on the walk back about how little they'd learned. Kiana had refused to explain her new hair to Aaron. Somehow, that had tickled Haddie. Even Dad had seemed amused.

Haddie understood Aaron's behavior. *I'm jealous*. He thought with his head, not his heart, and managed to keep out of the situations she ended up in. She could learn from that.

Her burner buzzed in her pocket.

Terry. He'd had gotten fired up after a chat with Aaron and kept texting Haddie updates. Most were about the lack of information from the local police departments, proof of the cover up in his estimation. When some social media queries about the gunfire disappeared, even Haddie had to admit that it seemed suspicious. *I'll message back on the ride*.

Crow smiled from the couch. "I thought I saw white hair poking out of that ratty wig." With his thick, tattooed arms stretched along the back to each side, he made the furniture look small.

He stood and gave Dad a hug.

Kiana turned from the window at the back of the room and strode toward Haddie. "No fire. Someone must have taken care of the carpet."

"What?" Had there been a fire? She remembered smelling smoke — and worse.

"Small one. Surprised there hadn't been more. Who's driving?" Kiana followed Dad with her eyes.

Crow clapped lightly on Haddie's good shoulder. "You look like your mom. Take care of T. Keep him out of trouble."

Dad called back from the entry. "Leave her be, Crow."

Haddie raised her eyebrows. *Crow knew my mom?* Kiana passed by, and Haddie found herself stumbling but following. She'd never met another person, other than Dad, who had known her mom. He winked when she looked back. She caught herself from walking into the wall and stepped outside.

One of the flowering plants or brush had a sweet perfume. The sky hung black with a faint haze of the city above. A cloudless night.

Crow knew Mom? She'd never thought to ask Dad. He always answered her questions quietly and thoughtfully, in a way that she knew it hurt to answer. Who else?

Haddie stumbled when she saw a small RV parked in front. An elderly couple, white-haired with broad smiles, looked at them through the windshield. She'd expected an SUV of some sort to be left in the driveway. Dad had just said he had a ride coming. She hadn't asked.

Kiana walked around the front to the passenger side where Dad waved on Haddie. With a Ford van front, the

RV extended above and a foot to the sides. She passed the elderly couple, returning a weak smile.

Dad smirked as he saw her face. "Don't worry, they've hauled worse than us. Lots of cash, no questions."

A wall had been placed between the drivers and the back of the RV. It smelled like coffee inside. Aaron had taken a seat at the table. Kiana slid in across from him. The only other seat was by the door.

"Get up on the bunk," Dad said from behind.

It did seem the most comfortable option, except for getting up there with her arm in a sling. Rolling onto her back, she took a deep breath. *I'll be asleep in minutes.* At some point in the morning, she needed to text Andrea, explain the broken elbow, and hopefully save her job. *Make up a lie about the broken elbow.*

She thought of texting David and stopped. She'd need a lie about the elbow first. Hiking accident? How did that tie into a trip with Dad?

Typing slowly, she began her lie with David. "Sorry for no call last night. Climbing out of the Jeep, I fell and messed up my elbow." So lame.

This early, he'd be home or at the gym. It took a while for him to respond. "Are you okay?"

"Yeah, good news is I'll be back tonight."

When he didn't respond immediately, she texted, "Are you at the gym?"

His reply came too quick, as though he'd been typing when she sent the message. "Can we talk Sunday? In person?"

Haddie's heart dropped. *He's dumping me.* She had caused this. The choices had been all hers. He'd left her two full days to agonize over the impending conversation. She wanted to text, to ask him if he planned on breaking up with her, but she just typed, "Sure. I love you."

She waited, but he didn't reply. Tears welled at the edges of her eyes as the door to the camper closed and the engine started. Haddie took small breaths, staring at her phone.

Aaron started talking as soon as the RV backed out of the drive. "What are we supposed to do now?"

Haddie rolled onto her good side. She couldn't imagine planning anything. She stared dully down at them.

Her back to Haddie, Kiana shrugged. "I still think we need to look at New York, but I'd prefer to go slower, as Thomas had first suggested."

Dad sat on the little chair by the door, his legs kicked up to Kiana's bench. "I'm happy to organize a few investigators for New York. However, I'll be busy for a while, setting up a new identity."

Kiana turned sharply at the comment. "Why?"

"Left the Jeep and a witness in the golf course parking lot. They'll have warrants out for me."

Aaron snorted. "They'll just cover it up."

"Worse," Dad said. "Whoever is covering it up — I probably don't want them finding me."

"What will you do?" Kiana tugged on her ear. She sounded concerned.

"I've got plans." Dad rubbed his head. "The two of you are welcome to keep working out of the eastern house and use the old Ford. I'll have some people watching Haddie, but she probably shouldn't head out there. Even if it's just the police, they'll expect her to lead them to me."

Haddie felt a chill along her neck. *I don't want him to leave.* He'd said they'd meet up, but that wasn't the same. Tears threatened, and she blinked hard against them.

"Ilsa and Rick will let me out in Bend. Haddie will get dropped off in a town called Sisters. She booked a room there last night. Her RAV4 will be at the hotel by the time she gets there. You two —"

"What?" Haddie leaned up on her arm. "How did that happen?"

Dad frowned. "Contingency. You would have had an alibi. Now we need it, the police will ask. I messaged to have your car brought out while you were in the shower. They're closer, so it'll be there when you arrive."

They. Dad had Biff driving Meg out to him. Haddie rolled back and closed her eyes. It had all gotten too real. Dad's leaving. *David too.* Tears welled up and she choked back a sob.

CHAPTER 48

HADDIE PULLED up to the front of the hotel and parked in the lot Dad had marked. It didn't look as big as he'd described, but the parking lot continued past the building. Rock leaned over onto her shoulder and checked it out through the windshield. She patted him on the chin with her good hand.

Sam rolled her shoulders forward. "So, this is where we start?"

Haddie nodded and sighed.

At Dad's suggestion, Haddie had offered Sam to come on a clandestine camping trip. It hadn't taken any persuasion. Sam had been frantic when Biff had come by at 2:00 a.m. Friday morning to pick up Meg, even after Dad called her. She didn't question any of the secrecy surrounding the trip, nor the long trip out to the eastern edge of Oregon. She *had* wanted to know about Haddie's elbow and accepted the slip and fall answer.

Liz had been more excited about the actual events around the new cast. She'd kept Haddie up until midnight with questions and theories.

Haddie carefully scoured the parking lot to see if she'd been followed. They brought nothing but backpacks. Sam and Rock followed her into the hotel. It looked more like a ski resort with all the windows and couches. The lounge had dinner going, from the smells of grilled meats and potatoes. She checked in and took the key before following Dad's instructions to the pool area in the back.

"Nice hotel," Sam said.

Haddie smirked as they exited. "Maybe we'll stay here someday."

The back lot had cars parked against another section of buildings that started to give Haddie a better idea of the size. The hotel spread along the Deschutes River on both sides. Her heart rate increasing, she strode across the parking lot quickly, toward the hotel restaurant that took up its own building.

They entered at the game room and walked past empty pool tables.

Sam kept close behind, Rock bumping against Haddie's legs. "I never played pool."

"Fun game. I'll teach you next time we're here."

Outside the back entrance, a bridge led over the quick running river to more buildings of the hotel. It was as large as Dad had said.

"Nice view. Not there yet, I gather." Sam reined in Rock as he moved from one side of the bridge to the next.

"Through this next building." Haddie walked them into the back of the building, paused inside the door, and watched the bridge for a count of thirty. Her heart still pounding, she walked them out the front.

Dad sat in gray Ford van with deeply tinted windows in the back. He motioned to the side door. Louis yapped from inside, and Sam stumbled as Rock pulled her forward.

Meg slid open the side door with a wide smile. "Rock. Sam." She held a squirming Louis in her arms.

Haddie raised her eyebrows. "And hello, Haddie."

Meg pouted. "Hi, Aunt Haddie." She frowned at the cast.

They climbed into the back, Haddie taking the front bench while Sam closed the door. Dad glanced back and smiled. "Look good?" he asked, putting the van into reverse.

"I didn't see anything." Haddie had looked for tails. Even knowing that Dad was having her followed, she hadn't spotted anything. If she had seen anything, then she might not have gone to see him. Not spotting his tail left her feeling inept.

Louis climbed under her legs from the back and wriggled against her. Rock had forgotten all about Haddie as he played in the back with Sam and Meg. She couldn't shake the sense of abandonment. Logically it all made sense that Dad had to leave, and Meg too. Inside, her chest felt tight, and she fought desperation. David's impending conversation waited for her tomorrow.

"It's going to be alright," he said.

Haddie looked away, through the tinted windows, fighting tears. "I'm going to miss you."

"We'll have our times, still. Like tonight. Camping like we used to. I love you, Haddie. Always will."

Meg sidled up to Haddie from the back, wrapping her arms around her. "Does it hurt?"

Haddie shook her head. "Not now. Not in the cast." Truthfully it ached, but her whole body did.

"Can we ask now?" Meg leaned up toward Dad.

He sighed, then spoke loudly, for Sam in the back. "We've moved onto a property west of Bend. Used to be an old farm."

Haddie smiled. "You're going to be a farmer?"

Dad shook his head. "I've enjoyed the work before, but not this time. They used to run a kennel out of it as well. They called it a doggie ranch."

Meg jumped up and down.

"Sit." Dad waited as Meg dropped down by Haddie, then continued, "Sixty acres, a lot of woods, and a pond. That's where we'll be camping."

"In your backyard?" asked Haddie.

"It's a big yard." He glanced at her in the mirror. "We'll be running the kennel and homeschooling Meg."

They headed north, the afternoon sun coming in the window to Haddie's left. It quickly turned more rural alongside the road, with businesses like Goshen. She could see why Dad liked it.

"What do you do for work, Sam? Besides walking Haddie's dog."

Haddie felt her chest grow hollow.

"Data entry. I have my grandmother's money too." Sam sounded excited.

"Want a job? You'd have to move."

"Yes."

The speed of Sam's reply stung.

Haddie leaned back as Meg jumped up, squealing. And now Sam was gone, too.

CHAPTER 49

HADDIE DROPPED onto her bed and Rock jumped up on the end. It had been a long trip back from camping. She'd been able to talk it through with Sam, who felt guilty but loved the idea of getting out of Eugene and working with animals. It made sense — even if Haddie hated it.

Someone knocked at the door and Haddie groaned. Rock jumped down and trotted for the door.

Then she sat up quickly, wincing as she jostled her arm. Liz planned on coming by later, for her usual bloodsucking. So, who was this? David had carefully avoided meeting at either of their places; she had two hours before they were to have coffee. The police looking for Dad?

She scooped up a pair of leggings and climbed in with one hand. Still hopping toward the door, they knocked a second time. Haddie slumped. It sounded like Detective Cooper.

He stood a pace back from the door. A scowl tightened his mustache under his nose. "Ms. Dawson."

Haddie blocked Rock. "Detective Cooper." She wondered sometimes if he were coerced. How had he known she just got home? "I didn't expect you to work Sundays."

"I work whatever days I need to." His eyebrows furrowed. "Did you hurt your arm?"

Haddie glanced down at the cast. Meg had signed it in bright pink letters and added a penguin by the campfire. Pretty good, considering the lighting. "Yes. Slipped hiking. Didn't think it was broken, but it was."

"Hiking?" He raised an eyebrow.

"Whychus Creek. Fell right in the water." She waited. Dad had said not to feed the information, but make the police pull it out.

Detective Cooper sighed. "Do you know why I'm here?"

"Not a clue. Why are you here, Detective Cooper?" She lowered her eyelids, trying to look bored or sleepy while maintaining eye contact.

"Your father. Were you with him Thursday night?"

Haddie raised her cast. "At the hotel, after hiking. Why? What do you need from my dad?"

"There's a warrant out for his arrest. You'll be involved if you're hiding him."

"A warrant. For what?" Haddie tried to match Cooper's scowl.

"Do you know where he is, Ms. Dawson?" Not to be outdone, his jaw tightened.

"Montana. He rides in the summer."

Cooper leaned his head back. "Where in Montana?"

"Campgrounds, parks. Roads mainly. What are the charges?"

"You know I'm under no obligation to explain that to you. May I search your apartment?"

Haddie tilted her head. "You know I'm under no obligation to let you in without a warrant. Tell me the charges, and I'll let you in."

"This isn't a game, Ms. Dawson."

"No, it's my dad." She made to close the door. "I'll find out on my own."

"That would be illegal." The door closed and he continued, "This isn't over."

Haddie leaned against the door. Rock nuzzled her hand. She waited, but Detective Cooper either had left or was standing silent outside.

Dad had been right about all of it. She'd been pouting, but he didn't have a choice. It would be worse if he ended up in jail or dead. If the police did watch her, they wouldn't for long. The FBI might be another matter. *I'm being a brat*. She had plenty of reasons. David surely planned on breaking up with her. Dad, Sam, and Meg were gone, and she had to play secret agent to meet up with them.

Her burner rang and she jumped, moving off the door.

Terry called. "Hey. I'm pissed at Aaron and you. He just told me that you got hurt. Elbow or something?"

"You can sign the cast next Thursday. Game night."

"You okay?" He sighed. "I feel like this is my fault."

"Your fault? How?" Haddie asked.

"Me and Aaron just wanted to get somewhere on the demons and the Unceasing. We pushed. I know he did, and I didn't try to talk him out of it. I egged him to go to New York. I even wanted to go myself. I'm sorry."

"Not on you, Terry."

"Okay, Buckaroo. Listen, me and Livia want to barbecue. We missed game night, so how about coming over tonight? About six?"

Haddie waved off Jisoo who howled in starvation when

she neared the kitchen. "Can't. Liz is coming by tonight to do her thing."

"Bring Liz for sure."

Drawing blood at a barbecue. That would whet everyone's appetite. Haddie stared at Rock. She'd have to find another dog walker, but she still had friends. Sam was still her friend. *Not the same.*

"Sure, see you at six." Liz would be up for it.

CHAPTER 50

HADDIE WALKED across the street with hot air swirling around her, but she felt as though a dark cloud hung over her, and she felt chills. As she opened the café door, conversations from the patrons embraced her, and strong coffee scented the air.

With his eyes on his espresso, David sat at a corner table toward the rear left side. He wore a light blue polo shirt for the meeting, not his usual weekend T-shirt and jeans. He'd been kind enough to order her a pot of hot tea and a glass of ice. His espresso was nearly finished, though she'd been intentionally early.

Bright eyes looked up as she approached. "Hey. How do you feel?" he asked, gesturing toward her cast. He didn't stand to kiss her.

Haddie sat on the opposite side of the table. "Nervous. Scared. You're upset about last week." She didn't touch the tea; her right hand shook too much.

David pursed his lips and nodded. "I don't understand. Portland. Whatever went on last week. You tell me part of it, then you come back hurt — I don't know what's happening — you won't tell me, at least not all of it."

"You knew what happened in Portland, I was getting Liz." She reached back for her hair.

David shook his head and drew a breath before speaking. "Okay. Ignore all the odd parts about Portland, how about this week?" He had never seemed angry to her, but his tone rose now.

"Something personal that involved my dad. I tried not to make the same mistakes that I did with Portland; I texted and called." She could hear the pleading in her voice. *I'm not going to beg.*

"How do you expect me to handle these secrets? Even now you avoid telling me anything." He gestured in the air, as if frustrated. "I want to be part of your life."

"I want you to be part of my life." She could see the truth in her statement. "But you'll have to accept me the way I am. That includes what I went through last week."

"I can't just —"

Haddie interrupted. "I don't intend to change just to make sure everything fits in a neat box for you."

David frowned. "That's not what I'm asking."

"I think it is. You like order, and I can be chaos sometimes. The police are looking for my dad." *Why did I say that?*

"What?" David's eyes widened.

Detective Cooper might question David. "As far as you know, I went on a hiking trip alone. Not with my dad. How's that for a little part of my life?"

David swallowed and stuttered. "You — you want me to lie?"

Yes, I do. Her entire life had been pulled upside down over the past year. She had friends like Liz and Terry who accepted her for who and what she was. Kiana had become her friend as well. Haddie had been protecting David by keeping him out of the mess. *I need time to deal with living without Dad and Sam.*

"For the moment, yes. If the police ask, I went hiking." Haddie poured the tea into the glass and watched it swirl through the melting cubes. "Let's take a little while. I need to adjust to some changes in my life, like my dad. You can work out if you're able to deal with who I am." She picked up her glass, somewhat surprised at her reaction. "I'm not going to change anytime soon." Haddie almost laughed. Instead, she took a sip of warm tea, her top lip against cold cubes.

She had tried to be more respectful to David by keeping her promises to a minimum and texting him. He could accept that, if he chose to. Aaron, Terry, and Kiana weren't about to back off, and Haddie had questions as well. Her life didn't look as though it would calm down.

"I love you," she said, "but I can't be organized like you. I'm a bit of a mess sometimes. We both need some time to work through things. Put them in perspective. I can't do that trying to be something I'm not."

David's eyes had widened, and he just stared at her. "You want to break up, or just take a break? For how long?"

Haddie put down her glass and stood. "A break. I don't know for how long. You might decide before then that you can't deal with my life." She pushed off the dread the comment made by taking a breath. She wanted to hold him, kiss him, but she shook her head. "I'll call or text."

David nodded.

Haddie turned for the door and tried not to limp as she walked away.

CHAPTER 51

Haddie pulled into a parking space outside Livia's apartment with Liz in the RAV4. The sun still seemed high for this late in the day. The parking lot had no shade. Dad's new place would be cooling off by now. Sam would need help packing later this week.

Liz pulled a strand of hair back, tucking it over her ear. "When can I talk to Kiana?"

Haddie shrugged, leaving the engine on. "I'll ask. You want to take her blood too?"

Jerking in her seat, Liz turned with a grin. "Do you think —?"

"I doubt it."

"I mean, think about it. What if the blood were affected? I have no baseline. We probably couldn't get records from her last physical. Maybe Terry could." Liz had nearly turned sideways in her seat.

"Better if we don't attract any attention. Please."

Liz pouted, then shrugged. "What did work say about you missing those days?"

"Andrea said she doesn't do liability. She could recommend a good lawyer. Be on time Monday."

Liz snickered. "She obviously doesn't want to lose a quality worker."

"I'm not sure that's it. I guess I'm trained." Had Josh shown up? She'd find out Monday. "Let's not keep them waiting."

Haddie had to reach under her cast to release her seatbelt. Warm air enveloped her as the door opened. The summer heat hadn't let up this early in the evening. She hoped they could sit inside on the couch.

The scent of burning charcoal had made it to the parking lot. Terry said gas ruined a barbecue.

Liz walked on Haddie's good side. "I get worried. About all this." She looked up, her sunglasses reflecting Haddie's stark white hair.

"Yeah, me too."

"I'm sorry about David."

Haddie winced. "Yeah, me too." Liz had been surprised, but so had Haddie once she'd thought it through.

They crossed the asphalt toward the grass just in front of the apartment. A neighbor carried takeout from the car. Already Haddie felt like she'd begun to sweat.

"You think Detective Cooper will bother you again? About T?"

Haddie nodded. "Likely. He doesn't like to let go."

"Your Dad's really just going to disappear, with Meg and Sam?"

"No good options." Haddie paused in front of Livia's door.

Liz frowned. "But taking Sam. That's rough."

Haddie shook her head. "Makes sense. For Meg. She needs someone and Sam does well with her."

Terry answered the door before Haddie could knock. "Buen provecho, ladies."

Livia smiled from inside, waving them in.

Haddie sighed, stepped inside, and smiled. *I need these friends.*

<<< The End >>>

ACKNOWLEDGMENTS

My wife April continues to support me in my writing career. That includes long hours listening to audible reviews and unending plans, ideas, and concerns that I might imagine.

Robyn Huss, my editor, has an amazing (magical?) ability to transform my words into a better version of my ideas. Because she doesn't have time to get to all my work, I've tried a dozen editors and she outshines them.

I will dearly miss a beloved and irreplaceable mentor, David Farland; our loss is felt around the world. Please pick up one of his books and enjoy the magic he endowed upon the world. Writers, study his lessons at Apex Writers.

Jody Lynn Nye's workshop does wonders for many aspiring writers. ♥

My writing groups from JordanCon, DragonCon, and Apex are fundamental in making sure I keep on track.

Thank you.

CPSIA information can be obtained
at www.ICGtesting.com
Printed in the USA
LVHW042305060322
712739LV00004B/195